A Divided Heart

ALESSANDRA TORRE

For Natasha Tomic.
Thank you for your early love for this book and for giving it wings.

I watched Molly's apartment, a Mediterranean-style mud brown complex with window boxes full of hot pink hibiscus. Lee's jeep was parked at a crooked angle in the front, a mud-spattered box of American masculinity in a neat line of Hondas, Toyotas, and Kias. Twenty-two minutes had passed since Lee had ambled down the sidewalk and into the front door, his hands dipped into ripped jean pockets, his jaw set. He'd turned the handle and stepped in as if he'd gone there a hundred times. As if he belonged there.

I tapped my pale pink nails against the gearshift. Closing my eyes, I let the air conditioner's breeze wash over me. I had a massage scheduled in an hour, so this situation needed to resolve itself soon or I'd be late for my date with Roberta's hands.

Movement in the right window of the apartment. Lee moved quickly past it, a blonde close behind, tugging on his shirt, arms gesturing wildly. I could imagine the words flying out of her mouth. *Lee, don't go. Lee, it isn't what you think!* I wondered if the word 'love' left her mouth; if their relationship had progressed to that point.

He disappeared out of sight, and I leaned forward, wishing I had a drink, something to crack open and enjoy while my hard work came to fruition. This had to work; this had to happen. She couldn't have him. He was mine.

The front door blew open and he stepped out, his steps fast as he wove between the cars and up to his Jeep. His face was tight, features hard, a look I hadn't seen on his face before but one I could embrace. Resolute. Decisive. I clenched my hands in excitement, watching as she came into view, her face blotchy, eyes wide, her mouth moving rapidly, giant breasts heaving out of the top of a skimpy blue tank top as she yelled something and grabbed at his shoulders. I wanted to roll my window down, just a peek, enough to hear this exchange, enough to savor the moment.

That's right. Watch him leave. He will no longer kiss your lips or make love to your body. He's mine, and I'm right here, ready to take your place.

I watched him get in, the door slamming hard enough to make her jump. And then, with the screech of tires—the best sound in the world, better than my fantasies—a sound of finality that left her standing in the empty parking spot, black mascara tears staining her cheeks, her scream loud enough to pass through my Mercedes's tinted windows.

Victory is mine. I grinned, giving myself a virtual high five, and put my SUV into drive. Pulling onto the street, I headed south. Maybe after my massage, I'd swing by my fiancé's office. Drop off a sandwich for him. Celebrate my victory with the other man in my life.

Go ahead. Judge me. You have no idea what my love entails.

I love two men. I fuck two men.

If you think you've heard this story before, you haven't.

Part One

This is a love story, but not one that is easy to read. It's dirty. It's sexual. It is, at times, rotten. Love can bring out the worst in someone and it doesn't always offer a happy ending.

Chapter 1

My life has always had a plan. I think my parents, pre-conception, sat down and planned it out. Drilled into me with constant reminders and a follow-by-example regimen. I was a child of wealth, expected to do nothing but also everything. A 4.0 was required, though I would never hold a job. Ivy League was mandatory, but only because that was where I would meet my husband. I would not carry any additional pounds, as that would be an embarrassment, but I could not show off my figure, as that would be classless.

My life plan was simple. Earn a respectable degree while being molded into the perfect wife. Marry quickly and to someone with at least nine figures of net worth. Support my husband while pursuing my other interests, such as charity work and running my staff.

I never liked the plan and foiled it in as many passive-aggressive ways as possible. At an early age, I learned to hide treachery behind a sweet smile and innocent façade. In my parents' eyes, I was behaving and thriving. Doing my part to turn into the woman their DNA deserved. In actuality, I was lying in wait, getting my perfect deceptive ducks in a row and ready for the day that mattered: my twenty-fifth birthday.

* * *

It was ridiculous that I was getting a birthday cake, a tradition that should die off by the teenage years. Yet, here it was, topped with twenty-five candles and carried by my mother's reedy arms. Looking at her was like staring into an image of my future, one with Botox and fillers, pinched lips, and over-plucked brows.

She placed the cake before me, and I smiled because it was expected. I let her sing the song, my father's voice falling off after the first few words, his attention caught by the ding of his phone. I beamed for the photo and blew out the candles, missing three on purpose, and Mother's eyes flickered, but her smile remained fixed.

She cut the red velvet cake with a pearl inlaid knife, the scent of Chanel No. 5 drifting over the table as she served me the smallest possible piece, a center cut, away from the decadent icing of an end piece. Then we ate, the three of us at the end of the dining room's twelve-seat table, the scrape of silver against china the only sound in the room. Father stood first, leaving his plate, and kissed the top of my head. "Happy birthday, sweetie."

Then there was only Mother and I, and the interrogation began.

"Are you dating anyone?" She set down her fork and pushed her untouched slice of cake forward. Her gaze darted to mine, and I placed my fork on the plate, tines down.

"Not right now." I smiled as I had been taught. Always smile. Smiles hid feelings.

"Why not? You're twenty-five. You only have a few good years left."

"Don't worry, Mother. I'll find someone."

"I think you should reconsider Jeff Rochester. You dated him for almost two years." Four months. Four months that we spun into a two-year relationship to keep my parents appeased and his gay lifestyle a secret.

I gave a regretful frown. "I've heard Jeff is seeing someone.

And to be honest, we really didn't have any chemistry." I picked up the fork and used the edge to section off another bite, enjoying the pain in her eyes when I brought it to my lips.

"Chemistry isn't important. He's from a good family—and he'll always be able to provide for you."

My trust fund would provide for me. I didn't need a physically stale relationship, a prison sentence that would paint a permanent smile on my madness and lead me into an early case of depression and pharmaceutical drug use. But I didn't want to mention the trust. Not when I was an hour away from finishing this party and heading straight to the bank. Let her think, for just a little while longer, that she had some semblance of influence and control.

"Janice Wilkins told me she saw you working downtown. Please tell me that's not true."

I smiled. "I have a degree in quantitative science. It's not unreasonable for me to consider using it. I'm doing consulting for a medical firm. Overseeing some FDA trials."

"Please don't. Work causes stress, which will prematurely age you. And you only have—"

"A few good years left." I finished her sentence, keeping my voice light. I took another bite of cake, then scraped every bit of icing off the plate and slid the fork into my mouth. Sucking on the tines, I killed a little of my mother's soul.

"We've worked so hard for you to have a good life."

"And I do. You've done a wonderful job, and I'm very happy."

"What about Ned Wimble? I heard he and that Avon heir ended things."

I placed down my fork and wondered how much longer this celebration would take.

* * *

Two hours. That's how long it took to sit through more stilted conversation and the opening of my gifts. Cashmere cardigan.

Sapphire earrings from my father. A Tracey Garvis Graves paperback from Becky, the maid who knew more about me than both of my parents combined. Becky had been the one who'd found me puking in the bathroom as a teenager and cleaned up the mess and nursed me through my hangover. She'd cleaned my room and kept her mouth shut on condoms, birth control packets, and vodka bottles. She'd held me to her chest when I suffered my first broken heart, courtesy of Mitch Brokeretch—who hadn't deserved my virginity, much less my tears.

I hugged both of my parents and closed the trunk's lid, hiding all of the gifts. My real present wasn't in the trunk. It was in today's date, the trust paperwork that had been completed before my first birthday. Twelve million dollars waited for me in a joint account that I had watched from afar for over a decade. And now, with the papers I was about to sign, I would be free from my parents and from their expectations and requirements that have held this money above my head for the last two decades.

I drove straight to the attorney's office and, within thirty minutes, was a free woman. As I walked out of the sleek glass building on Wilshire Boulevard, a genuine smile crossed my face. By the time I visited the bank and transferred the funds into a money market account, it had turned into a full beam.

Freedom. It felt damn good. I put down my convertible's top and screamed into the wind. That night, I celebrated with one of my building's valets—a twenty-one-year-old kid who only lasted five pumps, but he brought some good weed and laughed at my jokes.

It was a sad start to my new life.

Chapter 2

THREE YEARS AGO

I spent the first two decades of my life planning for the moment when I could be free. To have the chance to abandon my cardigan and manners and rush headfirst into life. Dance in the moonlight. Smoke a cigar. Ride a motorcycle and fall in love for a reason other than social standing. I had romantic notions of waiting tables, hitchhiking across America, kissing a strange boy, feeling a rush of unknown possibilities.

I had grown to hate every stitch of my privileged surroundings. I craved escape from the dinner parties, the ingrained disdain of others, and raised brows of judgment. I wanted the happily-ever-after of movies, the messiness of real life, the reckless enjoyment of impulsive decisions. And the day of my twenty-fifth birthday, I'd felt free. Filled with hope and possibilities. The first day of the rest of my life.

Yet, as I approached my thirtieth birthday, I was still stuck in the exact same life. I'd had a few wild nights. Screwed some strangers with calluses on their hands. Visited a 7-Eleven and bought a hot dog. Went to Tijuana long enough to realize I would never go back. Then ... like a migrating bird, I drifted home to this world and settled back into the nest without even realizing it.

I was still surrounded by the people from my youth. The friends who weren't friends. The parties where everyone smiled but no one had fun. The world where life was a constant race to one-up each other, and the prom queen was still the bitch no one liked, but everyone flocked to like maggots to meat. I needed to escape this life, I needed to find something different, I needed to make my own path, but I was stuck. Stuck on repeat. Stuck in hell.

The driver appeared in the doorway behind me, his cap in hand, and met my eyes in the mirror. "I'll be out front whenever you are ready to leave for the event, Ms. Fairmont."

"Thank you. I'll be out shortly."

He nodded, turning to leave, and my gaze returned to the mirror. My brown eyes were lightly outlined in a mint chocolate brown. As always, I wore enough makeup to hide flaws and gently enhance my features, but no more. *Classy, not trashy.* My mother had trained me well. I stared into my reflection and tried to find the person in it. The mirror showed the woman I had been raised to be. A couture gown that was dramatic yet sophisticated. A polished exterior, from my hair to my heels. I stared at my shell and wondered why I couldn't break from it.

It didn't matter. Tonight, of all nights, wouldn't be the start of my change. In two hours was the primary fundraising gala for the Homeless Youth of America, an organization close to my heart. An important event that shouldn't be missed.

Maybe tomorrow I could turn over a new leaf, try again to leave the nest, and live a genuine and unmoderated life.

I applied a coat of clear gloss over my lipstick and avoided my eyes in the mirror.

* * *

"Brant Sharp." He paused in front of me and extended his hand.

"Layana Fairmont." I shook it, intrigued. I knew who he was. Everyone in this room knew who he was, but I wondered how many would be able to point out and recognize the elusive billionaire. The billionaire with, according to rumor, a particular preference of women. Expensive, pay by the evening, women.

"I like your hair." His gaze drifted over the absolutely unexceptional French twist that was secured by a broach that once belonged to Elizabeth Taylor.

"I'm not a prostitute." I addressed the possibility directly, in case the rumors were true.

His mouth didn't change, but his eyes warmed. "I can overlook that fact."

It was the first five lines of our meeting, uttered two hours into the fundraising gala. Talk about an unromantic start to a love story. I can only blame my crude participation on alcohol, two glasses of wine already downed, my self-loathing slightly pacified by merlot.

Now, I studied the man, someone that I had followed ever since I got involved with the Homeless Youth of America.

Brant Sharp. Genius. Bachelor. Philanthropist.

He was even better looking than I imagined. The tiny thumbnail image used in press releases barely showed his features, and certainly hadn't done his looks any justice. But it was his intensity that really surprised me. He peered at me as if I was a problem, and he searched my soul for a solution. He also seemed inordinately pleased by my hair, his eyes frequently leaving mine to sweep over their dark strands.

I can overlook that fact. I laughed at the response, the sound one he seemed to enjoy, his own mouth twitching into something that was almost a smile. I liked that he was close-fisted with his smiles. It was refreshing.

"It's a pleasure to meet you. I'm a big fan of your work with HYA," I said. Homeless Youth of America was the only holdover from my mother's painful rearing—a charity she'd pushed me at, one that ended up gripping ahold of my heart and refusing to let go.

The amusement left his expression and when his eyes

darkened, they turned into molten heat. "I wouldn't call it work. My office cuts a check. Nothing else is done."

"The funds mean a great deal." *Funds* was putting his contribution lightly. Last year I raised half a million dollars for the charity, six percent of their annual donations. His check covered ninety-two percent. It was enough to make him the honorary Chairman of the Board, though he'd never shown his face at the facility or the board meetings. Beth Horton, the permanently dour head of HYA operations, had been the one to tell me about the escorts.

"There's been hundreds," she'd confided at last year's board meeting, wedging an entire powdered donut into her mouth. I'd watched closely, as interested at the prospect of her choking as I was in the discussion of Sharp's sex life. "My driver's brother is a doorman at his downtown condo and said the girls show up all hours. Beautiful girls, but clearly prostitutes. He never leaves with them, and they only stay for a few hours." I nod, half-believing the words. It would explain why he'd never publicly dated, a fact that drove the women of San Francisco mad and had sparked rumors of homosexuality. Those rumors never went too far. Too many women who had met the genius, worked for him, dissuaded them. I liked the idea of prostitutes, of the man unleashing holy hell on a woman of the night in the privacy of his Silicon Valley condo.

The funds mean a great deal. Sharp didn't respond to the comment, and it hung between us.

I took a sip of champagne. "I'm surprised to see you here."

"Why is that?" The laser focus of this man was unnerving. When he stared at you, there was no wavering, pure certainty that he was listening to your words and processing them accordingly. I tried to relax, the pressure of an intelligent response high, well aware that I was in the presence of brilliance. I'd never been a woman that found intelligence sexy. Four years surrounded by Stanford nerds would cure any woman of that misconception. But this man ... he had a combination of intelligence with confidence and intrigue, all mixed in a martini glass of strikingly handsome looks.

I shrugged and took another sip of liquid courage, wishing for something stronger than champagne. He moved closer, and I had the unnatural urge to lean into him and sniff. Maybe test the waters by placing my hands on his tux's lapels and tugging him in. Would he hold the eye contact? Would he step back? Or would he drag me somewhere private and fuck me senseless? My reckless confidence of earlier wavered in his presence. Ninety-two percent of the annual HYA budget. Ninety-two percent, staring at me as if he wanted to eat me.

I swallowed and tried to bring my mind back to the conversation. "Well, you're a recluse. Never photographed. The word on the street is that you have the social skills of a hyena."

The last statement was a complete fabrication, and I smiled to soften the joke. "And you've never come by the campus or attended a board meeting. I just assumed that the spring fundraiser would also be skipped."

"Hyena tendencies aside, Thomas Yand is on the guest list. I'm hoping to speak with him. He's been avoiding my calls."

"Ahhh..." I leaned closer and lowered my voice. "So this is an ambush."

"That was the plan. A conspirator would help." He raised his eyebrows at me, and every bone in my body came to attention.

Yeah, definitely not gay. I could understand why his female employees rushed to this man's defense. I'd spent two minutes in his presence and had experienced about nine spikes of arousal. I swallowed and painted a cool expression on my face. "What do you have in mind?"

* * *

He didn't need a conspirator. He was one of the wealthiest men in the world and as powerful as Zuckerberg in terms of the tech community. But we played our roles well. Flirted over cheese trays and whispered over champagne. Celebrated with conspiratorial smiles when Yand was cornered—me on one side, Brant on the other. I let their conversation take off, then stepped away. Retreated to the other side of the room, where Anne Waters, a bleach-blonde with double D's, pulled me into a chair at her table, licking crab cake off her fingers and diving into a long discussion over her spring shopping in the city. I nodded politely while my mind wandered, my resolution to live a different life strengthened with every unladylike lick of her fingers. I snuck a glance at Brant, who was focused on Yand, his face grim as he nodded at him.

Watching him, a surge of want curled inside my groin, surprising me. I'd always assumed, if I ever met the reclusive billionaire, that I would dislike him.

Reason #1: He'd been impossibly wealthy ever since he was a teen. With decades of being waited on and catered to—it was a tried-and-tested incubator for an asshole.

Reason #2: He was impossibly intelligent. I'd expected the ego to match the brains, producing a pompous, arrogant nerd, the type who'd spout off intricate facts while staring at my breasts.

What I didn't expect was everything that he was not. Quietly confident. Unassuming. Gorgeous, with intense interest that didn't play games.

He glanced away from Yand for a moment, and everything stopped as our eyes caught and held. He broke the contact and extended a hand toward Yand, ending their conversation with a polite smile. He moved toward me and I couldn't look away. I could only watch as he stalked across the room until he was standing before me, his gaze warm as I tried my best not to swoon into his arms.

His arrival halted the conversation at my table. I glanced at Anne, whose mouth was half-open, her crab cakes forgotten. "Excuse me, please," I murmured, rising to my feet as Brant pulled out my chair. The circle of vultures watched closely, hopeful for a scrap of gossip to feast on. Brant led the way and we escaped toward the rear doors.

"Thank you for your help with Yand," he said softly, his head lowered toward me.

"Thank you for saving me from those women," I whispered, smiling politely as I passed Nora Bishop, a woman I was fairly certain had spent most of the last decade on her back, beneath my father.

As we approached the exit, I realized how much I wanted this man. I thought briefly of the rumors—the prostitutes—and then the heat of his hand moved from the small of my back to my elbow. He controlled with courtesy, and I wanted more. Needed more. Then, we were outside and alone on the balcony, the warm summer night bringing a balmy breeze that smelled of ocean and summer. There, his hand left my arm, and I was able to have a moment of clear thought.

I rested my elbows on the rough balcony ledge, the cut of concrete comforting against the finery of ridiculous wealth. Every bit of this was such a show. We spent the entire year fundraising for children who would cry over the prospect of new sneakers, then shelled out a hundred thousand dollars on a party. I turned and looked back at the full-length windows that rose three stories and showcased the entire production in all of its false glory. Then I glanced at Brant, handsome elegance cased in tuxedo black, a picture that belonged to this world combined with a man I felt was above it. "Was it worth it?" I nodded at the party and glanced over at him, his profile strong, his eyes on the horizon, the glow of exterior torches flickering across the handsome shadows of his face. "Dealing with this crowd for a chance at Yand?"

"It was worth it as soon as I saw you." Soft words but with a dramatic impact.

I smiled and stepped up on the thin ledge, one that allowed me to lean over the balcony and put my face fully into the wind. "You don't know me." *I don't even know myself.*

"No, I don't." He said the words mildly, as if the concept was unimportant.

I turned and watched him. His features were calm, and he was so poised and undeterred. It was as if my attraction to him was unimportant, either due to confidence or because he didn't care if we ever saw each other again. The path of confidence was the option I preferred; the other was a problem. I was unaccustomed to denial, to losing; the thought of being discarded was difficult to comprehend. I didn't know who I was, what I wanted, but I knew I was desired by men. I had nothing, if not that self-assurance. I swallowed a foreign seed of insecurity. "Let's get out of here."

That turned his head. Hands in his pockets, he moved closer, enough for me to smell his cologne, an expensive scent that made me think of yachts and cigars. "Where do you want to go?"

I faced forward, closed my eyes against the ocean breeze, and exhaled. "Out of here."

Chapter 3

We hopped the balcony fence on the far end, where there was a staircase that was closed off for the party, the tiny act of rebellion perfect in its ridiculousness. I removed my heels, our dash down the stairs almost Cinderella-like in its execution, his strong hand pulling mine, our fingers interlocking when we reached the bottom. I tried to gather the bulk of my dress; the expensive fabric now ruined at the bottom. Giving up, I looked for my driver, the sea of mostly black cars in the lot signifying our lack of ability to diversify in any way. My Rolls rolled forward out of the pack as a bellman stepped forward and opened the door with a white glove. "Ms. Fairmont," the young man said stiffly.

I half-expected Brant to touch me in the car, his hand to steal onto my leg, his prostitute-loving self to put those beautiful lips on my body in some way. He did nothing, just settled into the seat beside me, his fingers drumming a pattern on the armrest as he stared out the window.

"My house, Mark." My family's driver, a man who has been in my life for over a decade, nodded, his eyes never flicking to the rearview mirror. My use of him and this car was rare, reserved for situations like this where I expected to imbibe. Despite my mother's neat signature on his paychecks, I had his loyalty. Who knew what secrets he kept for my parents, he kept a file cabinet's worth of mine. I turned my attention back to the mystery beside me.

I'd known plenty of geniuses. Stanford was stock full, so I had experienced every make and model. And, for the most part, they fell into a few standard types. There were the ones whose genetics had blessed them with intelligence but no social skills. There were the pompous, insecure men who feigned confidence by vomiting data and facts. And then there had been the kind who made me the most nervous: the quiet types who watched me while notating every nuance of my character for analysis at a later moment— Brant's type.

He glanced away from the window and studied me with open intensity, his eyes scraping open every damaged pore on my psyche.

"Stop," I ordered.

His mouth twitched. "Why?"

"Don't think so much. Your brain could probably use a rest." I smiled.

"Worried about what I will come up with?"

"No." *Yes.*

"Why'd you leave with me?" he asked, as if any woman needed to explain running off with a billionaire.

"I figured you should have one night with a woman that you didn't have to pay for."

His eyes crinkled at the edges. "I like paying."

"Why?" Now I was the curious one, and about every piece of this man. He was fascinating, the most interesting piece being his utter lack of concern about my opinion of his actions.

"It's less messy. I can dictate the night with no emotions involved."

"Emotions can make it hotter."

"And more painful."

"Have you been hurt?"

"Not yet." He stared at me so steadily, an odd emphasis placed on the words, as if he was giving his heart to me with both hands, certain it would lead to his demise.

I suddenly didn't *want* it. Didn't want the weight and pressure of that expectation. Didn't want to do anything but bring the light back into this man's eyes.

The car slowed, and I saw the gates of my home before us, moving slowly as we waited for entrance. I reached over, unclicked his belt, his gaze following my hand, his brows raising slightly. "We're here."

* * *

Mark dropped us at the front entrance, and I pulled Brant into the dark house and straight through the massive living space. The interior lights were off and the room's only illumination came from the view of the backyard, where uplighting highlighted traveler palms surrounded the glowing blue pool, my sliver of the ocean hidden by the night. I grabbed his hand and led him into my bedroom, my private oasis, which smelled of pears and sea salt, the bed already turned down, the lamp casting a soft, warm light onto the cream sheets. I turned my back to him. "Unzip me?"

There was a moment of pause, a moment where I tilted my head and waited for the pressure on my zipper. Then the slow drag of exposure, the fingers of his other hand following, four points dragging down my bare back as he took it down past the curve of my back, his breath changing in tempo, a deep inhale bringing a smile to my face. *So, he is human.*

His warm hands slid up and skimmed the tops of my shoulders, shedding me of the dress as the material fell down my arms and off my body. I turned, naked except for my underwear, and cast a mischievous smile toward his tuxedo.

"Strip."

"You do it." There was both a challenge and an order in his tone.

I shook my head. "I've got to break you of the habit of ordering women around."

He scowled and yanked his bowtie loose, then worked open the buttons on the front of his shirt. "When's the last time you did what you were told?"

I shrugged. "Hard to think back that far." I stepped out of my dress and faced the dresser. Behind me, there was the thud of his dress shoe as it hit the floor. As I carefully removed my diamond earrings, I watched him in the mirror. He shed his jacket, his shirt, then his pants. My eyebrows rose.

Dropping the large studs on the dresser, I moved toward my bed, my progress halted as he pulled me back and around into the hard surface of his chest. A full body press of his skin against mine, hard planes meeting soft curves. Nothing between us but my panties.

"Hi," I murmured, our faces inches away, his lit by the lamp's glow.

"Hi." He didn't kiss me, even though I lifted my chin, inviting the touch. His hand stole under the hem of my silk panties and cupped my ass.

"Your hands are warm," I said.

He slid his hand higher and gripped my waist. He gave me a boyish grin, then pitched me onto the bed.

There was a roll of naked skin, our legs tangling. The crawl of me along his body, our lips meeting, our first kiss born. His mouth was hesitant, his hands confident, and I wondered if he kissed the escorts before he fucked them. Then, the kiss deepened, our connection solidified, and I put the thought of prostitutes out of my head.

When he pulled away and sat back against the padded headboard, his hand slowly sweeping over the curves of my skin, there was a pause. A moment of indecision when he looked into my eyes, and his gaze held a question.

I didn't answer with words. I rolled over and off of the bed, then walked soundlessly across the thick rug and to the dresser, where I fished through panties and thongs until my hand hit foil. I pulled out a condom and walked back, my eyes taking an appreciative tour of his body as he lay on his back, fully exposed. His mouth curved; no move made to cover the impressive organ that lay stiffly against his thigh.

I didn't expect his confidence—most computer nerds are more bashful of their body, only arrogant of their mind. But then again, he hadn't quoted a single fact, hadn't brought up his company or money in any way. He wasn't trying to impress me. He was treating this the same way I was, two adults looking for a good time.

He took the condom and placed it beside him on the coverlet, his hand returning to grab mine. "Not yet. Come here."

He pulled me alongside him until every edge of us touched, a connection from head to toe. Turning to his side, he pressed a soft kiss against my lips, then straddled my hips. His fingers started at my shoulders and softly worked up the muscles of my neck, gently probing down the lines of my frame.

I closed my eyes, letting out a sigh as I relaxed against the pillow, and he slid his hands lower, palms flat on the swell of my breasts, his touch gentle as he spread his hands and took me into them.

"You're beautiful," he said, a whispered scratch in the tones. "I'm sorry if I'm ... I'm not used to romance."

I opened my eyes and let my own hands crawl down the strong muscles of his chest, the thick divots of his abs, a delicate exploration that was about to reach his cock. "I don't think I'm looking for it."

"I thought every woman was looking for it." He let out a guttural groan as my fingers wrapped around his stiff shaft and squeezed.

I looked up into his eyes, and he moved his body down, just out of my reach, so he could lower his mouth to mine. *This.* This was what every woman was looking for. A mouth that responded hungrily yet tenderly when kissed.

This. A firm drag of my body toward the end of the bed, eyes dominant, hands strong, as he pinned me to the mattress.

This. My hands in his hair, clawing at his shoulders, my body bucking underneath his talented tongue between my legs.

This. Our bodies entwined in my sheets, his weight on my wrists, the moment of primal connection when he spread my legs and thrust himself inside, moving with sure strokes, my cries of pleasure silenced by his kiss.

This. His body arcing into mine, his grip pulling me tight to him, the burying of his cock when he finished, gasping my name, the shudder of his breath against my mouth as he rolled me over and gave one final thrust.

This. This was what I wanted, what my new self desired. The romance, it could wait.

Chapter 4 – Brant

"You did what?" Jillian's shrill voice echoed in the large office, bouncing off antique desks and framed honors.

"I'm an adult, Jillian. I have every right to entertain whomever I wish."

"Layana Fairmont isn't a trailer park hussy, Brant. She's a respected member of society. Extremely intelligent, though you wouldn't know it from the life of leisure she lives."

"I would consider those marks in her favor. You're speaking as if you'd rather me date an uneducated redneck. I left her house last night and went home electrified. I worked all through the night and solved our issues with data recovery. The woman lit a fire in me."

His aunt stood, her pearls clicking, the fury in her eyes finding their mark and burning the skin they touched. "She's looking for a husband. A new last name, a finish line to the race of life that all of these debutantes live."

"I find it interesting for you to know so much about her intentions."

"You know me, Brant. I have nothing but your best interests in mind. Trust me when I say to let whatever happened last night be the end of it. You don't need a relationship and need to stay away from this woman. Next time you want to get your rocks off, let me call the service."

With a foot on the desk leg, he leaned back. "You realize how ridiculous it is for you to order me whores. Most maternal figures would be happy to see me taking out a respectable woman."

"Your mother would want this. Trust me."

He frowned. "I don't understand you half of the time."

She smiled at him with a hint of sadness. "Trust me, Brant. I could say the same about you."

Chapter 5

I woke up alone, Brant leaving the bed at some point during the night. I wondered briefly how he got home.

It was odd, that he had snuck out of bed in the middle of the night. Maybe that was the modus operandi with prostitutes.

I didn't like it. The sex had certainly been stay-until-the-next-morning-worthy to me. More than that, it had been incredible. Sitting up, I reached for my phone and checked my notifications.

No missed calls. 11:12 AM.

I rolled out of bed.

* * *

I ran along the surf, my tennis shoes squishing with salt water, the give of sand beneath my soles encouraging as I felt the muscles respond, jumping into action as I pounded down the beach. I increased my speed as my house came into view, the finish line in sight. I was wheezing when I came to a stop, my finger trembling as I stopped the timer on my watch. The burn of my chest matched the scream of my calves and the endorphin high made it all worthwhile. I forced myself to walk forward and my heartbeat calmed at the leisurely pace.

Two miles. Shorter than yesterday but at a faster pace. I glanced at my watch, at the frozen stopwatch there. 15:04. I cleared it, the time returning to the display, and started the uphill climb toward my pool deck, where a bench and shower station waited. There was a strange woman standing inside my gate and I paused at the sight of her—her rigid posture bringing back the memory of every prep school headmistress I'd ever had. I eyed her warily and continued forward.

"Is there something I can help you with?" I opened the gate to the pool deck. How had she gotten back here? I glanced toward the house, wondering if I had left the side gate unlocked.

Living on the beach occasionally brought trespassers onto my property, but this was something else, and I tried to place her as I sat on my bench and worked off my sandy sneakers. She looked familiar. Maybe the neighborhood association? Or one of my charity boards?

"Layana Fairmont, I assume."

I nodded. "That's me."

Whoever she was, we were currently a lesson in contrast. My skin was wet from ocean spray and sweat, and barely covered by a turquoise sports bra and spandex shorts. This woman wore a burgundy pants suit, a white turtleneck peeking out from her jacket. I had drops of sweat versus her pearl necklace. My wild brunette ringlets were barely contained by a headband and elastic, while her coiffed updo was barely shuddering in the strong wind.

I stood, my breathing now under control. "And you are?"

"I'm Jillian Sharp." She started to hold out a hand, her lips pursed, eyes sweeping over me, but then thought better of it, choosing to primly nod instead, as if she was the Queen of England and I should curtsy.

Jillian Sharp. My mind worked in overdrive as I swiped away a bead of sweat. So that's how I recognized her. She was the CFO of BSX, Brant's digital conglomerate, and the face of the company. She conducted all of the news conferences, interviews, and led their board of directors.

"I spoke to Brant this morning. He mentioned your little..."--she sniffed in a way I took to be disapproving--"*meeting* last night."

The polite thing to do would be to invite her in, but I didn't like her tone, or the sour look on her face. I decided to let her stand there. "And?"

She glanced around. "Maybe I should come in? This is, after all, a personal matter." She sniffed again.

"Sure." I finished peeling off my sweaty socks and stuffed them inside my shoes, then tucked them under the bench. "You've already trespassed into my backyard, might as well bring you inside my home." I reached for the shower's hose and washed down my feet, taking my time as she waited. Normally, in the privacy of the outdoor shower, I would have stripped. Scrubbed the sweat off my body and enjoyed the hot water on my tired muscles. That would have to wait, and my irritation at her intrusion grew as I walked around the edge of the pool and unlocked and opened the back door.

Inside the crisp air conditioning, I grabbed two bottles of water from the fridge and slid one across the granite island to Jillian, who inspected the bottle before setting it back down. She watched as I guzzled every drop from my bottle before wiping my mouth with the back of my hand.

Silence stretched, and I damn sure wasn't going to say anything. She was the surprise guest of the hour, a busy executive who probably had a list of things she should be doing. I could stand there all week without skipping a beat.

She delicately cleared her throat, and she pulled off elegance well, but I knew her background. She was one of the most powerful women in Silicon Valley, but she was--under all of those expensive clothes--straight middle class. She'd attended a community college and worked as a substitute teacher until 1997, when her nephew, one aforefucked Brant Sharp, built a computer in his basement. A computer that made IBM's latest creation look like a bowl of marshmallow pudding. A computer that made his parents drop every future plan and invest their savings in Team Brant. He was only eleven years old and needed a chaperone. So Aunt Jillian quit her job and hitched her wagon to Brant. She lived off food stamps and her savings in a spare bedroom with Brant's family for two years. Then she brokered Brant's first deal, and all of the Sharps moved their bank account balances seven decimals to the right.

"I'd like you to stay away from Brant." She raised her chin and it jutted out at an unattractive angle.

Well, that was unexpected. I'd half expected her to pull out an appointment book with plans to pencil in our wedding date while the summer calendar had openings. "Excuse me?"

"Brant doesn't need the distraction of a relationship right now." She remained in place, back rigid, a stick firmly wedged somewhere up her ass.

"That seems like a decision for Brant to make." I leaned my forearms on the counter and met her gaze squarely. "Last I checked, he's not eleven years old anymore."

Her dark red lips pursed together. "Don't assume that you know him or anything about me just because you did an internet search. He's not built for a relationship and doesn't have time for you. I'm coming here, woman to woman, to ask you to stay away."

"And I'm telling *you*, woman to woman, that it's none of your business." Any interest I had in Brant was skyrocketing with each word out of her mouth. I had obediently colored inside the lines for decades. I was looking for any opportunity to rebel and kicking this schoolteacher to the curb would be a fun start.

She unclasped her purse, a cream Hermes that I owned in green, and reached inside.

A laugh bubbled in my throat when I saw her withdraw a checkbook. "You're going to try to *bribe* me to stay away from him?"

She ignored the question and placed the book on the counter, her jaw set as she clicked a pen into action and bent forward, writing my name onto the first line.

"We spent one night together. He's not preparing to propose."

"It's better to be safe than sorry," the woman said stiffly. "Plus, at this point, there are no emotions involved. Walking away should be, in your case, a breeze. You're a smart girl. I'm sure you'll make an intelligent decision." She completed the amount, then signed her name and ripped it from the deck. She dropped it onto the granite, then used her pen to slide it across the island toward me as if it might burn her fingers.

I ignored it. "I appreciate the visit, but I think it's time for you to leave."

She didn't budge. "It's for your own good, sweetheart. You don't want Brant. He's damaged goods." The cruel words were said with affection, the tone not minimizing the truth in her eyes. She believed it, and I had only spent a few hours with him, but *damaged* was not the word that I would have used. She returned the pen to her purse and buckled the gold clasp.

"I don't want your money."

"A million dollars never hurt anyone, dear."

I dropped my eyes to the check, surprised to see her name across the top. *One million dollars.* To me, it meant an extra vacation home. Maybe a condo in Colorado. Nothing that would change my life. But it was still a significant amount of money, especially to be written off her personal account. "It's worth a million dollars to you for him to stay single? Or is it me that you have such personal disdain for?"

Her eyes flickered, and there was a tropical storm of emotions in this small woman. "Trust me. I want what's best for Brant. And, for you."

I pushed back the check. "No thanks. And it has nothing to do with Brant. I'm not going to be bought off from anything."

She chuckled, and the sound was anything but jovial. Instead, it scraped long, dead fingernails down my spine, reducing me, in one squeeze of her vocal chords to a misbehaving child. "Oh, how easy it is for a child of wealth to take the moral high ground. I imagine, if you'd had to work a single day in your life, that you would react differently. If it were your money that built this house and purchased your ocean-front view, you'd be taking my check and thanking me for it."

She was probably right, but that didn't mean I was going to let her stand here and lecture me. She wanted to buy my distance, and I didn't want to give it. I tore the check into two and let the two halves float to the counter.

"Fine." She shrugged. "You don't want my money? What about HYA?"

My fingers tightened on the counter, and everything changed between us with that question. She wouldn't. She couldn't. "What *about* it?"

"Last year BSX donated..." She moved her gaze around the kitchen, as if there was complex math being done in some corner of her mind.

"Seven and a half million dollars." I found my voice—it moved out of my throat without invitation. *She wouldn't.*

"Seven point six," she corrected me, her voice hard. "I head our charitable contributions team, along with twelve other departments at BSX. Step away from him, or I'll pull this year's donation."

My world grew a little smaller. Donations were due next month. We were asking BSX for eight million, which would, in addition to normal expenditures, pay off the existing debt on three new homes we put under construction during the last year. Without that donation, the organization would have to cover both mortgages for a full year. An impossible task. And, honestly, with my poor fundraising skills ... I couldn't make up that deficit. No way. I could barely raise the outside three hundred grand I had recruited last year.

I swallowed and stared at this evil woman who suddenly held a full house in her deck. A full house of homeless kids. "Get the fuck out of my house."

And just like that, my relationship with Jillian began.

Chapter 6

I didn't react well when being told what to do. I was also selfish. Both of those arrows pointed in the direction of calling Brant and planting myself front and center in his life in any way I could.

But I couldn't ignore the kids. The ones I spent my Tuesdays and Thursdays with, the one break from my superficial life, the one peek I got into a difficult existence that HYA brightened in so many important ways. Jillian was right about one thing. There were no emotions attached at this point, no reason why I couldn't just walk away from Brant. Walk away and allow thousands of children to have a little brightness in their lives this year. Would I take that away from them just to spite Jillian Sharp?

Yeah. Probably. I never claimed to be a saint. Manipulation should never win. Plus, I should never lose. My new mantra was to do as I wished, not as society expected or wanted. On that note, I was almost obligated to give her the proverbial middle finger.

I dumped a liberal amount of Kahlua in my coffee, sat down on my sofa, and stewed over the decision. Stewed over why Jillian was so dead set against a possibility that hadn't even become a possibility yet. Was it me? Some hatred of a stranger she'd never met? Or was it any woman who might interrupt the flow of

Brant's life? How many kitchens had she stood in? How many checks had she written, foes had she faced?

Two hours later, I was slumped low on the couch, the pillow imprinting expensive designs in the side of my face, when my phone rang. I jerked to life and up to my feet, trying to regain my bearings. My ringtone sounded again, and I stumbled toward the kitchen and found the cell on the counter beside the bottle of Kahlua.

BRANT displayed on the screen. I silenced it, stumbled back to the couch, and collapsed facedown.

Think of the children.

* * *

My second nap was ended by my hunger, which punched incessantly through my alcohol-induced slumber. I made it through half of the steps involved in a chicken salad sandwich before I was reminded of Brant's missed call. I picked up my phone with mayonnaise-covered fingers and opened my voicemail.

I had one new message, received at 3:07 PM.

"Layana. This is Brant Sharp. I enjoyed last night - sorry to leave without saying goodbye. I'd like to take you to dinner tonight to make up for it. Let me know if you're free."

I tossed down the cell and finished fixing my sandwich. I stood at the counter and ate it, a frown pinching my features.

* * *

He called two more times that week. Left two voicemails.

The next week nothing.

The next week nothing.

The fourth week he sent a large arrangement of orchids. The card simply said, "Call me."

I didn't.

On day thirty-four: BSX wired their annual donation, meeting our request of eight million dollars.

On day thirty-five, I called him back.

"Hey," he said. There was total silence in the background. No hum of machinery, no busy San Francisco street.

"I'm sorry."

"Trust me, I won't leave in the middle of the night again. I learned my lesson."

His wry tone made me laugh. "It wasn't that. Truly. I just needed to get some things in order before I saw you again."

His next sentence was a grumble of words. "Let me guess? Clear the bench?"

More like wait out a contract. "Something like that."

"So ... your bench is available?"

I laughed. "As unsexy as that sounds, yes. It's wide open."

"Good. I'd like to take you to dinner tonight."

I smiled. "Pick me up at seven."

Chapter 7

Jillian must have had a direct line to Brant's brain. She called within three hours. The number unfamiliar, I answered it while folding laundry, whites laid out across my sofa like flags of surrender.

"I didn't expect you to be a woman who would renege on a deal." No polite words of greeting or introduction before diving into the meat of the issue. I recognized her voice instantly and my smile widened as I got a month's worth of pleasure at the irritation in her voice.

"All's fair in love and war, Jillian. We have a year before BSX's next donation to HYA. That should give us both enough time to sort this matter out."

"I don't expect to remember your name in a year."

I clicked my tongue at her. "Word of advice, Jillian? Don't push back. It'll only cause me to pursue him more."

"Word of advice, *darling*?" She dunked the last word in poison, drawing it out in a manner that made my brow arch in admiration. "Realize when someone is trying to do you a favor."

I didn't have a witty comeback for that one. Didn't really understand it enough to respond. I swallowed, folded a white tank top over twice in my hands and added it to the pile. "Don't worry about Brant. I won't hurt him."

"That isn't really what concerns me." She hesitated, and there was a catch in her breath when she spoke again. "Call me when you find out what does."

I didn't talk to her again for nine months. I called her the night I discovered his secret.

Chapter 8

Wealthy men were a breed I knew well. I was raised by one, my opinion of him formed during brief moments of notability during my first eighteen years. I'd dated the young versions, ones who had been born into the world of trust funds, Harvard legacies, and country clubs. Their sense of entitlement had been seconded only by their undeserved egos. Then, I graduated college and moved into the world of men, older versions who reminded me too much of my father, men who took rather than asked, and who expected subservience from anyone with breasts.

Wealthy men had their benefits: the jets, vacation homes, power, and exorbitant gifts. They also had their shortfalls: arrogance, unfaithfulness, an impossible schedule, and, more often than not, an opinion of women that left much to be desired. But hey—that was the rare thing I'd had in common with most of my dates, a mutual lack of respect. And probably the reason why I'd never had a relationship that bloomed to fruition.

Brant was completely different than every other wealthy man I'd ever met. He listened when I spoke. He looked into my eyes and not at my breasts. He asked my opinions and valued my intellect. He approached our new relationship in the cautious way that a cat approached food, pushing delicately before gaining footing, his steps as new and explorative as my own. We danced around each other, our moves becoming stronger, more sure-footed with each passing day. Together, we created and explored our roles; sex was the only area of our life where no practice was needed.

The man was a sexual animal. I sipped my coffee and shifted in my seat, the sore ache of my body reminding me of a few nights before, his skillful manipulation of my body that had brought me to orgasm four, five ... then six times. I twisted slightly, watching Brant as he stepped into the coffee shop, his eyes finding me as he walked over and brushed a kiss against my lips.

"Been waiting long?"

"Five minutes. Here." I pushed across his coffee. "Straight black, you unexciting man."

He settled into the seat, picking it up with a dignified scowl. "It's manly. Puts hair on my chest."

I laughed into my cup. "I don't want hair on your chest. I prefer it as is, perfectly manicured by your team of beauticians."

That earned me a real scowl. "I don't have beauticians. They're..." My eloquent man seemed suddenly at a loss for words. I laughed, pushing gently on his cup until his coffee was out of the way, then leaned across the table and stole another kiss. He grabbed the back of my neck, pulled my mouth harder to his, asserted his masculinity in a rough moment of passion. I pulled off, blushing as I sat back down, a passing woman glaring at me as if we've just screwed on the coffee shop's floor.

"I'm sorry about yesterday." The joviality was gone from Brant's voice.

I shrugged. "It's not a big deal. I shopped and ran some errands while downtown."

"I've been fighting a deadline on this wireframe overhaul ... sometimes I get in a work zone and lose track of time."

"It's *fine*. I was just worried. I'm not mad—just hated bothering Jillian about it." Hated bothering Jillian was a mild way of putting it. Brant and I'd set dinner plans: 6 PM at Alexander's.

I'd waited at our table for a half hour before leaving, my calls to Brant going unanswered. I had hesitated to text Jillian, my fingers finally moving across the screen purely out of concern—in case something had happened; in case he was missing. I half-expected a snarky response, something that referenced how unimportant I must be to him. But she had responded quickly and professionally.

> He's here at the office. Will probably work late.
> No doubt lost track of time. I'm sorry.

The fact that she had been civil in her response only irritated me more, tipping the scales a bit in her favor, setting precedence for an act of similar civility on my part. I broke off a piece of muffin.

"Let me make it up to you."

I watched him while chewing, blueberries mixing with sugar and flour to make a delicious combination in my mouth. "Go ahead," I mumbled.

"Today, I'll blow off work. Be all yours."

I swallowed the bite. "But you're under deadline. You've been working for three weeks to make—"

"I don't care." He reached over the table and gripped my hand. "You are more important, and I've set aside a full day of groveling to make up for last night."

I raised an eyebrow. "A full day? That's a hefty commitment, Mr. Sharp."

He met my eyes. "One I'm ready to make."

I leaned over and lowered my voice. "And what do you have planned in this full day of groveling?"

He tugged my hand up to his lips. "I thought I'd start by us dropping by my condo. I have some ideas of ways to make it up to you."

"They'll need to be very persuasive ways."

He pulled on the back of my neck until his mouth was against my ear. "They'll be ways that will make your legs tremble around my neck. Ways that already have me so hard and ready that I may not make it all the way there. Ways that will have you screaming my name and—"

"Let's go." I jerked to standing and the legs of my chair squeaked as they slid across the floor. Pulling on his hand, I beelined for the door.

Chapter 9

Brant's downtown condo was his sex den, the place where high-class hookers had satisfied every carnal desire he'd had over the last two decades. I stood in a living room where other women had moaned his name, serviced his cock, and I couldn't care less. Because the man standing before me, his eyes dark as he stripped my clothes off? I could see into his soul, and he didn't have eyes for anyone else in the world. He wasn't thinking, picturing, wanting, anything but me. He lifted me up and set me on the dining table, his hands sliding my shorts down my legs and removing my sandals, caressing my skin as his hands journeyed back. He knelt on the floor, looked up into my eyes, and pushed on the inside of my knees, spreading my legs until I was open, his gaze dropping.

"Brant," I moaned, the exposure too much, the open stance causing air to hit places that were typically hidden.

"Be quiet." He slid his hands up my inner thighs, and I dug my fingers into his thick head of hair and bit my bottom lip as his right hand brushed over me. I opened my legs further, and he groaned out my name as he ran a finger over my sensitive lips, outlining the folds with a whisper-soft touch, his teasing brush causing my body to react, to cry for him in the only way it knew, moisture collecting, his breath hissing as he pushed a finger partially in. He met my gaze as he pulled his finger out and tasted my juices, his eyes closing briefly in reverence. "God, I can't wait to bury my face in you." His touch returned, teasing the outside of me, soft strokes breaking me apart as he caressed every part of me, the pad of his fingers exploring, testing, circling, and pushing, my back arching, mouth dropping as I stared at him, helpless to look away from the scene.

When I couldn't take it anymore, I pulled his mouth to me, my body shuddering when his hot mouth enveloped me, his tongue dipping inside before covering my clit and starting a wet suction and play of stimulation that had me gasping into the air, my nails frantic in his hair, my gaze catching on the faint reflection of us in the window, the picture it showed one of desperate need. I clutched the edge of the table and pushed at his head, unable to—I bucked underneath his mouth, a babble of incoherent words coming out—then I screamed, my hips grinding a frantic pace against his mouth, his hands gripping my hips, pinning me down, keeping his mouth on me as I broke apart.

He relaxed his tongue as I came down, keeping the movement but softening it, the orgasm stretching out beneath his tongue, my breath coming hard, my arms giving out. I collapsed on the table and my legs went limp.

* * *

He carried me to the bedroom, my limbs struggling to reawaken, his deposit on the bed gentle, his hands moving my arms and legs into place. He undid his belt and the drop of his pants revealed how ready he was. "Wow." My arms worked enough to prop me up, my eyes flicking from his arousal to his face, catching on the half smile that tugged at his lips.

"You are so beautiful right now," he said, ripping open a condom and sliding it over his shaft, the bob of his sheathed cock tempting, the level of his erection mouth-watering. I bent my knees and spread my legs, giving him the carnal view I knew he wanted, a low swear emitting from his mouth as he kneeled on the bed and ran his hands along my legs before positioning himself for entrance. "Tell me if it hurts," he murmured, moving forward, the head of him pushing inside, the girth causing a pleased moan to slip from my lips, my gaze drinking in the gorgeous sight of my pussy's lips wrapped around his cock.

He was thick. Cut. Groomed. Beautiful. He pushed slightly in, then out, several more inches still unused, the condom slick with my arousal, my sparse hair wet and matted, framing his cock as he took his time, letting me adjust, the slow drag of him so ... everything. I lost intelligent thought, broke from my view of us and looked up to him, his eyes on mine, the look on his face so vulnerable, so raw. He stared down at me as if I was his world, as if our month-long courtship was so much more, as if I already had his heart and he had mine. He worshipped my face with his stare, and the only movement was the rise and fall of his hips as he thrust and pulled at my self-composure. The moment when he fully pushed inside, when he broke past the sweet and moved to the painful, the moment when my body fully adjusted to his length and girth, the need as great as the satisfaction ... I saw it. We said it through our eyes, the words unnecessary, our bond completed as he lowered his mouth to mine and stole a piece of my soul.

I love him.

Chapter 10

I rolled into his chest, my touch finding its way over his stomach, the lines of his body, his abs jumping beneath my fingers as he exhaled. My hand moved lower, sliding under the sheet, a growl coming from his throat as I closed my hand around him, the thick muscle awakening underneath my touch. "Don't start unless you want more."

"Of that?" I teased. "I'll always want more." I gave him a final squeeze and then released, dragging my hand back up to his chest, wanting a few more minutes of this moment. Brant was relaxed, his intensity subdued, his eyes closed, the only movement the rise and fall of his chest underneath my hand.

We lay there in silence for a bit. I closed my eyes and replayed the sex. I didn't enter this relationship a virgin. I'd had seven or eight lovers. I'd had orgasms. A few freaky nights where I'd walked on the wilder side of the sheets. But I'd never experienced this kind of sex. A full session with Brant was one where the entire focus was on only one thing: my pleasure. His orgasm came, it always occurred as the final act, but it was a side effect, not the goal. Brant's goal, each and every time, was to leave me sated, every possible orgasm pulled, tugged, and yanked from my body with his talented hands, mouth, and cock.

I wrapped my leg around him and pulled tighter. His hand squeezed my ass in response. "Tell me about the escorts." I didn't know where the request came from; it jumped out without warning. Beneath me, I felt his body tighten, his hand stopping the lazy exploration across my skin.

"What have you heard?"

"That you've hired hundreds and that they come here, not your home."

"This is closer to the office. And ... I have too many valuables at home, plus my work is there. This worked better."

"But you've taken me to your house," I pointed out.

He chuckled. "Yes. I trust you not to rob me blind while I sleep."

I propped my chin on his chest and watched his face, his dark brown eyes flicking to mine. "Hundreds?" I asked.

He frowned. "No. Over the last twenty years..." He shrugged. "There have probably been thirty."

I digested the number. On one hand, it was more than mine. On the other, it was less than I had expected. "And ... why prostitutes?"

He blushed, something I had never seen from him. "Pleasing a woman ... it's important to me. I wanted to be taught, by a professional."

"Taught?"

He moved a curl of hair from my cheek and wrapped it around his finger before tucking it behind my ear. "I was young the first time. Seventeen. I'd never even kissed a girl before; my whole world pretty much confined to my computer in the basement. I wanted to date, my hormones were going nuts, but Jillian and my parents didn't want me running around town flagging down the first girl I saw."

"So they ordered you a prostitute?" I pushed up off his chest, the motion causing my breasts to move, and his gaze dropped to them, a deep exhale easing from his chest as he took a moment, his hands sliding up my back and curving forward, cupping my breasts with reverence. "Brant," I said as he shifted total concentration to my chest. "Brant," I repeated. "Your parents got you a prostitute?"

"No," he mumbled, trying to pull me higher, so his mouth could reach my nipples. "Jillian got me Bridget, an eighteen-year-old girl straight off the pages of my fantasies."

"A prostitute," I repeated, sliding lower, moving my breasts farther away. I grinned despite myself.

He finally looked up. "Well, I didn't know she was a prostitute. Jillian had her knock on the door one day when I was home alone. The girl pretty much dragged me into my bedroom. She gave me my first blow job and made me forget all about computers for a good three minutes."

"Isn't that ... illegal? You were seventeen. Jillian's your aunt! That's creepy in so many different ways I can't even name them all."

He laughed. "It was the best thing they could do for me at the time. And I didn't want to leave the house, didn't want..." He looked down, busying himself by pulling our sheet higher. "I understood them keeping me close. Protecting me. I didn't know she was a prostitute. I thought she liked me and had just moved in nearby. She hung around for two years and took me from a boy to a man. Then she was gone."

"What happened?"

He shrugged. "Moved away, got a boyfriend? I don't know. I was heartbroken. You know teenagers. I'd thought we were meant to be, and then Jillian told me how the girl was interested in getting paid and nothing more. She said I should concentrate on the good and what I had gotten from the relationship. I was pissed off and didn't talk to her for a few days. I'd moved out of my parents' house by then and was living here at the condo. A few days passed, then she sent over a new girl. I understood the test. I couldn't be pissed at her for giving me something I wanted. So, I could turn away the girl, knowing she was a prostitute, or take her and accept the reality." He looked at me. "So, I fucked her. And it was different than with Bridget because I understood the dynamic, and I could control the situation. So, I focused on getting what I wanted—the ability to please a woman. And I figured, one day, I would have a woman worth using that ability on."

I winced and wrapped my arms around his neck. "I'm sorry."

"Don't be." He kissed me on the lips.

"You realize," I said slowly, "that stories like this are your skeletons. You're supposed to keep this stuff locked away, behind a wall of impenetrable masculinity."

He laughed and rolled us over until he was on top, and his cock was still hard, still begging for attention. "Well, then there you have it. My skeletons. Will you still have me?" He nibbled a path along my neck, and I giggled beneath him, reaching a hand down and gripping the part of him I couldn't get enough of. "Skeletons?" I mused. "Well, I do like a good bone."

He groaned into my neck as he thrust into my hand. "That was so cheesy."

I laughed. "Good cheesy?"

He shook his head against my curls. "Bad cheesy."

"I like bad," I whispered, my hand tightening, his hips fucking his cock into my grip.

"God, woman." He stretched across my body and yanked at the handle of the bedside table, his hands knocking over items in his haste. "I don't know what to do with you."

"Really?" I teased. "You don't know what to do with me?"

"Correct that," he rumbled, lifting off me just long enough to put on a condom, his hands slightly shaking in his urgency. "I know exactly what to do with you."

Then he was back atop me, and then he was inside of me, and then he showed me *exactly* what his plans entailed.

Chapter 11

Jillian and I engaged in a silent battle, one where she pushed in every passive-aggressive way she could, campaigning with all her strength against the relationship that Brant and I were forming. It was a battle without words, but through the man she loved, and I had fallen for.

I met her next roadblock on a Tuesday morning which was dedicated on my calendar to HYA. Pulling through the organization's painted red gates, I was greeted by a shiny male specimen, complete with a genuine six-pack, blinding white smile, and rugged good looks that a model scout would trip over herself to snag. He jogged across the grass, lines of dirt smeared across the ripped muscles of his chest, a trio of kids tailing after him, their arms outstretched for the football he carried. I watched him run toward me and wondered who he was and what he was doing inside the HYA sanctuary.

Employees and volunteers at HYA were carefully vetted. Background checks, drug tests, and references were required. We'd had the same staff, give or take, for the six years I'd been involved. A new face wasn't often seen and was typically discussed well before recruitment. I parked in one of the volunteer spots and watched as his head lifted, his hand raising in greeting.

I smiled at the kids, who detached themselves from the stranger to run toward my convertible. Opening the door, I was accosted with hugs, a volley of questions, and one helpful boy who closed my door with a solemn responsibility.

"Thanks, Lucas." I put a casual arm around his shoulders and hugged him briefly.

"They like you." The stranger stopped before me, legs slightly apart, the football jumping a lazy trip between his two hands.

"Honestly, they like everyone." I smiled and extended a hand. "I'm Layana."

"Billy," he said, holding the handshake a bit longer than necessary.

I disentangled my hand, turning to the children to disguise the motion. Reaching out, I snagged the closest body and pulled her to me, tickling the little girl briefly before twisting toward the main house and sprinting forward. "Race you guys to HQ!"

My tennis shoes tore across the damp grass, the squeal of voices in pursuit causing me to increase my speed. I glanced over my shoulder, seeing the new guy—Billy—staying close, a flirtatious grin shot at me.

I ignored the look and focused on the hill before me, my legs pumping up the embankment as I slowed my stride a bit to give the kids a fighting chance. Reggie, a ninth-grader who'd come to us three years ago, his torso already marked with gang ink, passed me, his long legs eating up the distance. I let him go, casting a quick glance around me to find the other kids. I slowed a little more, then let out a yell of mock frustration when the race ended with me as the loser.

I bent over, breathing dramatically, my back patted consolingly by Hannah, my personal favorite at the HYA compound. I turned to smile at her, my eyes catching on Billy, who watched the exchange, an interested grin on his face. I looked away.

* * *

"How long have you volunteered here?" The question came from the other end of the main house's kitchen. I didn't stop my PB&J production, didn't turn, knew the source of the manly drawl without looking.

"Five or six years. I'm only here twice a week." I unscrewed the lid to the jelly and avoided looking at the man who I was pretty sure just moved closer.

"I'm new." *Duh.* "Just a volunteer."

"How'd you find out about HYA?"

"HYA?"

I paused my jelly application and glanced over to see the man lean against the counter, then straighten. "HYA. Homeless Youths of America."

"Oh." He let out a short laugh. "I read about it online."

That was a negative. We were a privately funded organization, run by internal and corporate donations and one that intentionally stayed off the public radar and as discreet as possible.

"Who was your referral?" I abandoned the sandwiches and set down the knife. Turning to him, I rested a hip against the counter and managed—somewhat successfully—to avoid staring at his abs, which were still on full and sweaty display. The man, apparently, had not brought a shirt.

"My referral?" His grin grew strained.

"New volunteers require a personal referral from someone inside the organization." I kept my voice mild, as if I wasn't handing him a noose, certain that he would use it to hang himself.

His eyes darted to each side like ping-pong balls. I knew he had a referral. He had to have. Otherwise, he wouldn't have gotten through the gate, wouldn't have a name sticker, which was currently affixed to the front of his workout shorts.

"Oh." He looked around, as if for rescue. I tilted my head and pinned him in place with my gaze, my suspicion growing the longer he wrestled with the question. He swallowed, and the bulge of his Adam's apple moved painfully across the tight stretch of his neck. By the time his mouth finally worked open, I was ready to crawl into his throat and pull the words out. "Jillian Sharp."

I should have known, should have expected the name. A handsome stranger at HYA, tripping over himself to make my acquaintance, with every firm muscle on full display for my eyes. I smiled. "Jillian," I drawled. "What a pleasant surprise." I studied his face, a handsome canvas that looked as if he might vomit in the closest trashcan. "You seem like a nice guy, Billy. Don't take it personally that we can't, and will never be, friends."

His brow knitted. "Never?"

I chuckled. "Never." I moved around him and toward the walk-in cooler. A final thought came to mind, and I spun, pointing a finger at him. "Oh Billy?"

"Yes?" he asked weakly.

"Don't hurt these kids. They fall in love easily. I don't give a damn if you stay or go, but don't hurt them." I stared him down until he nodded, held the eye contact until I was sure he understood, then I pulled open the door to the cooler and stepped in.

Chapter 12

Three months after our first official date, I ran my hands lightly through Brant's hair, his steady breathing forecasting a better night of sleep than I would be getting. He was beautiful at rest. The thick brush of his lashes. The bones of his face that created the perfect canvas. Brilliance and beauty all rolled into one.

I didn't understand why I was his first relationship. Once he completed his journey into manhood, why had he continued to use escorts for sex? Why didn't he have any friends, any real ties to anyone other than his parents and Jillian? It didn't make sense, especially because he seemed custom-built for a relationship.

He wasn't perfect. I'd found some flaws. He got distracted, didn't always listen to conversations, or plans, had a memory that would qualify him for pharmaceutical help. Just last week, he'd missed another date. Just hadn't shown up at all, his cell phone going unanswered until the next morning, when he provided a weak excuse about falling asleep at his desk. A different man, I would have suspected of cheating. But Brant made it clear early on where his focus lied. Work and me. Nothing else, no one else. The man's dedication was impressive, might have even been alarming, had I not been gunning for a relationship with both throttles wide open. I had no other men waiting in my wings. I'd ended any casual flings after our first real date. Every tool in his shed was superior by two to any other suitor. And my interest had been heightened by the fact that his aunt would pay seven figures just to keep me away.

I loved that he was different than the men of my past. He didn't have the cloak of aristocracy, wasn't aloof or snooty, and didn't care if we played by society's rules or wrote our own. In three months together, we had created an igloo of sorts in San Francisco society. Our relationship was a haven of two, a place where I felt comfortable saying 'screw it.' My world was expanding, my boundaries blurring, and I was moving in the right direction toward happiness. Brant, in his oblivion to anything but work and us, was pulling me there.

Love? The word hadn't been verbalized yet, but it was coming. In our eyes, touches, in the affection. But both of us were cautious, guarding our virgin hearts with ineffective hands. I kept reminding myself that it had only been three months since I'd finally returned his call and we'd both dove headfirst into this relationship.

I rolled to the side, breaking the view of his beautiful profile and turned around until my body fit into the curve of his, his arm tightening around me as he sighed into the back of my neck.

It didn't make sense. He was too perfect. How was I the first woman to tie him down?

In the morning, we were driving two hours up the coast to meet his parents. Maybe *they* were the reason my perfect boyfriend was still a bachelor. Maybe they were satanic and would ask for a sample of my skin. Maybe they were doomsday preppers who would teach me to can vegetables and show me their collection of guns. Brant didn't say much about them, his primary point of contact being Jillian. The internet provided even less. But maybe they were the reason for his singledom. I pressed a soft kiss to Brant's forearm and tried to go to sleep.

* * *

"Would you care for more lemonade?" The delicate lilt of Gloria Sharp caused me to lift my eyes.

"No, thank you." I took a sip and set the glass down, trading glassware for silverware, and cut a small piece of chicken and placed it in my mouth.

Food. The excuse we all had to avoid talking. I chewed slowly, grateful for the action. To put it mildly, the Sharps seemed unaccustomed to company. They stared at me as if I was a new species, on display at a museum, and looked frequently between Brant and me, as if trying to put the pieces together in a puzzle that didn't match.

Brant stood, his plate in hand, and leaned over to kiss the top of my head. "Excuse me for a moment."

I looked up with a polite smile but begged him with my eyes to stay.

He ignored the request. "Restroom," he explained.

I watched him as he headed out of the dining room, mentally pulling on his red polo shirt to no avail. I turned my gaze back to his parents and found both of their attention on me. Not chewing, just staring. I cleared my throat. "I love your home. The fact that this is where Brant—"

"Ms. Fairmont," Brant's father spoke in a thick and strained voice, one of a man older than his years.

I smoothed my napkin in my lap and waited for him to continue. Smiled. God, I hated using that smile. "Yes, Mr. Sharp?"

"You should probably know that we don't think it is a good idea for Brant to be in a relationship. You seem like a very nice girl, but you should think about moving on."

It was a good thing I'd mastered the expression. Knew how to keep my eyes relaxed, my face muscles loose so the smile looked natural, not forced or tight. You could tell so much about a person from the way they smiled. But not me. My smile gave away nothing and it now worked in overtime to maintain my composure. "Why is that?" I asked lightly as I cut another wedge of the chicken and glanced at Brant's mother, whose gaze was now down, her hands fighting with her napkin.

"Brant's done better in life when he hasn't had a girlfriend."

Brant's a grown man. I kept the smile in place but brought it down a level, so I didn't look deranged. "I care very much for your son. He's a brilliant man. You should be very proud of where he is in life."

His father gave me an exasperated smile, as if he was ready for the bullshit to be over. "We'd just like it if you could keep your distance. Restrict your time with him to a minimum. Let him focus on work. He does best when he does that."

There was the sound of a door and then the soft thud of Brant's steps. When he re-appeared in the doorway, I placed my fork down. "Dinner was delicious, Mrs. Sharp. Thank you both for having me over. Brant?" I met his eyes. "Do you mind showing me the basement? I'd love to see your old workshop."

His mother's mouth twisted, his father's hardened, and they could both kiss my ass because Brant was an adult, one more intelligent than the rest of this house put together, myself included. The woman rose and snagged my plate, a glance at my half-eaten meal not going unnoticed.

Brant seemed oblivious, breezing through the room and grabbing my hand on his way. As we walked through the living room and down a short hall, I tried to understand why this family seemed to dislike me so much. Was it me? Or just any woman in Brant's life? Had Jillian gotten to them? Did they know about the unaccepted bribe? He swung open a door and gestured me forward. I stepped down a dusty flight of stairs and into the basement.

It was small—roughly six hundred square feet of dimly lit space, the back wall illuminated by a single fluorescent. An unimpressive setting for impressive feats. He sat on a stool and spun to one side as he stretched out his arms and leaned back. "This is it. My home for almost a decade."

"Fancy." I walked slowly along the counter, a drag of my finger bringing up enough dust to choke a horsefly. I looked at the wall, which held a meticulous system of cubbies and cubes, but no photos or mementos stuck to its hole-dotted surface. "Has this place changed since you lived here?"

Looking over the room, he shook his head. "Looks about the same." He ran his hand over the grid work of storage. "I put all of this in place. Looks like Dad hasn't touched it." Reaching out, he patted the worn wood counter. "This is where I built Sheila."

"Sheila?" I grinned at the fond look in his eyes and took a seat on the stool next to him. The room felt good. Lived in, despite its decades of unuse.

"Sheila Anderson. The prettiest girl in my third-grade class. I thought building a computer would get me girls like her."

I moved my chair closer. "Did it work? Was she impressed?"

He wiped his hand over the surface as if memorizing the lines in the wood. "Ah, I don't know. I never had a chance to show it to her." The stool squeaked as he rotated, facing me fully. Reaching forward, he dragged the stool until I was between his open legs.

I tilted my head and gave him a mock frown. "I'm a little jealous of this Sheila girl."

He worked open the front of my shirt, unbuttoning one, then two, then the entire row of buttons, the fabric gaping open, a sigh coming from his mouth as he slid his hands inside. As he cupped my lace bra, my skin awoke underneath his hands. "You have nothing to be jealous *of anyone* about."

"I don't know..." I whispered. A small groan slipped out when his fingers pulled down the cups, my breasts falling out before him, hanging heavy with need, the brush of his hands bringing my nipples to full alert. "She did have a computer named after her..." I left my hands on my knees. Did nothing to stop him as he took his time with my skin, the brush of his lips soft as he leaned forward and tasted my neck. Thumbed his tongue along the hollows of my throat as he gently pulled on my nipples, then moved to squeeze the weight of my breasts.

"That computer was a piece of junk," he whispered, moving

his head back and taking my mouth with his. "I'll build you a universe." His kiss was soft, his movements slow. He sucked on my bottom lip and teased my mouth. I gave up my grip on my knees and threaded my hands through his hair. Pulled him closer.

"How many girls have you kissed in here?" I asked against his mouth.

"Hmmm..." His lips moved, kissed a soft trail along my jaw, his hands taking liberties with my breasts that would make Sheila Anderson blush bright red. "Do you count?"

"No." I pulled his head by his hair. Guided it back to my mouth.

"Then none. Unless you count the Farah Fawcett poster I professed my love to."

"Shhh. You're ruining this with your talk of senior citizens."

He laughed and went for my belt. There was the creak of a door, and I stiffened, pushing him away. Behind us, there was the flip-flop sound of his mother's steps. "Brant? It's getting late."

His eyes stayed on me as his mouth curved into a boyish smirk, his gaze dropping to my exposed chest, my shirt still hanging open. "All right Mom. We'll be up in a second."

No response from her, just the retreat of footsteps and the click of a door. I clamped my hand over my mouth as a ridiculous giggle erupted out. He gave me one last grope before standing and pulling my shirt closed. "Button up my little minx. Let's get out of here before I take you on this desk."

I fumbled my way through the buttons, certain that my flushed cheeks and his smile would give away our actions. But when we made our way through the house and back to the table, his parents seemed none the wiser.

Dessert, a lemon pie that would put Marie Callender to shame, was more pleasant, and conversation moved at a steadier clip. If I had to guess, Brant's mother had given his father a stern warning during our basement time. The man seemed contrite, and Mrs. Sharp kept sending me apologetic looks, every time our gaze met over the table. When our plates were emptied, I rose to help clear the table.

I followed Brant's mother through a swinging door and into a small kitchen. It was dated, with white appliances and old tile countertops. I scraped plates into the trash and the small space was quiet with our sudden isolation from the men.

"I'm sorry," she blurted out, her voice soft. "For what Spencer said. About you not dating Brant."

"It's fine. Really." I didn't want to talk about it, didn't want to give the hundred nosy questions inside me an opening to spill out. My prying would only damage this fragile connection. I looked for a safe topic. "It's wonderful that you allowed Brant, at such a young age, to take off school to build Sheila."

"Sheila?" Mrs. Brant looked over from the sink, confusion clearing from her face when she understood my reference. "Oh-- the computer. I'd almost forgotten; it's been so long since it was referred to as that. It was kind of a memorial thing ... the name didn't stick. Apple didn't want the negative connotations attached to the project." She turned off the faucet and took the plates from my hand and slid them into the soapy water.

"Negative connotations?"

She glanced over. "Oh – I forgot – you were too young. Sheila Anderson. The little girl who was murdered all those years ago. It was the summer Brant started working all the time. They never found her killer – or her body for that matter. Just..." Her voice faltered. "Just her clothes. Bloody. Not far from here. A few girls disappeared that summer, but she was the first. And ... Brant had always had a crush on her. He took it hard. That was around the time ... well." She paused, glancing over her shoulder. "Hi Brant."

He moved up behind me, his hand wrapping around my waist and pulling me into his body. "Mom putting you to work?" He planted a kiss on my head.

"Barely. She was just telling me about –"

"Old memories," she interrupted. "Thanks for bringing her

by, Brant." Grabbing a hand towel, she wiped at her palms. "It was a pleasure to meet you, Layana."

I smiled. "Thank you. It was wonderful to meet you both."

"You leaving?" The large body of Brant's father closed off the doorway, and the small kitchen was suddenly claustrophobic with the four of us inside.

"Yes. Thanks." Brant clapped his father on the shoulder, and we squeezed our way out of the kitchen and escaped.

I was quiet during the ride home, my mind walking me back through the evening. I wondered at the reasons behind Jillian and Mr. Sharp's aversion to our relationship. Wondered whether Mrs. Sharp had agreed with her husband, despite her apologies for his statement. Wondered about Sheila Anderson and why Brant didn't mention that she had died. I could have asked questions. But I didn't. I looked out the window and thought.

My upbringing had taught me to be cautious, especially in matters dealing with family. But I couldn't. I was hooked on this man, and love had a strange way of bucking restraint.

Chapter 13

"Bonjour." I stuck my head in Brant's office.

His head lifted, his fingers continuing to move across the keyboard as he smiled in greeting. "This is a nice surprise."

"Don't get too excited yet," I teased, walking around the desk as he continued typing at a rate faster than humanly possible, his gaze glued to me, his mind capable of more simultaneous action than mine. "I'm kidnapping you."

"Sounds..." He finished his typing, then swiveled in his chair to face my approach. Reaching out, he pulled me onto his lap. "Interesting. Where are we going for this kidnapping?"

I shook my head. "I'm not telling you that. It would ruin the fun. How much time do you need before we can go?" I glanced at the three side-by-side monitors on his desk, two that displayed file downloads in progress.

"I'm yours. Steal me away before Jillian reminds me about the budget meeting that starts in fourteen minutes."

"Hot damn." I hopped off his lap and snagged my purse off the floor. "Then let me get you out of here."

"You're turning me into a rebel." He clicked his tongue.

"Oh yeah," I giggled. "Skipping budget meetings. You can get fitted for your leather vest now. Stick with me, and soon you'll be going to bed without flossing. Getting really crazy."

I waited for him to join me at the door, then peeked out into the hall with an exaggerated gesture before turning back and putting a finger to my lips. "Run on three," I whispered. "One...two..." I opened the door and we sprinted.

* * *

"Here?" Brant looked out the window at the homes as my car rolled to a stop in a front parking spot. "I've been here before."

"At the ribbon cutting. I know. This will be a little different. Come on." I opened my door and stepped out. Stepping onto the grass, I scooped up an empty gum packet and looked back at Brant.

His posture was awkward as he stood beside my convertible, his gaze sweeping over the compound. It held five brick homes, each nicely spaced out on the large, fenced-in estate. Three kids were clustered in the shade of an oak, and an overweight mutt sniffed the edge of the fence and eyed us as if wondering whether to attack. He recognized me and wagged his tail. Squeezing through the gate, I knelt, running my hands over the dark grey dog. "Hey Buster." I ran him through his three tricks: sit, shake, and down, glancing over when Brant entered the yard and crouched beside me.

"Buster, huh?" He reached out a hand and scratched him behind the ears.

"Yep. Meet the most loved dog in the Greater Bay area."

A patter of steps came from behind me, and I turned in time to see a small body fly through the air, knocking me into the soft grass.

"Miz Lana!" Hannah, my six-year-old bundle of trouble, squealed and squeezed my neck tightly enough to restrict airflow.

"Hey sweetie," I gasped. "Let me up a minute so I can introduce you to someone." I put a hand on the grass and hoisted us both to standing, flashing a smile at the two other kids, ones I'd never seen but would guess to be a few years older than Hannah, the close press of their bodies indicating a sibling familiarity verified by the twin shocks of red hair both possessed. I readjusted Hannah's weight until she rested on my hip. "Hannah, this is my friend Mr. Brant."

"Hi Mister Brant." She extended a solemn hand.

Brant shook it with equal seriousness. "It's nice to meet you, Hannah."

I turned to the others. "You guys must be new. I'm Lana, and this is my friend Brant."

"I told them all about you," Hannah said with importance, her thin arms tight around my neck.

"Well ... tell me about them then, since you know everything," I teased.

"This is Samuel and Ann. They're from Boatland."

"Oakland," the boy corrected, glancing at his sister.

Buster nudged my leg, and I reached down to pet his head. "Welcome to the house, guys. Which one are you in?" The houses were named after states, HYA's goal to have fifty built within the next five years. We were currently looking at a lot in Sacramento for more homes, as well as spots in San Jose and Los Angeles.

"Georgia. Though they said we have to split up next month." A worried glance shot between the two faces that were too young to have these concerns.

"Don't worry about that." I readjusted Hannah on my hip, her weight tiring. "By next month you guys'll have so many friends here you'll be begging for time away from each other. And the separation will only be at night. Days and meals are all free-for-alls between homes, so you guys will have lots of time together, if you want it." I gestured to Brant. "I've got to take Mr. Brant inside, but I'll see you guys again before we leave." I gently set Hannah down, giving each newbie a high five before looping my fingers through Brant's and pulling him toward the main house, a large structure on the rear of the property, where meals were served, sleepovers and movie nights held, and general bedlam occurred all day.

"This place is amazing," Brant said, glancing around, the basketball court filled with action, a bevy of girls sprinting around the corner of a nearby house and flying past us.

"It is." I nodded. "And all made possible by your donation."

"Maybe I should increase it."

I grinned. "That may have been my ulterior motive in bringing you here."

He pulled me to a stop. "You don't ever need motives, Layana. Anything you want, anything that makes you happy ... just ask."

"I know." And I believed it. I truly believed he would give me anything—do anything to make me happy. "But I figure you might as well see the impact of your money." I continued forward. "Come on. I want to show you the main house."

* * *

We toured the common areas and the work areas, then stopped on the third-floor deck, an open area scattered with outdoor furniture. To our right, a group of teenage girls laid across hammocks, their voices low. From this height, you could see the entire campus, and we leaned against the railing and looked down on the common lawn. "How many kids live in this house?" he asked.

"None. This is the social hub, where everyone eats, plays, and studies. The houses are set up for breakfast and sleeping, little else. That system seems to cut down on temper tantrums over who is in which house."

"I can't imagine that the kids would ever want to leave. This place is like summer camp."

I watched as Trenton, one of my favorites, climbed onto the first limb of a live oak. "Every kid wants love. To have parents whose focus is on their happiness. We can't do that for a hundred kids. We try, but we can't. They'd all leave this in a heartbeat for a chance to feel wanted and loved."

"You weren't?"

I laughed, pushing on his arm. "I was talking about homeless kids, not my parents. My parents gave me everything I ever wanted."

"Money and presents don't equal love. I live in a huge house that doesn't hold a bit of love. I know what emptiness feels like. It's one of the reasons I hate living alone."

"My parents loved me." The words had to be true. Parents love their children; they just choose to show it in different ways. Mine chose to love by expectation.

"I love you." He turned to me, and his hands settled on my waist. "You, Layana Fairmont, are impossible not to love."

I scoffed. "You don't know me enough to love me." Thirty years old and it was the first time a man, including my father, had ever uttered those words. It was a sad truth, one made possible by my talent to alienate every man other than the one who stood before me, pulling me closer, owning me. I had given him my heart and was terrified at the prospect of what that might mean.

"I love you. Every dark and light piece of you." He lowered his mouth, but I stopped his kiss, pressing a hand on his chest.

"There's no kissing on campus," I whispered. "HYA policy."

He frowned. "Don't I hold an office of some sort in this organization?"

"Board president."

He grinned. "I hereby, and for the next five minutes, strike that rule from the books." He pulled me closer and pressed his lips to mine, a soft sweet brush of commitment, one that changed, grew more passionate and possessive, his hand moving to cup the back of my head, his mouth sealing the deal, catching my heart as it jumped over the edge of forever.

I loved this man, and when the kiss ended, I told him as much. He grinned and recaptured my mouth, his kiss deepening as he pressed me against the railing.

There was a gasp from our right, and I pulled away and saw Hannah, her eyes huge, her face alarmed at our flagrant breach of the rules. She pressed a firm finger to her lips, then made a zipper motion, doing a solemn and careful pantomime of locking her lips and throwing away the key.

Then, her face broke into a grin, and she tore off into the house with a squeal.

Chapter 14

Two months later, I pulled up to Brant's house, the entrance lights illuminating the path as they sensed the presence of a vehicle. More lights came on, palm trees and stone appearing in an orchestration that must have set Brant back a fortune. I pressed the remote, and my bay in the garage opened. Pulling in, I parked and waited for the door to shut and stop the cold Bay Area wind from whooshing in.

Inside, I removed my shoes and left them by the door, conscious of Brant's level of OCD cleanliness. The house was silent, and I walked into the three-story entranceway and paused at the base of the stairs, listening. There were no sounds from above. He was probably downstairs.

I took the elevator, the doors quietly opening to an underground computer lab that rivaled Ironman's in both size and capability. The air was cooler down here and there was the hum of computers throughout the rooms. I checked the server rooms, then found him in the far room, at the long workspace. His back was hunched forward, his skin bare under the fluorescents, blue pajama pants low on his hips. Straddling a stool, he worked over a pile of wires, his tools lined up before him in neat order. I took the leather chair in the corner of the room. Tugging the blanket off the back of it, I wrapped it around my body and settled in to watch him work.

"Hey baby." He didn't turn, the clink of tools the only sign of his activity.

"Hey love."

"I'll be done soon."

"Take your time. Mind if I put some music on?"

"Please. I adjusted the play tracks. Let me know what you think."

I picked up the Laya, Brant's latest prototype, a tablet that wouldn't hit markets for another year. Opening the music center, I was instantly impressed. He had done more than adjust play tracks. The layout of the music center was completely different. I chose my mood: lazy. Drawing an abstract sketch with my finger, a lazy swirl with an occasional dot or skip of interest, I clicked play. It knew my touch, recognized fingerprints in a millisecond. And, within seconds, it was playing the exact song desired—a song I didn't even know, but it was exactly what I wanted. Coldplay. The music flowed through speakers hidden along the walls, and a light display began to dance over the walls.

I loved his house. It was such a stark difference from the condo—which was luxurious efficiency and nothing else. Here, there was life in the walls. Places like this one, with his stamp on it. This was a place I could imagine having a family. A dog. Christmases and holidays. Home-cooked meals.

I curled into the chair and thought of his bedroom upstairs, of the massive walk-in closet and pictured moving in, of waking up each morning in this house, of sitting right here, each evening, and watching as he changes the world.

My hesitancy of love, my fear of it, had vanished. I truly loved this man. I couldn't imagine a life without him. He was the complement to my fears, a man firmly set into the wealth I desired but with the independence and confidence to build his own world of it. Together, we had created a simple life of elegance, exploring the nuances of each other without caring what anyone thought. With this man, I could see the possibility of a family. A genuine life. Being married *and* happy, and not as a trophy wife.

"Do you approve?" He didn't turn, his work continuing as he spoke.

"I approve," I said softly. "You are brilliant, baby."

"Thanks, love."

I watched the flex of his back, the way his muscles yawned when he ran his hands through his hair. Listened to the soft mutter of his words as he spoke to himself. Smiled as the room went dark, crescendos played against my skin, and I fell asleep against the soft leather.

* * *

I was woken by kisses. The drag of his hands across my skin as he pulled me down in the chair, my legs nudged open, the burn of his skin as my bare knees bounced against the hard muscle of his thighs. He shouldn't be muscular. Shouldn't have tan skin, cut arms, a defined chest. He should be pale and scrawny. He spent ten hours a day under fluorescents, before computers. But I didn't question how God had blessed him, especially not in moments like this.

He pulled me forward until I was lying on the seat of the chair, my butt hanging off its edge, his touch soft, probing, lifting my legs to the sky and pulling the soft silk of my shorts, the scratchy tease of my thong's lace moving up and then off my legs. And then I was bare before him, his hands pushing up the cotton of my tank, over my breasts, his body stilling when I was fully exposed before him.

"Perfect," he breathed. He ran his hands lightly, from breast to thigh, back and forth, side to side, just the skim of fingertips across skin, just light enough to make me arch into his touch, begging for more with my eyes. I waited. Breathed. Parted my legs before his eyes and lifted my knees until my feet rested on the edge of the chair, and I was fully exposed before him. His gaze dropped, focused on the place between my legs, a soft groan coming from his mouth, his fingertips dragging lower and running softly over my sensitive lips.

"Perfect," he repeated, his fingers brushing up and down over *that* spot, not pushing, not spreading, just a gentle caress that had me lifting my hips, his name whispering from my lips, wanting, needing more.

Then he pushed a finger inside, and everything changed.

"God..." The curse, tumbling from his lips, as his mouth lowered to mine. Stretching his body forward, the hard muscles of his chest pressed against mine as he kissed me. I wrapped my legs around him, pinned his hand inside me, the gentle movement of that finger causing my breath to catch, my mouth to freeze on his.

"Yes, Brant. Oh my God, yes."

"I love you so much," he whispered, his lips leaving mine, dropping to my neck, his hand pulling my legs apart as he moved down my body, his mouth soft on my skin, a delicious journey downward as his finger continued its perfect tease inside my body. It was amazing what a finger could do. Such a small digit, but able to go exactly right *there*. My back came off the leather, my breath arrested as he touched some place that made my world go dark. "Don't stop," I whispered. "Oh my God, don't stop."

I couldn't keep my eyes open, but I wanted to. Wanted to see the look on his face, the dark intensity that stole over his face when he watched me. Wanted to see the moment he pulled out his cock, wanted to see the firm head of it, his hand wrapped around the base, the rough stroke across the tight skin as he worked it over.

This was his favorite moment—watching me come. It made the skin on his cock stretch as he hardened to a level past belief. It caused his eyes to darken, his breath to hitch. The muscles in his chest tightened, his hands quickened, my name a broken moan on his lips. And I knew what was coming, what would happen as the shudders ceased, as I tumbled down the delicious hill that was my orgasm. At that moment, the most perfect moment my body would ever know? That was when he would remove his fingers and push himself inside. That was when he would fill me completely before starting a rhythm that would trump whatever ecstasy I had just experienced.

And the knowing, the expectation ... opening my eyes and seeing him prepare himself, his own excited anticipation at what was about to happen—his heavy gaze and pant of his breath as his finger continued its delicious work inside of me—I bucked against his hand and came so hard I broke.

Waves upon waves, the sounds from my mouth senseless, unmeaning. I arched against his hand, humped it like an animal in heat, my body exploding around his finger, the perfect flick of his fingers making my legs kick out, the glimpse of his face, dark intensity, his cock, hard and ready, and I tried to savor it as it stretched, beautiful insanity that turned my world into stars and my body into a constellation. Before I fell from the sky, at the moment when my breath began to catch and my eyes flicked open, he shoved inside of me, and I lost it again.

Hard, fast. He fucked me as if he hated me, but the words spilling out were nothing but love. He bent over me and dug his hands into my hips, holding me tightly in place. As he pumped away, the urgency in his movements carried me higher, spurring my pleasure. This was for him, and that made it for me, knowing that the loss of his control was a gift, a rarity that only I could see. I wrapped my legs around his waist and dug my heels into him as I raked my nails across his chest.

When he came, it was intense, one hand tight to my neck, the other squeezing the meat of my ass, pulling me tighter, as if he would never get enough—be deep enough, be one enough—of me. He thrust fully in, moaned my name, and shuddered through the final fucks of his orgasm.

"I love you so much," he whispered and lifted me, keeping his cock inside, spinning with me until he was on the chair and I was on top, stretched out over his body, my chest against his chest, the quick beat of our hearts off sync.

"I love you too, baby."

Outside, I heard the roll of thunder. A storm was coming.

Chapter 15

"When's the event?" Brant took a sip of ice water, his eyes catching the waiter's, the man scurrying to his side with the bill.

"Next Tuesday. I'll call you that afternoon and remind you." Jillian set down her fork, relaxing back in her chair, her hands smoothing the napkin on her lap.

"I'm not sixteen. I can remember a dinner. Though, if you let me have an assistant, you could stop worrying entirely. She could tie my shoes *and* get me to work on time."

His aunt's face softened. "You know you're forgetful."

"You don't have time to keep me organized. You're a busy woman. The company needs you more than I do." He pulled a credit card from his wallet and dropped it on the bill, pushing the folio to the edge of the table.

"You're not busy enough to need an assistant. And I don't want some stranger thumbing through the details of our lives. You and I have looked after each other for twenty years. No need to change any of that now."

Brant looked away from her as his mind wandered and was brought back to square one by her palm, which hit the linen tablecloth with enough force to cause him to jerk.

"Stay with me, Brant," she said sharply. "You're getting distracted, and I need to run. Dinner, next Thursday. Be there."

"Layana will remember. Email her the details." Brant's brow creased when she frowned. "You still hate her."

"No," she spoke sharply. "I never hated her and don't now. Layana is fine, she's just not what you need."

"You don't know what I need. You've never even seen us together. You should come by the house sometime and join us for dinner."

The woman shook her head stubbornly, the glint of light reflecting off her large diamond earrings. "I appreciate the offer, but no." She smoothed her hands over the linen napkin on her lap and lined up her wine glass with her unused dessert fork. "I don't think she would particularly want me there."

He laughed. "Layana? See, you really *don't* know her. She'd love to get to know you better."

There was another uncomfortable shift from Jillian.

His eyes narrowed at the tell. She was hiding something. But then again, he always got that sense from her. "What?"

"Nothing. Any plans for this week?"

"Layana's planned something. I'll need the jet."

If possible, she grew even more tense. "For how long?" She pursed her lips and the wrinkles around her mouth grew into tight spiderwebs. He had begun to notice, after Layana pointed it out, how attached Jillian seemed to be to him. He had always considered it normal, but maybe it wasn't. Maybe this stubbornness against Layana was in protection of their relationship, but that was bullshit. He could be close to both of them.

She was still waiting, and he refocused on her question. "We'll be back by Monday. Don't worry, the work won't suffer."

"It's a very busy time, Brant."

He frowned, thinking over the projects in process. "Not really. No irons in the fire. And you've done a good job of quieting any issues."

"The board meeting is Monday."

"And I'll be back for it," he repeated firmly, watching as she rose to her feet with a quick jerk.

"Please don't forget the Rosewood event. I'll have my assistant send her the details."

Her. He didn't think Jillian had ever muttered Layana's name. A small snub, but noteworthy. Jillian was more of a mother to him than his own. It was important to him that they got along.

Chapter 16

Jillian didn't give up; I'd give her that. From the start, she had laid down a battle line in front of Brant and prepared for war. Every one of our dates had despite her best efforts, his schedule often disrupted by "emergency items" stuck in on a day that should be free. Twice during the preceding months, he had completely stood me up, Jillian texting with a bullshit excuse after repeated calls to his cell went unanswered.

The worse part, Brant let her do it all, and dismissed her actions with a shrug of his shoulders. He wouldn't even tell me what the emergencies typically were. Everything fell under the confidentiality needs of BSX, and I had stopped asking questions, frustrated by my inability to get information or be intelligent enough to understand it.

We were at Nightbird, four courses into their dinner menu, at a coveted table by the window. I waited until a waiter passed, then spoke. "I don't understand why she hates me."

"Jillian's just protective," he explained. "And stubborn," he added, using the edge of his fork to cut into a lightly crusted scallop.

"Protective? Why?" I stared at him across the table, his features lit by the glow of the candles around the restaurant. He wore a loose white V-neck tee paired with designer jeans and the watch that glinted off of his wrist had been a thirty-fifth birthday present from yours truly. He looked every bit a California playboy. What he didn't look like was a genius. Geniuses weren't supposed to come in perfect packages with straight teeth, movie star looks and a muscular build. They were supposed to come with pocket protectors and acne scars, horrible table manners and obnoxious egos.

The beautiful man before me shrugged and took a sip of ice water. "She's always been worried about a woman going after me for the wrong reasons."

I nodded. "That's reasonable." I didn't know a wealthy man who didn't share the same concern. But those same men still ate up the benefits of their wealth and went through twenty-year-old cocktail waitresses like they were Kleenex. Brant ... well. Everything Brant did was different. "Does that worry you?"

He stopped chewing. "Worry about you?" He sounded genuinely confused. "Dating me for my money?"

"Or your brain. Or that cock." I raised my eyebrows suggestively at him, but his serious expression didn't change.

"It's never crossed my mind."

I ran my fingers over the back of his hand, and it rolled under my touch until our palms met. He brought it to his lips and placed a gentle kiss on my fingers.

I smiled. "Thanks for the vouch of confidence."

"Thanks for sticking with me," he said, as if it was a chore.

"We're still on for this weekend, right? You, me, and Belize?"

"Wouldn't miss it."

Our connection was broken by the wait staff, who brought our fifth course, which looked like stuffed goldfish crackers on a bed of stones. They presented the plates as if it they were gold, then quietly left. We picked up our chopsticks and our conversation moved from Jillian to Christmas and how we would divide the holiday between our two families.

But his aunt didn't leave my mind. I understood

protectiveness. I felt the same emotion where Brant was concerned—a fierce need to protect what was mine. The problem for Jillian was that he was *mine.* Not hers. An aunt didn't have any property to protect, no claim over which to assert her dominance. And it was too late. I had him—had never been so sure of anything in my life.

As it turned out, I was a stupid, self-assuming girl, sitting at that table, so smug in my confidence.

I'd never been so wrong.

I didn't have him.

I only owned half of him. The other half? It was a living a life I knew nothing about.

Chapter 17 – Brant

I'd been with a hundred women, but never loved one until her. I could be with a thousand more and never find another Layana. She was beautiful, classy, but with a sharp edge that defined her personality, a thread of dark that complemented all of her light. One that would cut you should you cross her. One that would fight for her wants, her needs, her opinions. She stared in my eyes and loved me with a vehemence all her own. A scary, passionate type of love. One that ripped away all pretenses and allowed us to love each other bare and without consequence.

I understand that my parents were scared. That Jillian fought against Layana with claws out, terrified that her involvement in my life would cause a repeat of the past. But I was stronger now. A man, not the boy of before. I'd never felt so in control, so grounded. It was as if all of the madness, the colors, the insanity, had disappeared. Maybe it's from the medication, maybe it's from maturity. But I wasn't gonna risk it; I'd continue the medication until the day I died. It balanced me, kept me sane. It kept my relationship with Layana safe. With its help, she'd never know.

True love made a person reckless, made them take risks and make sacrifices. True love tested the boundaries of our person, made us yearn to be better and fight for the ground we stand on. I would fight for this love. Lie for it. Steal for it. It was worthy of that. On paper, we were a horrible match. I had no light; she brimmed with it. I was serious; she was fun. But off paper, that was where our magic occurred. I wanted to be more like her. I wanted to listen to her laugh and have had something to do with it.

I loved her completely.

She returned the love wildly.

This love was worth the unsaid truths.

The hidden lies.

Chapter 18

I knew the moment his cell rang, it's rattle against granite, that it brought trouble. I stepped to the island, flipped it over, and saw JILLIAN on the screen. Silencing the call, I returned to my celery sticks and listened to the static of Brant's shower. My bags sat by the door. Brant's were being packed as I chewed, the task handled by two girls who seem well versed in all things travel. I needed to borrow them for the next trip. Hell, with their level of efficiency, I should just move them into the guesthouse. They'd solve half of my organizational issues in a month.

I chewed as zippers sounded and drawers opened, then the two women wheeled a single suitcase by, polite smiles nodding my way. I let them out, returned to my chair, and heard the tone of a voicemail sound against the counter.

The damn woman called back within ten minutes at the inconvenient moment when Brant stood in the kitchen, leaning against the counter, an apple in hand. He stepped forward, picking up the phone. "Hey J."

His eyes caught mine and he pulled the phone away from his ear, pressed a button and the speakerphone came on, Jillian's reedy voice filling the kitchen.

"...maintenance crew has it now. They might need to order a

part; they're running diagnostic tests now. But there's no way it is flight-worthy."

Bullshit. My eyes flicked to Brant's. He said nothing, rubbed his neck as he stared at the phone.

Her sigh crackled through the phone. "I'm sorry, Brant. I hate that this ruins your trip. The plane should be back in order in a few weeks. Maybe you guys can reschedule after Vision 5's launch."

"It's fine. Nothing you can do about it. I'm glad you caught us before we headed to the airport." He reached forward, took the phone off speakerphone, and ended the call with a few short words. Then he tossed the phone on the counter, glancing at me with a wry look. "Sorry babe."

I shrugged and squatted down to unzip my bag and unpack any liquid contents in excess of three ounces. "No big deal. I'll grab my laptop. See what flights are open."

He frowned. "Flights?"

I straightened. "Yeah. Commercial flights."

"I ... don't fly commercial."

I laughed as I rose to my feet. "What do you mean you don't fly commercial? Your body doesn't physically have the capabilities?"

His eyes hardened. "We'll just go another time."

"No." I stared him down. "You'll push it off and we'll never go. I've already set everything up for this trip. You and I have never gone away together. Something always comes up. We're going."

"Commercial." He said the word like it physically tasted bad on its way out of his mouth.

"Yes. First class. Toughen up." This was interesting. Five minutes earlier, I would have said Brant didn't have a snobby bone in his body. Didn't need any of the trappings of wealth and luxury that he spent all day ignoring. Maybe I was wrong. Maybe he gripped all of this as tightly as I did. Maybe he'd be lost in a world that didn't include massages and concierges and enough money to last the rest of our lives. I opened my laptop and placed it on the counter. As I brought up flights to Belize, I cursed Jillian's hand in this. It takes a meddler to know a meddler, and I'd bet ten thousand bucks that there was nothing wrong with the BSX jet.

* * *

"This is bullshit."

"This is normal. Welcome to life." I stared at the back of a Hawaiian shirt, the tourist before us, one who misunderstood San Francisco weather when making his travel plans, anticipating a sunny climate in which sandals and short sleeves would be appropriate in April. I knew this information from his wife, a scrawny woman with sharp elbows and a voice that carried, a voice that had lectured him on his packing choices for the last twenty minutes. In that stretch of time, we had moved half of the distance toward the security gate. Twenty more minutes behind this couple. The flare of Brant's nostrils warned me he wasn't going to make it.

He wasn't handling this well. He'd balked at the long-term lot we left his Aston Martin in, not liking the looks of the parking attendants. He'd been less than crazy about wheeling his bag the half-mile stretch to the terminal. And he hadn't understood, upon our arrival at the Delta counter, that the line of bodies stretching through the space all belonged to people ahead of us in line.

I was sick of his bitching. Hell, maybe this was the reason Jillian didn't expect us to last. Maybe *this* was the deep, dark secret I had anticipated for the last nine months.

Brant was a public transportation pussy.

My brain winced at the crudeness of my inner thoughts, glancing around casually to make sure my obscenity wasn't telegraphed.

Nope, all clear. The line ahead of us shifted and we took one step forward. I glanced at my watch, worried about the time. Too late, I yanked my wrist down and tried to hide the motion with an elaborate yawn.

"We late?"

Brant had become obsessed with the time; certain we were going to miss the flight. He'd checked his watch and calculated our rate of airport progression so many times that I'd taken away his watch and stuffed it into one of the inner compartments of my Jimmy Choo hobo bag.

"Nope," I lied. "We're good."

"I don't think we are. There are 121 people between the first security checkpoint and us, and they're processing individuals at a rate of fifteen to twenty seconds per interaction. If you take an average of eighteen seconds each person, that's twenty-two hundred seconds. Thirty-six minutes. Given that I can't see the next stage of the process, we can only guess at the duration of that wait. But our tickets indicate that boarding ends fifteen minutes before departure. So, unless it's earlier than 3:12, which would only give us a window of twenty minutes for the next stage of the security process, we're going to miss the plane." He stared at my wrist as if the power of his stare alone could force the bones to turn and reveal the time.

I tucked my hands in my hoodie pockets out of pure stubbornness. Why couldn't he be normal? The type of boyfriend who glanced at a watch and stated some unfounded prediction that we might miss our plane? I didn't need intelligent foundations for my worries. I just wanted to move obliviously toward my demise.

The chatterbox in front of us had stopped talking about clothes and had moved into our space, gawking at Brant like he was an informational display, her pokey elbows jabbing into the girth of her husband. He noticed and I stifled a laugh at the alarm that crossed his face.

"Looks like you'll have to recalculate," I whispered as a new line opened to the right, catching the attention of our entire section, heads snapping, feet scurrying, as everyone did a jerky dance where they tried to decide to take the new path or stay in the soon-to-be-shorter current location. "Do we move?"

He watched the traffic, his eyes bouncing, mind ticking, then shook his head. "No."

I stayed in place, stepping forward as our line thinned considerably.

"I'm not sure you were right," I said a few minutes later, watching the speedy pace of the new line.

"About what?" He seemed calmer; the clench of his jaw less noticeable.

"This line being faster."

"It's not."

I looked over at him, pausing in my search for a mint in my purse. "What?"

"This line's not faster. It's going to take an extra five to seven minutes in this line."

I whipped my head right, looking in exasperation at the new line, Hawaiian shirt guy and his loud wife a good ten people closer to security than us. "Then why'd you tell me to stay here?" I couldn't help it. I looked at my watch. 3:19 p.m.

"I watched her." He pointed to the wife of Hawaii. "Then decided on the opposite course of action." He met my glare head-on, and the corner of his mouth crooked slightly.

I couldn't stop my laugh; it burst out with enough force that I had to sit on the top of my rolling suitcase, all of the day's stress leaving in that one moment. Suddenly, it didn't matter if we made the plane or not. If the weekend was a disaster or saved. All that mattered was that I was with him.

I contained my laughter as he leaned down, tugging on my ponytail as he kissed me. "I really do love you," I whispered against his mouth.

"You have no idea how happy that makes me," he replied, and took another kiss. Behind us, an exasperated sigh sounded, followed by the irritated tap of a ballet flat.

Brant pulled me to my feet, his other hand scooping up my suitcase and moving us a few steps closer to takeoff.

I was so happy. So oblivious to the secret hidden in his kiss, the secret that was following us to Belize.

The secret I discovered that first night in paradise.

Chapter 19 - Belize

I woke up to the sound of curtains moving with the ocean breeze. The crash of waves put me in my bedroom but the air was wrong. It wasn't the icy Californian chill, but a balmy caress, warm enough to comfort but cool enough to enjoy. I sat up, my eyes adjusting to the dark, the white linen curtains billowing in the wind, the ocean sparkling under the glow of the moon through the open doors. I relaxed back against the sheets and rolled, stretching out my arm, but the other side of the bed was empty. Stilling, I listened, lifting my head when I didn't hear anything. "Brant?"

Dead silence. No one in our suite but me. I slid off of the bed and felt my way out of the bedroom and through the suite, to the kitchen. My purse was on the counter, and I found my phone inside it and powered it on.

We were staying at an eco-resort that didn't believe in electronics; their website had described a tropical "unplugged" paradise that was distraction-free. It was one of those concepts that seemed like a great idea until we arrived. It only took two hours to realize our attachment to air conditioning and internet, our technology withdrawals peaking at the moment when we failed to find in-room electrical outlets to charge our cells. I flipped on the bathroom light and watched my phone go through its opening scripts, the time finally displaying. 1:22 AM. *Late*.

I called Brant's cell, realizing, as it went to voicemail, that it was off, its battery-saving mission more important than my own. I stepped over to his suitcase, unzipping its top and dug through it, looking for the device. What I wasn't looking for, tucked underneath underwear and swim trunks, was the ring box.

Oh no. My hand froze, as I stared at the black velvet box. *No. No. No*. A woman got proposed to only once, assuming she played her cards wisely. It should be handled perfectly, the correct amount of delighted surprise filling her eyes. This discovery could ruin my reaction. I softly brushed my fingers over the velvet top and fought the urge to pull it out of the suitcase. It would be so easy to flip it open. Take a little peek.

I pulled back and carefully placed his clothes back into order. Zipping the suitcase closed, I stepped away from it and turned off the lamp. I could still be surprised. I hadn't seen the ring. I'd just practice my shocked face. Make sure it wasn't grotesque or too exaggerated. I spotted the bulge of his suitcase's side pocket and unzipped it, finding his phone. I grabbed it.

I placed both cells on the entrance table and took a chance, walking to the back balcony and stepping out. As I scanned my eyes over the beach, moonlight reflected off waves, the sand pristine and unmarred. No billionaire in sight, nothing but nature. Yeah, it was pretty. Big deal. I would have traded it all for a television with HBO.

Granted, it was the perfect place for a proposal. Mrs. Layana Sharp. The name alone put goosebumps on my skin. Was it what I wanted? Absolutely. No question. My biggest complaint with our relationship was that I wanted more of it. More time with Brant. More insight into the beauty that was his mind, so many pieces of him hidden behind his commitment to work. I wanted a partnership, wanted children, wanted to move into his home and fill it with memories. Be his wife. Grow up and have a purpose.

Tomorrow, it seemed, I might have it.

I scanned the beach one last time and then returned into the suite and closed the doors, the sound of the ocean muted. I glanced toward the bedroom and contemplated returning to bed.

I was used to waking up alone. The few nights I had spent at Brant's, he often got up during the night. Headed down to the basement to work or drove to the office. It didn't bother me; I wasn't someone who needed a full night's commitment to feel secure. But here, in this resort, with no work in sight, where was he? And why didn't he leave a note? The questions kept me from returning to bed.

Instead, I went into the closet. The hotel had fluffy cream robes and I pulled one over my silk pajamas, loosely tied the belt, and worked my feet into the matching slippers. I put both of our phones into the pockets with my room key and a handful of cash. Still smiling from the ring box discovery, I schooled the goofy grin away, then stepped out of the suite, tugging the door closed.

I went downstairs to find my future husband.

It didn't take long. It was a small resort—another issue that ensured we wouldn't be returning. There just wasn't enough to do here, especially not for a man who got his kicks off on things that beeped and lit up.

Ten minutes after leaving the room, I walked into the place I should have started my search at—the hotel bar. Brant didn't really drink, certainly didn't seek out social mingling or groups of people. But, at almost 2 AM, it was one of the only places open inside the resort's gates. I walked into the large outdoor tiki hut, scanned the crowd, and saw him at the bar, his back to me, in a cluster of people I didn't recognize.

I smiled, relief washing through me. I didn't know what I expected, what the tight knot in my stomach had anticipated, but the tension eased at the sight of him. I made my way past the steel drum band and toward the bar, my pajamas out of place, a few women at small tables by the dance floor giving me snide looks that deserved a sharp word, but I continued forward. As I moved closer, I fished his phone out of my pocket and powered it on. I'd give him his phone, kiss him goodnight, then make my way back upstairs. I didn't need to stay down there; I wanted to go back to our bed, and he could call me if he got drunk and needed help finding his way back. I smiled at the absurd thought of a drunk Brant and moved closer.

A few steps away. Bodies moved aside, gave me a better view of him.

Closer. My slippers caught on the tile, and I tripped slightly. I caught myself, my face heating.

I heard the murmur of his voice and reached out. Placing my hand on his shoulder, I pulled gently.

He spun on the stool, glancing over his shoulder as he came full circle to face me.

In the next few minutes, everything about our relationship changed.

I had fallen for him. Planned our future, already mentally accepted his proposal.

It turned out I didn't even know him.

Chapter 20 – Brant

I'd intended to propose in Belize.

Cancelled that plan when the jet was nixed.

Reestablished that plan when Layana bullied us into commercial.

Then our trip had a hiccup; she got sick, and the moment never happened.

Tonight would be my second attempt. I shook a pill out, placed it under my tongue and tried to relax. Swigging ice water, I stared at the back wall of my office, a wall of windows offering a million-dollar view of the city.

Everything should be exact. Everything perfect. She deserved nothing less. This would be the moment that solidified our future. A story we would tell our children's children. She was already a loose cannon and will no doubt foil tonight's plans in some impulsive way, but everything is in place to minimize the impact. All that mattered, at the end of the night, is that I would have the ring and could articulate a question. The rest would sort itself out.

She would say yes. It was a given, one that was statistically certain. We loved each other. The bond between us was unquestionable. My personality had needed a quantitative analysis to make my decision, but she wouldn't need anything other than her emotions. The urges that made her throw her arms around me and kiss my neck. The grins I watched streak across her face. The smolder that burned in her eyes when we made eye contact across a crowded room.

She was committed. We were in love. Marriage was the next step to forever. I pocketed the ring and checked the clock, reaffirming that I was on schedule.

Three hours to forever.

* * *

Two hours to forever. I watched her fasten her earrings, the stance before the mirror one of casual elegance, yet sexual all the same. Slightly spread legs, her hip cocked, head tilted, all of her curves present before me. I settled in behind her and our eyes met in the mirror as I pulled her an inch back, the press of her fitting into me perfectly.

She was nervous. There was a darkness in her eyes, a tremor in her hand as she pushed the diamond stud through her earlobe. Something was off—from the deep inhale of her breath to the smile she gave me. It's not the false front she served out to others, but it wasn't the smile I knew. It was a distracted mix of the two. Something was on her mind. Something in her eyes that she didn't seem ready to talk about. I bent forward, inhaled the sweet scent of her as I placed a kiss on her collarbone. "Would you rather stay in? We don't have to go out." It was a question that could ruin tonight's plans, but I didn't want a reluctant companion. Not tonight, at the official start of our life together as one.

Another smile that was off. "No, we should go. I want to." Her breathing was quicker than usual. Maybe I should pull her into the bedroom. Slide up her dress and connect with her. Lose both of our senses in the hard press of our bodies. Reassure myself that she is mine and she is happy.

Instead, I held open her coat, letting it fall over her shoulders and opened the front door for my future wife. Suddenly, everything I knew felt up in the air.

Maybe not tonight. Maybe I'll wait until this funk passes and she's back to normal. I watched as she took the steps down toward the car and followed.

* * *

One hour to forever. She didn't question the helicopter or that night's unorthodox use of the car and my driver. Tucked under my arm, she looks out the helicopter's window, the rooflines of San Francisco tiny against the shoreline as the chopper moved steadily through the sky. As I followed her gaze, the reflection of the setting sun shone off the peaks of rocky waves.

"I love you," she said softly, the words coming through my headset as if she were whispering it in my ear.

My arm tightened, embracing her. She loved to be held; a part of her always hungry for the physical confirmation of our bond. "I love you too."

She tilted her chin up and met my eyes. "Forever," she said firmly.

"Forever," I repeated, leaning down and pressing a kiss against her exposed forehead. The copter shifted and I tightened my grip. "Hold on. We're landing."

Forever. It had sounded ominous on her lips.

***

Despite the wind, the helicopter set down easily on Farallon Island. We opened the door to two men in tuxedos, waiting with outstretched arms to help us out of the chopper and along the irregular ground. Layana immediately took off her heels, and her bare feet were nimble on the uneven surface, a genuine laugh spilling from her as she gripped my arm tightly and climbed over the small hill of rocks, the slick surface of my dress shoes making the journey treacherous.

Just what I needed. I could picture the headline: COUPLE

STUMBLES TO UNTIMELY DEATH JUST MOMENTS BEFORE PROPOSAL. Not that there had ever been a timely death.

It was all worth it when she cleared the rocks. I heard her gasp at the sight of the small table, set on a flat rock with white linen, candles, and champagne. The table was framed by a landscape of rock and sunset-tipped waves, the sunset all purples and pinks above the jagged skyline of San Francisco.

Sitting, we accepted flutes of champagne as a small fire was lit in a pot beside the table. It was all just as I imagined, the small island was a perfect, private sanctuary for this moment.

"Wow. You went all out." She smoothed her fingers over the white linen tablecloth, staring down at it.

"All out would have coordinated a whale sighting. Their union wouldn't agree to my offer, but I'm hoping we see some tonight." I nodded to the waves. "I was told this is the spot to see them breach."

A moment of silence fell as she wrapped her coat tighter and looked out over the water. I wished for a whale, for nature to prove its support of our union with one dramatic show of grace. In my right pocket, folded and unfolded a hundred times, was my speech. I didn't need the paper. I knew the words, had recited them perfectly this morning while shaving. I'd changed the order ten times, the wording twenty. The weight of the paper had been comforting all day, yet suddenly the speech seemed wrong. I threw away the plan and reached for her hand. "You know I love you."

Her gaze moved to our hands. "I know."

No. I needed to see her eyes. To have that connection, to read her. The Layana I knew didn't avoid eye contact and I forged on despite her meekness. "You know that I will do anything for you to make you happy."

She finally looked back up. "I know."

Standing, I moved next to her chair and knelt, pulling out the box that held our future. "I love you with every piece of my heart and vow to spend every day of the remainder of my life making you happy. Let me do that for you, Layana, and please do me the honor of spending the rest of your life as my wife." I cracked open the box, and even in the dusk, the blue diamond glimmered. I held it out, realizing—as soon as I saw her face—all of the red flags in this situation.

The flush of her cheeks.

The tremble of her lips.

Regret in her stare.

Moisture glistening in her eyes.

She closed her eyes tightly, and a lone tear dripped down her cheek. I stared at her face and felt every piece of my carefully constructed world break.

* * *

She wouldn't give me a reason. Wouldn't do anything but cry as I studied every line of her face before she covered it with her hands. She gave a stiff shake of her head, and I closed the lid, putting the ring box back into my pocket, a place that had already grown cold in the last few minutes, the scrape of my knuckles against the cashmere of my coat a sickening texture. Something was wrong. Something had happened and broken the perfection of us.

I needed to find out what has happened. This was a problem. An equation. One to be fixed. We were fixable. Nothing would change that.

I would wait however long she needed. I would fight, until the day I died, for her.

For us.

There wasn't, and would never be, anyone else for me.

Our relationship had been perfect. He was a gorgeous, brilliant man, one who loved me with every spare inch of his heart.

Spoiled me.

Listened to me.

Valued me.

And I loved him—still loved him—passionately in return. I'd already made plans for us. Big plans that sucked up large parts of my heart. Plans involving a house full of children, us growing old as one, a joining of our lives that would never end.

Then, our trip to Belize. One night and every fantasy I had of happily ever after, of children and marriage: gone. I was faced with a hole of deceit and had to decide if I wanted to jump in or walk away.

I could have ended everything.

Broke it off and continued on—tried to find another love, a different happy ending.

Instead, I stalled. I went back and forth over the line of indecision, even while turning down his proposal. I waffled, I moped, I drank. And then ... finally? I squared my shoulders and stayed.

I didn't let on that I knew his secret. But that day in Belize, when my fairy tale died? I lost my trust in him and in our relationship. And a few months later, I met Lee.

Part Two

Lies. A mountain of them between us.

Chapter 22

TWO YEARS AGO

A few months after Belize, I was in a convenience store in the bad section of 82, examining colorful rows of candy and trying to decide which one was worth my change when he walked in. I was out of my normal neighborhood, having driven down to Palo Alto to drop off a package at Brant's office.

He walked behind me and then paused, his presence uncomfortably close, and I turned my head to see who it was.

His stare was like a baby's, so direct you wanted to break contact but I didn't. The aggressive eye contact was so unlike Brant's that I mentally stuttered, caught in this moment in time where we both held the stare, and then he smiled.

Wow. Cocky. Confident. Sexual. Again, so different from the fixed intensity I was used to with Brant. I was drawn to it, and my own mouth curved in response.

"Hard decision," he said, nodding his chin to the shelves.

"Yeah." I nodded like a marionette doll; my goofy expression still painted in place.

"Wait, I know you..." he said slowly, genuine recognition dawning in his eyes.

I stiffened, dreading yet curious about whatever words would come next.

There was an 'aha' moment when he made the connection. "Brant Sharp's girlfriend, right?" He spun to the left and scanned the magazine rack behind us, his hand skimming over the glossy covers and then grabbing one. A groan vibrated through my clenched jaw at the selection.

It was *Wired Magazine*—the go-to for geeks in America—which had just crowned me Tech Hottie of the Year, an "honor" that should have gone to someone actually in the tech industry, not just a girlfriend of this century's brainchild. They'd plastered my image on the cover—a provocative shot where I was naked, covered in artfully arranged wires, a keyboard held over my breasts. And there, in giant letters across my midsection, my photo's validation: "Lucky Layana: where Brant Sharp gets his creative inspiration."

I snatched the magazine from his hands, took four steps to the side and stuffed it behind a few issues of *Martha Stewart Living*.

"Well now, that just answered my question," he said with a smile, putting a hand on the rack and leaning in just enough that I could smell the scent of fresh grass coming off him.

It was a good smell. I stole a discreet sniff and then stepped back. So ... he didn't *really* know me. He'd just recognized me from the magazine, either the *Wired* cover or another one. Over the last few months, Brant's media machine had gone into overdrive and put me on seven of them, the PR campaign headlined by Jillian, a woman who had jumped fully onto Team Layana. On the night I found out Brant's secret, we mended fences in our common goal to keep it. The stiffness was still there, but with the secret now shared between us, she had moved her energy onto things other than ending our union. Her recent efforts centered on pushing me into the spotlight. I knew what she was doing. She wanted the focus off Brant; his privacy left intact while the vultures feasted on me. It'd been working. I'd done five feature interviews so far. In a decade, Brant hadn't done one.

The media machine had coined me Lucky Layana, due to my supposed inspiration for Brant's last creation: the Paya. The Paya had doubled BSX's bottom line that quarter, all thanks to me, according to the media's mind. Ridiculous.

"So are you?"

My candy selection was looking like a lost cause. "Am I what?"

"Lucky." His voice grated with intentions, desire, and dropyourpanties sex.

Our eyes met, and I inhaled at the heat in the contact and the draw I felt to him. This was nothing like how it was with Brant. This was electricity and danger and raw need. I should have looked away. I should have turned and left. Instead, I stepped closer, until we were almost touching, and looked up into his face. "Why don't you try me and find out?"

He chuckled and stepped back, the yellow suede of his work boots creaking on the linoleum floor. "You're not that kind of girl."

I swallowed the apprehension that rose in my throat. This was wrong. This was bad. I should run home, wait for Brant, and forget this had ever happened. My voice disobeyed, coming out cool, confident. Exactly as I'd always wished a flirtation to sound, yet *this* was the time when I finally nailed it. "I'm not that kind of girl? Then you really *don't* know me."

"Anybody can talk big in public." His cocky smile was back.

"Then take me somewhere private." The challenge was clear and confident, even as my conscience screamed through my bones.

Private turned out to be the back of the store, a gravel lot enclosed on both sides with a privacy fence and junk cars, an abandoned bucket and empty cigarette packs that littered the ground. He shoved me against the wall of the store, pulling my red sleeveless tank down over my shoulders, the linen neckline popping as it stretched beyond its means, his strong hands ripping the fabric until the pale top of my breasts were exposed, peeking out of the cream lace of my bra. "Nice," he murmured, and I sank against the concrete at the approval in his voice.

He yanked my bra down until my breasts hung free in the warm sun. His rough hands cupped and squeezed them as his pelvis pressed against me. His chin lifted and our eyes met.

Everything paused, and in the moment, my sanity screamed at the top of my lungs.

I needed to get out of there. Push him aside. Sprint to my car. Gun the engine and tear out of the lot. What was this risking? Anything? Everything?

He broke my thought process with a low chuckle. "What are you doing with me, Lucky? Aren't you late for afternoon tea?"

I growled at him and leaned forward and bit into his neck, the taste of his skin one of sweat and salt, dirt and want. A far cry from the cologne and professionalism which I was accustomed to. "I thought you were a man of action. You nervous? Worried you can't compete?"

His hand fisted my hair, and he pulled my head back until I was staring full force into his eyes. They were now dominant and hard, the playfulness gone and nothing but competitive forces at play in their depths. I'd seen that look in Brant's eyes before when he was attacking a problem or going after a competitor. Never when he stared at me.

"I'm worried I'll fuck you so well I'll ruin you for life."

I liked it. I wanted it. I wanted that intensity to fuck me until I couldn't walk.

And that he did. Right there in that overgrown parking lot. Exposed to anyone who would have walked back there. Against the wall, my shoulders rubbed against the concrete. When he bent me over the hood of an employee's car, my bare breasts dragged back and forth against the warm metal. Heaven cursed my soul while I spread my feet and let him take me deep with a cheap condom on his cock.

It was hard and dirty and hotter than I'd ever gotten it before, including from Brant. He fucked me to use me, his focus on his pleasure, his attraction to me not filtered in any way. It should have felt wrong, it shouldn't have been hot, but it was, and I came hard, my hands gripping the rough surfaces, my legs shaking, the pleasure ripping a forbidden path through my body.

He finished a minute later with a roar, not attempting to quiet his voice, his cry whipped by the wind, my own moan loud against his neck, his hands tight on my ass, pulling me into him, the gasps and pants letting me know how long, how good, his finish was.

"Damn," he swore and pushed away, his cock dropping out of me, one of his hands hard against my shoulder, keeping me pinned to the car as he stripped off the condom and tucked his cock back into his pants. He zipped up his jeans with one hand and let out a hard laugh. "So that's what the other half gets."

"Screw you," I shot back, with as much challenge as I could, given that my white shorts were stretched tight around my ankles, my expensive tank top stretched to pieces, my tits hanging out. A strong breeze gusted, and my nipples responded, the skin tightening, my body still humming with arousal.

He squatted and gripped the top of my shorts, working them up my legs. I moved my feet closer together to help, my jeweled sandals scraping against the gravel as the heat of his fingers dragged up my legs. As he rose, his gaze held mine, the direct eye contact more invasive than his cock.

At my navel, his knuckles brushed against my soft skin as he fastened the button, then he slid his hands higher, brushing over the curve of my breasts, my breath hitching as he turned his hands over and squeezed them almost hard enough to hurt.

I felt every single finger as they spread across my chest. He alternated the pressure, and I would have laughed except that I was on the edge of asking him for round two.

Abruptly, he pulled my bra into place and my shirt higher. With clothes between us, we suddenly had less in common.

"Get back to his mansion, Lucky. I'm sure he's waiting."

"He's not."

He grinned again, this one less playful, harder, cynical. "You always fuck strangers within five minutes of meeting them?"

"Did they leave that fact out of the article?"

"I guess high-class bitches like cock just like any other."

"I guess lowlifes don't know how to take a girl on a date."

A catch in those eyes. A slow nod, the corners of his mouth turned up a tad, a dimple breaking through. Brant had a dimple, though I hadn't seen it in months. "Then let me take you to lunch."

I glanced at my watch, the Tag sparkling brilliantly against the afternoon sun, framed by California-kissed skin. "A little late for lunch."

"Then beers. Unless that's too lowbrow for you."

I shrugged. "I can fuck in a parking lot, so I think I can down some dollar wells."

His face darkened, and I had already seen more emotion from him in thirty minutes than in the last month with Brant. Ever since my rejection of his proposal, he had withdrawn into his work and into himself. It was the first time I'd seen his feelings hurt, and the result was a prickle cactus in a frozen desert. This man, on the other hand, was a ball of fire. I couldn't step away from the flame.

We got in his vehicle, a Jeep with an attached trailer that was full of mowers and tools. My eyes skipped over the contents, inventorying everything, and his eyes caught the movement.

"Sorry. Left my Ferrari at home."

He drove with one wrist resting on the steering wheel. The seats were vinyl, and I ran my fingers over a crack in the seat. It was maddening, the urge to pull open the glove box and check the registration, to put a name and some bit of understanding to the man who sat beside me. The Jeep hitched, then jerked, throwing me against the door as he tore out of the parking lot, past my white Mercedes.

"What's with the tools?" I had to yell over the music, some

country song about broken hearts and Texas, and his hand left the shaky shifter to turn the dial down. It shouldn't have been a sexual movement, the easy way his hand gripped the shift knob—but it was. I forced myself to look away and tried to figure out what the hell I was doing and where this would go.

"I do landscaping. Cut, trim, edge, plant. Hard manual labor." He glanced over. "That work for you?"

"It doesn't need to work for me." I gripped the seatbelt. Hoped his next tight turn didn't tumble us into the ditch. Whoever decided on pulling the doors off of this vehicle was a lunatic. Wasn't the safety rating and rollover risk of these through the roof?

"You always such a bitch?"

I laughed. Shook my head. "No." Brant would never call me a bitch. Didn't use words like that. Thought of them as unintelligent, a waste of syllables when there were so many more appropriate terms.

"So, I'm just special?"

"You're ... different," I mused, unsure how to say all of the things I didn't need to say.

"I'm just ordinary, Lucky. That's not necessarily a bad thing."

No. A piece of us all yearned to be ordinary. I'd like to escape into it myself sometime.

He pulled up to a bar I had never seen, in a part of town I have never visited. Toasty's was sandwiched between two larger bars that probably served food and had waitstaff and a sanitation rating above a D. But we walked into Toasty's, and the bartender looked up with a familiar smile and greeted him by name. *Lee.* Wouldn't have guessed that. Lee fit strangely on him, would take some mental adjustment. Guess we'd missed introductions in our romantic rush to the back lot.

The first stool I sat on wobbled badly and an attempt at stool #2 was also a failure. I accepted my fate and hooked my feet on the rungs and looked over into the bored face of the bartender.

"Whatcha want?"

"What do you have?"

"Millers, Buds and Pabsts."

Super classy. "Miller Lite, please. Bottle."

I got a draft two minutes later, the glass looking less than clean, a plastic cup more welcome, had one been available. I took a strong chug of the beer, happy to find it cold, then set it down, feeling his eyes on me. I glanced over at him and damn...

His smile was my kryptonite. It was shy in the way that only a confident man can pull, a slow drawl of a mouth that asked you for permission to step inside and fuck your mind.

I took another sip of beer, and he studied my mouth. Even when his smile stopped, it continued in his eyes. He fucked me with those eyes. I felt them pull off my clothes and push me back, climb on top of me and make me his. I couldn't look away; I couldn't help but smile in return. I should be confident, I should hold the cards, but instead I blushed and lost track of thought. This man, he could be the death of me. The risk pounded through my mind. I should stand up, leave—but I couldn't budge. With everything with Brant so off-kilter, it might be worth losing our war for time in the battle with him.

He wiped his mouth with the back of his hand. "Anyone ever tell you you're weird?"

"In what way?"

He laughed. "Every way." He took a deep sip of his beer, then reached over and grabbed my stool in between my legs, his hand brushing against the crotch of my shorts as he gripped the wood and pulled it, my hands gripping the bar for balance as he dragged the stool and me toward him, stopping when I was in between his legs, his hand on my bare thigh, sliding confidently up the muscle until he reached the hem of my white shorts.

"You're pretty weird yourself."

"You don't know me yet."

He was right about that. This man was a complete mystery to me. "I have a pretty good idea."

"I'm glad one of us does."

I stared at him, fascinated, by the way his fingers dipped under the line of my shorts, how he was sexual and frank, yet aloof. He showed disdain and attraction for me all at one time and acted as if it was completely normal. But most fascinating, most tempting: all of the ways he was different from Brant. He tipped back his head and emptied his glass and there was pure masculinity in every movement, even the scent of him—one of earth, grass, and sweat. And he had doubled down on the vibe with how he had fucked me against the wall. Right there in the open with hard, invasive thrusts, as if he was marking me with his cock. He was the type of man I'd always run from but might be the type I'd always needed.

He pulled me to the edge of my stool and lifted one leg over his, then the other, until I was all but straddling him, the push of his jeans against mine maddeningly stimulating.

"Kiss me." He pulled the beer out my hand and set it on the counter. Facing me, he cupped my face and stared into my eyes. I closed my eyes and exhaled.

A long moment passed, and nothing happened. I cracked an eye open.

He was smiling at me. "I didn't say, 'be kissed.' I said, *'kiss me.'*"

Huffing in frustration, I fisted his shirt and yanked him toward me, the force of it pulling me off the edge of the stool and onto his lap. I attacked his mouth, surprised at how soft and supple his response was. His hands curved down my back and pulled me tighter to him.

God, I loved my mouth on his, the flex of his tongue under mine.

He rotated on his stool, taking me with him, pinning my back against the bar, his mouth breaking from mine long enough to speak.

"You want more?" he whispered. "Cause my dick wants to feel the inside of your mouth before I send you back to him."

"I want more," I gasped.

Two minutes later, we were in the bar's bathroom.

It was cramped, a tiny cube with a pedestal sink screwed to the wall, condom dispenser on the wall, sticky tile beneath my feet.

He forced me back against the door, and it slammed shut in the frame. He tasted like beer and kissed me deeply, frantically. He pulled away long enough to work my red tank top over my head. He unhooked the back of my bra and skimmed the straps off my shoulders.

A heavy sigh tumbled from him as he scooped my newly freed breasts into his hands, his hold tender. "God, these are beautiful." His gorgeous mouth nibbled the delicate skin, and I inhaled deeply as his tongue circled my nipple, then sucked it into his mouth.

The back of my head dropped against the door as I heard the metal ting of his belt against the tile as his jeans fell. I skimmed his shirt off his muscular torso and then he was fully naked. His eyes, when they met mine, showed the breaking point of his control. And God, he was hard. I could see it in my peripheral vision, felt it as it bumped against me.

"Get on your knees," he rasped.

I had no interest in getting on that floor. I'm pretty sure it hadn't been cleaned in months. But I had every interest in taking him in my mouth. Every interest in making that raw look in his eyes continue. I snagged his pants, created a pillow for my knees, and dropped down.

Even though I'd done this a hundred times, it felt different. Opening my mouth, wrapping my hand around the complete stiffness that was his cock, licking my lips and hearing him inhale ... I'd never been this wet. Never wanted this so much. I craved his hard hand on the back of my head, the impatient thrust of his hips, needing to look up in his eyes and see both disrespect and desire in one heated stare. I dove down on his cock, pumped my hand, inhaled through my nose, and took as much of him as I could, gagging at times, my mouth finding a rhythm, the groans from his mouth letting me know I was doing it well.

I sucked him until my jaw ached. My movements slowed and he pulled me up. Reaching down, he pulled at my shorts, the button popping off, and then I was also naked. He spun me around until we both faced the dirty mirror.

We both looked like wild animals, our eyes wide, chests heaving. He reached down, digging through his pockets and I put my hand up on the mirror, needing to prove to myself that the naked woman in the dingy bathroom was me, that this was actually happening, that we were about to have sex in a bar bathroom. Something bumped against the outside of the door, and I heard a new song start on the jukebox.

"Bend over," he growled in my ear. I obeyed, leaning against the sink and watching our reflection as he looked down, wrapped his cock in a condom, tested my pussy, and then shoved inside.

I gripped ahold of the sink and tried not to scream, but ohmygod I was addicted.

Chapter 23

We returned to the bar where two warm beers waited at our spots, the bar twice as full as when we left, meaning six bodies now filled the tiny space. He picked up the glass, downed the drink, then pushed the empty glass forward. "Thanks for the beer."

I raised my eyebrows and ignored my own. I checked my phone for any missed calls. None. "Thank *you* for the beer."

He shook his head. "Naw. I'm pretty sure your drinking and fucking budget is bigger than mine. I'll be outside." He swung by me, shaking a few hands and slapping backs on his way out, his stride relaxed and confident. Apparently, he was well known here. Had he christened the bathroom before? The thought made me sick.

I looked back at the bartender, who gave me an expectant look. "He got a tab?"

"Not one he's paid recently." The man reached for our glasses, raised an eyebrow at my full one, then dumped them both out.

"Figures." I dug in my pocket, came up with a twenty, and placed it on the counter. "So, he comes in a lot?"

He shrugged. "Once a week, sometimes two."

I glanced around the dingy place and wondered why, of all

places, he came here. I nodded toward the cash and swallowed all of the questions I wanted to ask. "Thanks."

"No problem. Always great to see one of Lee's girls."

I paused, turning around to glare at him. "I'm not one of his *girls*."

The man snorted back a laugh, shrugging as he plucked up the twenty and stuffed it in his front pocket. "Whatever."

One of Lee's girls. The words screamed through my head as I pushed out the door and walked toward his Jeep. My stomach tightened with anxiety at the sight of him in the driver's seat, his fingers tapping on the door sill to some rock song that had a bunch of screaming. *Rock.* Brant liked Andrea Bocelli and I winced as a loud expletive crackled through his speakers. I crawled up into his jeep and quietly suffered the ten-minute car ride back to the convenience store, the wind whipping my hair as his speakers pumped and the vehicle bounced and rocked over the uneven road.

He came to an abrupt stop behind my car, his eyes sweeping over my convertible. It had been a Valentine's Day gift, one that had put Brant back six figures. "I assume this is you, Lucky."

"It's Layana." I grabbed my purse and unclipped the seatbelt.

He flipped open the ashtray and fished out a business card, the edges worn and bent. "I'm not crazy about that name."

"I'm not crazy about Lee."

"Whatever. Call me if you want another round." He grinned at me and held out the card. Revved his engine as if he was ready for me to get out.

I took the card and stared at its cheap font. *He has a business card.* The fact was both ridiculous and endearing. I wrote my name, number, and home address on the back of a Burger King receipt that was on the floorboard and passed it to him. Then I got out.

He pulled off without saying goodbye, and the trailer's tires sent a cloud of parking lot dust into my face. I got into my car dirty, my hair wild, my shirt stretched out, my shorts still missing its button.

I pulled over three exits before home and parked in a grocery store lot. Locking my doors, I lowered my forehead to the leather steering wheel and began to cry.

Chapter 24

I stripped as soon as I entered my bedroom, needing the shower but reluctant to wash off his scent. I smelled like Lee. Oil and grass and dirt and sex. It was out of place in my world, in my bedroom, in my life. So different from Brant, so outside our box. I liked the different. I wanted more of it. More than I could get from Brant, more sides, more than the man who put me on a pedestal and engaged me intellectually and proposed to me in the moonlight.

I turned on the shower but didn't step inside. Instead, I put my leg up on the tub's edge and pushed my fingers inside. I closed my eyes against the soreness there. What would it feel like after an entire night with him? Would that—could that—ever happen? Pulling out my fingers, I opened the door and slowly stepped into the hot stream of water. I cried again as I washed every part of the day off my body.

I stayed in the shower for over a half hour, then slowly turned off the railhead, then the body jets. Grabbing one of the white fluffy towels from the warmer, I wrapped it tightly around my body and stepped out.

I had to finish. I had to get dressed. I was having dinner with Brant that night, assuming he showed up.

* * *

Lies. There was a mountain of them between us, the linen tablecloth too pure and small to hold them all. They tumbled down the sides, spilled around and crowded the twin lobsters before us, the melted butter catching some of them in its flame.

I had many; he had few. I was fully aware of my deceit, and I could only guess at his. We'd talked for hours in this relationship, but had said little that wasn't, in some part, a lie.

"I heard that you're honoring your parents at the Xavier Event," I said.

He nodded as he cut a piece of asparagus. "I've decided to name the new building in their honor." The building was a hundred-million-dollar investment, one that would have their names on the top. A kind gesture, but a frequent one. Three of them on BSX's campus already bore my name, the challenge of a new employee finding his way to the right one becoming a hazing practice among veterans. Other boyfriends gave roses; Brant gave buildings. Literally gave them. My name was on the property deeds, his companies now paying me handsome rent each month.

I took a sip of wine and savored the taste for a moment before swallowing. It was a 1961 La Mission Haut-Brion, and it was perfection. "Are you giving the building to their foundation?"

He nodded and cut a piece of steak. "Tomorrow, can you get with Jillian? Look over the foundation's endowments this year and see if you agree with where they are going."

It was a process that I would normally embrace, but I winced at the thought of the hours it would require with Jillian. I forced a smile. "Sure. I can prepare you a summary of the organizations and the impact—"

He waved off the offer. "It's fine, as long as you're happy with them. What'd you do today?"

An abrupt change of conversation was typical of Brant, yet I felt thrown onto the stand. "Ran errands. Took a nap." Liars elaborate. My tongue was proving the fact true and itching to get creative. I set my jaw.

Brant reached over and gently touched the top of my arm, a habitual gesture, one I loved. A mini-connection in our love life. "Sounds nice."

"Maybe you can take off tomorrow," I suggested. "Spend the day in bed with me."

He shook his head. "Not a chance. I'm close to breaking the battery capabilities of Onyx down to a fifth of current levels. Which could mean—"

"That you're brilliant," I interrupted with a smile.

He shrugged. "That I'm lucky."

I shot him a wry look, and reached across the table, spearing a piece of his meat and bringing it to his lips. "Promise me after you crack the battery issue that you'll celebrate with me. Give me two days, wherever I want to take you."

"I promise." He took the food offering and chewed, settling back in his chair as the tuxedoed waiter approached.

* * *

Two weeks later, he completed the build of a battery slimmer than the closest competitor by half, one that would run for nine days without charging. I planned a vacation to Colorado. Booked a house. Scheduled the jet. But we didn't go. And I understood.

Chapter 25

I tucked Lee's business card into the frame of my bathroom mirror. I eyed it while applying mascara and lipstick. I memorized it as I brushed my teeth and flossed.

When I closed my eyes at night, I thought of him. When my hand stole underneath the covers and pressed hard against the ache between my legs, I thought of him. I watched the sunrise over my lawn as I sipped coffee and considered hiring him to cut it. Then I thought of all of the ways this would crash to the ground.

I knew that I shouldn't call him, but I couldn't stay away.

I lasted a week, then I called him. He didn't answer and there was no voicemail setup. I waited a week, then called again. The third week, nothing. I grew frantic, then panicked. I had wasted our time together with sex—but damn, the sex. And now, I knew nothing about him, and the harder I looked for him, the less I found.

I tried to push him out of my mind and focused my attention on Brant. I moved more of my items into his house. Took a second office near his lab. We bought a house together in Hawaii. Spent a day at Big Sur. I tried, desperately, to forget Lee. Tried to find parts of him in Brant. Failed miserably at both.

I started to call Lee again. Week seven passed. Then eight. Still no voicemail, still no answer. I went back to Toasty's. Twice. I asked too many questions but got no answers. He was a ghost to them as much as he was to me.

And then, four months after our first meeting, I found him.

Chapter 26

FOUR MONTHS LATER

"What are you doing here?" Lee came to a stop beside his Jeep and flipped his keys in his hand as he stared at me. The man was not afraid of eye contact. While Brant's eyes were constantly on the move, following his mind, this man's gaze glued and rooted me in place, his focus unnerving. Maybe because his mind didn't move, didn't function enough to wander.

"I saw your Jeep. Thought I'd say hi." I gave a breezy smile and tucked a runaway strand of hair behind my ear.

"Just driving by?" His eyes flicked over the street. Found my car, then returned to my face. "Doesn't seem like your neighborhood."

It wasn't my neighborhood, but the hardware store was less than a mile from where we met. Two blocks from the bar where he ordered me onto my knees in the bathroom. I shrugged. "I was visiting a friend." *Stalking you.*

"Still that rich dick's bitch?" His gaze didn't leave my face when he said the crude words. They rolled off his tongue like marbles, smooth and glib, and the heat of his gaze was causing arousal to coil in my belly. Damn, I wanted him. His stance, legs slightly spread, full masculinity on display, the strength of his body showcased in the tight shirt and worn jeans, work boots on his feet.

"Yep." I stepped closer, my heels crunching on the gravel, and his dominant stare journeyed down the length of my body, a smirk forming at my red pencil skirt and white button-up top. "Still want to fuck the rich dick's bitch?"

His smile fell and he reached forward and hooked his large palm around my waist and pulled me flush against him. I stumbled, my heel turning in the gravel, and I grabbed his strong arms for balance. He leaned back against the Jeep; his mouth hard as he kissed me hungrily. My hands tangled in his shirt, prodding, feeling, and he hissed against my tongue when I found and gripped the crotch of his jeans.

"God, you are one fucked up woman." He placed his hand over mine and let me feel his hardening erection, the emerging push of it against his jeans. I squeezed, savoring the feel of him.

"Okay, stop," he muttered, pulling his mouth off mine as he pushed my hand away. "Fuck," he swore, rubbing a hand over his mouth and studying me over his knuckles with a wary glance. I stepped back, sensing his trepidation, unsure what was prompting it. "Fuck," he repeated. "You are crazy."

I met his gaze and said nothing. I was crazy. Being here, looking for him, falling right back into his arms without asking any questions ... it was all crazy, especially the way my body was crying out for more, more, more. It wasn't like this with Brant. I didn't know why it was so different, didn't understand it, but regardless of the reason, my sexual connection with Lee was so much stronger. He had to feel the electricity between us. His eyes said he did. They were steady on me as he chewed on his thumb, thinking.

"I have a girlfriend," he said finally and dropped his hand. He pushed off of the Jeep and lifted his chin. "Is that a problem?"

The moment froze and crystallized, like shards of ice on a pool, spiderwebbing and crinkling underneath me until the statement slammed, full force, into the center of my heart. *I have a girlfriend. Is that a problem?*

I tried not to let my face show the war of emotions that were throwing a panic party in the front living room of my head. This was bad. Horrible. Heartbreaking. "No," I whispered, and I cleared my throat. "No," I repeated, hoping he couldn't hear the lie in it.

"Well." He climbed into the Jeep and glanced over at me. "It's a problem for me. So, I guess I'll see ya, *Lucky*." He sneered the nickname, as if I was anything but, and the tone hit like a slap in my face.

I was still standing there, heels askew on the gravel, my face red, panties damp, mind whirring, when he floored the gas and left me in the middle of the hardware store parking lot. His head didn't turn, and he didn't look at me when he drove past. He just left, and probably to go to *her*.

I have a girlfriend.

My hands curled into fists and anger took center stage over my hurt.

* * *

Brant didn't come home that night. I used my key to let myself into his house, telling myself I was staying there to surprise him with breakfast, not because I wanted him to hold me all night and reassure me that I was loved. Instead, I spent the night alone in his bed, hugging a body pillow and trying not to let my mind wander to Lee and what he was doing.

I closed my eyes, pulled the blanket tighter around me, and wished it was Brant's arm. Finally, around three in the morning, I fell asleep and didn't wake until noon.

Chapter 27 - Brant

When you truly love someone, you cannot walk away. No matter what they do. No matter the lies from their mouth, or the actions from their bodies, you tie yourself tightly to their sail and vow to be there through thick and thin. Let the wind blow you where it may. Even if that place is a crash. Even if that place tears you apart and kills anything good.

Layana was always a storm, but one I entered without hesitation.

Chapter 28

"Her name is Molly Jenkins. She's a med student at UCLA. Dean's List there, was a scholarship athlete until she damaged her ACL." The private investigator delivered the information along with a dark blue folder, which he set in the middle of my desk. We were in my home office, the location chosen with discretion in mind.

"What sport?" I opened the folder and flipped through its contents, each image of the athletic blonde making me grit my teeth harder. She was prettier than me. Younger. Perkier. Was *this* what Lee liked?

"Gymnastics."

I sat back in my leather desk chair, taking my time with the information, which was divided into tabs. Rotating slowly in the chair, I scanned her transcripts, social media posts—even her college application essay was here. I didn't see what I wanted, and I looked up at the man, whose name had slipped my mind. "So, what's wrong with her?"

"Excuse me?"

"I don't want her resume. I want her weaknesses. Does she do drugs? Have a kid? Attend orgies on the weekend?"

His eyes darted to the folder. "My report is very comprehensive, Miss Fairmont."

"And leaves anything negative out." I sat back in my seat. "Where's the dirt?"

"I didn't find any." He drummed his fingers on his knee. "She's young. Too young to have skeletons. Seems like a sweet kid."

Oh great. Hot and sweet. A gymnast, so she could probably bend in ways that would kill a normal woman. "Where does she work?"

"Olive Garden. The one in Stonestown."

"I need a copy of her schedule, what days she works."

He nodded and the downward tilt of his head revealed the hair plugs that dotted his scalp. "Anything else?"

"No." I sighed. "Not yet."

I pulled out my desk drawer and withdrew a checkbook. I quickly wrote out a check, selecting a generous amount that would properly incentivize the man. I carefully pulled off the check and stood, holding it out. "Please call me when you know more."

He grinned, revealing a row of crooked teeth, their tips pointing in more directions than a pencil holder. "Yes, Ms. Fairmont."

I gave him a polite smile and picked up my cell. As soon as my office door closed behind him, I made my call.

Chapter 29

I'd never taken down a girl before. My prep school didn't have the Gossip-Girl types who killed hopes and dreams while modeling couture. My high school friends were nerds. The women at Stanford were laser-focused on grades, internships and futures, no spare effort available to be wasted on things like boys and rivalries.

So, I was entering this game a virgin. But, in my own estimations, a well-equipped one. Financed and intelligent. And ... as a small point for my side ... I'd already screwed her boyfriend. I had some inkling of what he liked and had confidence in his attraction to me, despite the fact that she looked nothing like me. It was as if he'd visited an encyclopedia, scrolled to the section 'Opposite of Layana' and selected her photo. Go figure.

I also had the element of surprise on my side. I was alone in this battle, with no one aware of my scheming, no one's defenses raised. I'd be attacking a sleeping kitten. An innocent, fragile kitten. Ripping her away from Lee and severing any chance of their reconnection.

I should have felt guilty, should have had compassion, but I didn't. Lee was, or would be, mine. No matter what.

* * *

I stood in the steam shower, my muscles tight from my morning run, the strum of hot water lulling them into submission. I inhaled the thick, moisture-filled air and wondered what Brant was up to. He had cancelled our dinner last night and hadn't responded to my texts this morning.

From the teak shelf by the door, my phone lit up with a notification. I twisted all of the knobs to OFF and selected a towel from the warmer. I picked up the cell, my damp finger dysfunctional on the screen, a few attempts needed before I could unlock and view the message, which was from the private investigator.

He's with Molly Jenkins now. Panera on 43rd Street.

I quickly texted back.

Ok, let me know if they leave.

I checked the time. 11:04 AM. I was supposed to be having lunch with Brant at noon. Placing the phone on the white marble counter, I moved into the smaller walk-in closet that was off the bathroom. Flipping through the jeans, I selected a dark pair and pulled them out.

43rd Street was a fifteen-minute drive, if I caught the lights and didn't hit traffic. If I hurried, I could make it there before they left

I dressed quickly, left my hair wet, and took my makeup bag with me. I was in my car within a few minutes, and made it to 43rd without delay, pulling into the shopping center at the same time that Lee's dark green Jeep pulled out. I braked hard, craning my neck to see more of the blonde head in the passenger seat— but then it was careening into traffic and pulling away. My car's display chimed with a text from the P.I., one that displayed on the interior screen.

They're leaving. I'm following.

I pulled a U-turn and then was stuck, a minivan taking its sweet time in making the right-hand turn. I drummed my fingers on the steering wheel and glanced at the dash clock. 11:28. I shouldn't even be here. If Brant found out ... what would I say? How would I explain this? Another text chimed through the car's display. This time, from Jillian.

Brant won't make lunch. My apologies.

Shocker. The minivan pulled out and I gunned the accelerator and wove through traffic, intent on catching up to Lee's Jeep. It took four blocks, but then I was behind them, his open-air vehicle making my surveillance painfully easy.

He drove like he fucked—with reckless accuracy. He hung one arm out the window and his head was often turned in her direction, every glimpse of her smile a knife in my heart. At one stoplight, he rested a hand on her headrest and leaned over, their mouths meeting for one horrible moment before my hand misbehaved and hit the horn. Her head jerked away, and he looked into the review mirror.

I inhaled, wondering if he would recognize my car. The light changed and any connection—if there was one—was lost as he floored the gas.

I hung back, letting a few cars get between us, and tried to figure out where they were heading. We entered the Belmont area, and, with my luck, they were heading down to Los Angeles, and this would be an overnight trip.

It wasn't, because just a few miles later they stopped at a park. I drove past the entrance, then circled around to the other side, idling beside a food truck and watching as Lee got out.

He waited for her at the front bumper and held out his hand, hers fitting into it, and they walked toward the lake, a blanket tucked under her arm, a bag slug over her bare shoulders. She was in a bright blue tube dress that showed off her tan, her blonde hair in French braids, cheap white sunglasses perched on her upturned nose. I pulled out the binoculars I'd ordered online and adjusted them, homing in on the couple.

Hello stalking, I'm Layana. Pleased to make your acquaintance.

* * *

When she ran, he chased her.

When she napped in the sun, he ran a hand gently through her hair.

When he pulled off his shirt and stretched out to enjoy some rare San Francisco sun, I saw the desire on her face.

He was so different with her than he'd been with me. There was none of that dismissive attitude, no cocky arrogance. With her, he was tender and sweet—a playboy tamed.

It was a problem.

I sat in my car and steamed. My hand grew tired of holding up the binoculars, so I set them on the passenger seat. I growled into a handful of pistachios as I saw hints of what might be love. I finished my bottle of water as he laid down on the blanket and pulled her over to him. She straddled him and I focused the binoculars on them, watching as he ran his hand up the front of her dress and groped her breast, right there in the middle of the park. She laughed and I could hear the faint sound of it, even through the windows and way over here. A deep grumble of thunder sounded, and I glanced up at the sky. To the south, a dark cloud dissected the sky and I looked back to the couple, who was also looking up. They kissed, then she stood and he followed suit.

I didn't follow the Jeep when it pulled out. I knew what foreplay looked like. I didn't need to watch them enter a house to know more. The idea of sitting in a car outside and knowing that they were fucking ... I would go nuts. A surge of emotion swelled in my chest, and I swallowed it down. Frustrated, I grabbed the gear shift and yanked the car into reverse.

I needed a plan. I had seen enough. What I needed to figure out was how to destroy them.

Chapter 30

"I was thinking about us heading to the island for a week." Brant spoke across a decadent table full of fruit, quiches, breakfast meats and breads.

I lowered a toasted baguette topped with smoked salmon, pleased at the suggestion. Brant never brought up travel. He was normally so buried in work that I had to drag him, kicking and screaming, away for fun. "Sure, when would you want to go?"

"Maybe Saturday. We just finished the design phase of the photo frames. It'll take the tech team a week or so to get me initial mockups."

I took a bite, chewing slowly as I thought through the timing.

This Saturday, for a week. It was smack dab in the middle of Operation Remove Gymnast Barbie. The timing wasn't ideal, but it was a week with the man I loved. Twenty-four hours a day of Brant and any bit of fun that I could coax out to play. He needed this. WE needed this. It'd been three or four months since we had gone anywhere, his full focus on the last development, then the new one, and soon the next. He lived to build, to improve. And it looked like, for the next week, his focus—his project—would be us.

The island he was referring to was our Hawaiian home, which wasn't its own island, just a private peninsula that jutted off of Honolulu. The property held a twenty thousand square foot vacation home, with private pools, a full-sized gym, spa, library, and theatre. We'd purchased the property last year and had yet to visit it since the closing. We were overdue for this trip, and it would be good to get away. My sabotage of Lee and Molly could wait.

I smiled at him. "Sure. I'll coordinate with Jillian and get it set up."

Finishing his coffee, he wiped his mouth with a white linen napkin and stood, leaving his plate with a half-eaten bagel still on it. He walked over to my seat and leaned over, placing his hand on my knee as he pressed his lips to mine. "I love you."

I looked up into his face and smiled, happy. "I love you too."

"When will you let me be your husband?" There was a quiet husk to the words and a raw need behind the question. I glanced around his dining room, making sure that we were alone. His personal chef was back in the kitchen, and I met Brant's eyes. He was one of the most brilliant men in the world, a man whose fortune was unparalleled, but he was still—in so many ways—a lonely little boy who played in his basement while every other kid was outside. I hated to tell him anything other than 'yes' but I couldn't, not with all of the lies between us, accept his proposal.

"One day," I said quietly.

"A man might get tired of waiting." The curve of his mouth belied his words.

I gripped the front of his shirt and pulled myself to my feet. Wrapping my arms around his neck, I pressed against him. "Well, then maybe I should give you another reason to stay."

He took my kiss and deepened it. He tasted like bitter coffee and I loved the bite of it. I yanked his shirt loose from his pants and undid his belt as he walked me backwards, into the sunroom. He sat on the couch and I was right there, straddling him. As the morning sun streamed through French doors, I distracted him from thoughts of marriage and reassured him of my love in the way I knew best.

Chapter 31

New fact about Molly Jenkins: she liked to drink. In my home office, I looked at the most recent PI report, and page 9 included an inventory of her trash can.

12 empty bottles: Smirnoff Ice
4 empty cans: Bud Light
Tags from an article of clothing: Gap. $24.99
Dry Cleaning receipt: One Price Cleaners
Empty bottle: Kahlua
Empty bottle: Absolut Vanilla Vodka
Thank you card and envelope from 'Mom' (see photo)
Monthly statement from Capital One credit card (see photo)
Empty Bag of Nacho Cheesier Doritos
I called him and he answered on the second ring.
"Yes, Ms. Fairmont."
"Is this normal, all the alcohol?"
"I'm not sure. It's the first bag we've inventoried. It's from last week. I left off all of the food items, but if you'd like we can also include those."
"Food items?"
"You know, banana peels, coffee grounds, leftovers, eggshells—"

"No," I interrupted. "I don't need all that. Just items like this. When will you have the rest of the bags done?"

"I can put someone on it today, if you think it'd be important."

"Yes. Please send me all of the reports as they are done. As soon as possible."

"I'll pull someone off another project and get it to you quickly."

"Thanks." I hung up the phone and looked at the list again. I flipped to the image with her credit card statement. It felt ridiculously invasive, spying on her spending habits, and it was wild how much of her life could be exposed by her trash. I spun in my chair and looked at the silver can that sat a few feet away, under my desk. Wonder how much of my life could be told through its contents. I made a mental note to invest in a shredder. And a trash compactor, if those were still in existence.

I looked back at the credit card statement and tried, between the purchases and the trash, to find an opening, an opportunity. Something to exploit and use. Something to take her down with.

* * *

The P.I. didn't waste time, and sent me four more emails that afternoon, each with a different trash bag inventory from Molly Jenkins' house. Trash pickups at her house were weekly, so unless she missed a pickup, this was a week's worth of garbage.

Amidst the unimportant items, there was more alcohol. I counted six full-size liquor bottles and thirty empty beer cans. If it was all hers, she was an alcoholic—at least by my standards. If she'd had friends over, it was the normal evidence of a party. She was in college, so a party was likely. I sighed, then perked up at the other attachment in his new emails. A bank account statement. I put it side by side with her credit card one and compared notes.

According to the printouts, she frequented The Ginger Break. Had been there five times in the last month, four times on a

Wednesday, once on a Friday. A Google search told me that The Ginger Break was a bar a block from her apartment. Another search told me that Tuesday was $5 Martini Night.

I clicked my pen into action and examined my calendar. Tuesday was three days away. Doable. I leaned back in my chair and stared at the ceiling. Pulling scattered thoughts together, I came up with a semblance of a plan.

First step: Find bait.

Second step: Sequester Lee.

Third step: Watch and enjoy.

Chapter 32

I looked over a pomegranate martini into a pair of deep blue eyes. The modeling agency had chosen well. Marcus's brow furrowed in a way that was gorgeously masculine. His eyes were intelligent, but compassionate. His dark navy suit was tailored and fit his strong athletic build perfectly. He looked like the sort that rescued kittens from trees after listening to your problems. His mouth was full and twitched when he smiled. After delivering the lost kitten, I bet he'd carry you to bed and fuck away any concerns. He set down his beer and studied me. "Why are you doing this?"

I shrugged. "I have my reasons."

He leaned across the high two-top table and lowered his voice. "You seem a little old to be playing games with some adolescent." He tilted his head down to the restaurant's lower layer, where Molly was seated at the bar, reading a thick paperback novel. We were in the upper level of The Ginger Break and had spent the last fifteen minutes getting acquainted and going over the job.

I met his gaze. It was direct, so much so that it ate holes in the dark parts of my soul. *A little old to be playing games.* Yes, Compared to Molly, I was ancient. "Let's go back over the plan."

Marcus sighed, leaned back and stretched his arms out, regarding me with a bored stare. "I know the plan. You go down there, then I go down there. We drink, you leave. More drinks, we leave. I take her home, fuck her eight ways to Sunday, then head on my merry little way."

I shifted, and the knot of guilt in my stomach tightened. "Yes."

He leaned forward, his knee bumping mine, and gently touched the top of my hand. "You know, you have nothing to worry about with her."

I moved my hand away and picked up my martini. "In what way?"

"You're a beautiful, sexy woman. She..." He glanced down at the blonde head that all of this was about. "She's a girl. She can't compete." He leaned closer and winked.

I glared at him with the frostiest look I had. "I didn't hire you to fuck *me*, Marcus. I'm in a relationship. Taken."

He chuckled softly. "Forgive me, Layana, but you're here. You don't look taken to me."

I drained the martini and stood. "Save your lines for her. I'm well-taken care of." I picked up my purse. "I'll see you downstairs in twenty." I counted out a handful of bills for the waitress and placed them on the sticky wooden top and headed for the ladies room.

* * *

I took a deep breath and stared into the mirror. I looked so different thanks to the wig, which had transformed me into a strawberry blonde, one with a short, blunt-cut bob. I'd spent over a thousand dollars on the hot and itchy hairpiece, but the disguise was well worth it. I hoped to never see her again, but I couldn't be too careful. And heaven forbid she recognized me from a magazine cover.

I tucked a fake strand of hair behind my ear and smiled into the mirror. The gesture looked friendly, but my eyes... they gave away the possessive hatred in my heart. I closed my eyes and took a deep breath and tried to release all of the anger I felt for her.

Exhaling, I opened my eyes and tried again. This smile was better —less deranged and more genuine.

It would have to work. Straightening my green sleeveless tank into place, I opened the door and headed for Molly.

* * *

The stool over beside her was open and I took it, ignoring her as I caught the bartender's eye. "Flirtini, please."

I felt her soft touch, a gentle tap on my arm. "Flirtini? That sounds good."

Wow. That was easy. I looked over my shoulder and gave a small smile. The P.I.'s report really skipped over how pretty she was. Her blue eyes sparkled. They were open and genuine, her smile not forced or fake. Her tan was natural, her breasts looked real, and I could literally smell sexuality coming off her. I had a brief glimpse in my head of her and Lee fucking and pushed it away. "It's great. It has champagne in it." I nodded to the bartender. "Here, let me get you one."

"Get me one? Oh no, you don't have to do that." Her eyes widened, as if buying a discounted martini was a generous gesture.

"I don't mind." I shrugged. "I could use the company." The bartender placed two drinks before us, and I pushed Molly's in front of her. "Cheers." I held up my drink. "To taking opportunities."

She giggled and followed suit. "To taking opportunities."

We clinked glasses and then sipped. "I'm Britney," I said.

"Molly."

"You here alone?" I asked, looking around.

She gave a shy smile. "Yeah. I like to get here early on Martini Night. Otherwise, it gets too crazy."

"I can understand that. I like a quieter scene."

She took another sip and her blue eyes widened. "Wow! This is great."

So easily impressed. Maybe that was what Lee liked about her. I couldn't deliver that naive appreciation, no matter how hard I tried. I gestured to the bartender to bring us another round. *Drink up, baby. Drink up.*

She was a friendly and talkative drinker. By the time she finished the second flirtini, I steered the conversation toward Lee.

"Any hot guys come in here?" I looked around as if I cared.

She shook her head. "Not really. I mean some guys, but probably too young for you."

I swallowed a snarky response. "I don't know about that. You have a boyfriend?"

"Oh, yeah." She smiled, as if the thought of Lee appealed to her.

I ground my teeth. "Where's your man tonight?"

She shrugged. "I'm not sure. He's flaky. Sometimes he makes it by, sometimes he doesn't." She tapped the cover of her book, which she'd set on the bar when we started talking. "But that's why I bring a book."

Oh, I bet he's flaky. Tonight, his absence had been carefully calculated. I had a team of three keeping him away from this side of town. I sipped my martini and kept my voice mild. "That sucks. But you know men and their work... " I grinned. "He's probably working hard to spoil you rotten."

It was a carefully executed jab that hit home as her smile dimmed slightly. As if on cue, Marcus entered the bar, our eyes meeting over the crowd, and I leaned forward, gripping Molly's arm with false urgency. "Oh my God," I hissed. "My ex just walked in."

Her head snapped up, female bonding in full force, and craned her neck. "Where?"

"Tall, blond, and gorgeous." I ducked forward and kept my hand locked on her wrist. "Do you see him?"

"Sex in a suit?"

I fought a smile at the unwavering lock of her stare. "Yes. *Please* tell me he isn't headed this way."

"Not yet." She reluctantly pulled her gaze back to me. "What was wrong with *him*?"

"Him? Nothing. His residency was in San Diego, and I might have strayed a little during the time apart." I groaned again for good measure.

"Residency?" She bit on the bait without hesitation.

"Yeah. He's a cardiologist. Plus, an absolute freak of nature in bed." I hopped off the stool and slid two hundred bucks across the bar. "I'm gonna run before I lose my self-respect and beg him to take me back."

"You're leaving?" She shot me a wide-eyed look. "You don't want to talk to him?"

I shook my head. "No, the last thing my heart needs is to be reminded of what I screwed up." I shot a glance over my shoulder, then held out my arms and went in for a hug. "It was really nice meeting you," I said in her ear. *And taking you down.*

"You too. Maybe we'll see each other again? Oh, and thanks for the drinks."

I held the hug for another moment, just to make sure the knife was firmly in her back, then let go. I gave her a regretful smile, then made my way toward the exit.

Marcus would succeed. He was charming and sexy and—as far as she knew—a doctor with the sex skills of a porn star. I nodded to another member of this team, a man whose Google glass, in combination with my downtown condo's security cams, would properly document the entire evening.

I pushed through the revolving door of the bar and stepped out into the cool California night, a genuine smile lighting up my face.

Maybe she loved Lee. Maybe he loved her. But he was mine, whether they knew it or not.

Chapter 33

I was ready for the call when it came. Feet cocooned in a moisture wrap, propped on my coffee table, a Hulu-binge in full effect, my phone rang. I glanced at the clock and answered Marcus's call. "Give me good news."

"She didn't do it." He sounded defeated.

"What?" I sat forward, my feet coming off the table. "Why not?"

"I don't know. She just didn't. I didn't push it, stopped when she said no."

I rubbed my forehead and glanced toward the bedroom, where Brant was sleeping. "How far did you get?" I asked quietly.

"She came back to the condo. We kissed ... her shirt came off. Not much else."

"I thought your skills were better than that," I snapped.

"You should have tested them out." The playful lilt of his sentence pushed me over the edge of poise.

"Fuck you, Marcus. This is bullshit. It should have been child's play."

"She's committed to her boyfriend. She started crying, saying she was making a mistake. What was I supposed to do, unzip and pull my cock out?"

I huffed in annoyance. "No. You did the right thing. It's just ... whatever. Let me know if she calls you. I'm gonna check the camera footage. Unless I say otherwise, carry on with the plan."

"Will do." He paused. "Either this guy's one in a million or you're a psychotic bitch."

I gave a sad smile. "Or both."

"Yeah. Or both." There was a pause and I hung up before he said anything else.

* * *

As Brant quietly snored from my bedroom, I logged into the security app for my downtown condo, a three thousand square foot palace I rarely set foot into. Starting the download of the evening's files, I called Don, the P.I. who had trailed the couple all evening.

He answered with a yawn. "I'm downloading the images from my camera now."

"Got anything good?"

"A few you'll like. I'll email them to you within the hour."

"The sooner the better."

I ended the call, tapped on the downloaded video file, and sat down to watch Marcus's failure.

He had tried, that was for sure. Done everything right. Hadn't chased, had let her come to him. Been aloof, yet sexual. Hadn't bragged about the condo but let her ooh and ahh over the place. When she had crawled onto his lap, he had fisted her hair in his hands, ground her hips into him enough to let her feel his arousal and his equipment. They had kissed ... she had been horny ... it had been close.

And then... I saw the moment he lost the war. Her brain and guilt had kicked into action and she had stiffened, then pulled away, moving into a chair. Lots of crying and hugging herself and rocking and all sorts of ohmygodwhathaveIdone drama. Marcus had stood awkwardly, at one point glancing toward a ceiling cam with a grimace. Then he sat next to her, pulled her into his arms and smoothed the top of her hair. He'd let her cry into his chest until she calmed.

Then, damn her to hell, she had stopped crying and started to talk to him about me. Tried to talk him into taking me back, said I was so nice and missed him and blah-blah-blah. I closed the video before my guilt took over.

Ugh. Why couldn't Molly have been a normal twenty-one-year-old drunk girl who succumbed to the sexy doctor with the big cock and fancy condo? She was dating a yard boy for heaven's sake, one who was flighty and irresponsible and MIA half the time. This should have been easy; I should have won.

Good thing I didn't need her mistake. I only needed the illusion of one.

I restarted the footage and watched again, taking screenshots of the moments that mattered. Then, I reviewed the still shots, confidence growing with each isolated image. Yes. I had enough. And that was without even seeing Don's images.

I sent an email to my graphic designer and attached the images. Don's email popped up and I forwarded that also. The designer would know what to do, which ones to pick, and by the time Brant and I returned from Hawaii, everything would be ready for execution. I closed my laptop and waddled to the bathroom where I unwrapped my feet and rinsed off the moisture treatment.

Soon, everything would be fixed. Soon, Lee would be fully mine.

* * *

The weapon of my plan — a newspaper proof — was beautiful. I scrolled down the long image, checking the title, date, and the side copy that framed either side of our deceit. It was all legitimate and accurate. Should she feel the need to check on the publication, she'd find what I've placed in easy reach.

The beauty of the proof was in the center of the page, the main event. The headline was in giant letters across the top:

AREA SURGEON'S WIFE FILES FOR DIVORCE AMID CHEATING SCANDAL

Then, the photos. Crisp black and whites, one a respectable newspaper wouldn't print, but in this deception, spoke louder than any words ever could:

Molly and Marcus. At the Ginger. His hand on her leg, his mouth to her ear, a smile I'd seen her use with Lee screaming from the page, her features easily recognizable.

Molly and Marcus. In his car, her mouth on his, the press of her hand silhouetted in the window.

Molly and Marcus. In my living room. On my couch. The zoomed-in photo only showed her bare back, leaning over him, his eyes burning up at her.

Molly and Marcus. My favorite. His hands digging into her back, her mouth at his neck, his head back, eyes closed. The crop made it look like he was inside her, getting the ride of his life.

The copy was short and beneath the photos.

One of the city's most respected cardiologists received divorce papers today in what could be the ending of a five-year union. The good doctor was captured in several incriminating photos with an unidentified young woman. There's no word on how long their dalliance has been going on. The majority of the photos received were too inappropriate to print. For questions and leads, please email Don Insit at don@newseagleprint.com or call 415-323-9811.

The page looked stunning, the photos leaping out from the page in a manner that was unavoidable. He would stare. She would stare. He would accuse. She would object or confess. Either way, they would be done. I approved the work, then called Don and verified the plan. He'd print two copies of the full-length newspaper spread. Next week, I'd replace the paper's cover sheet with this one. I'd leave it on her front step with a nasty note, in a place that Lee would be sure to see it. They could fight over the photos, and I'd reap the rewards of my labor.

The plan was flawless and intelligent. I gave myself an awkward pat on the back and hung up with Don. Then I hurried to the closet and took out my Prada tote. We were wheels up in two hours, but I didn't need to pack much. Our Hawaii closets were full, the bathrooms and kitchens stocked by a staff that was expecting our arrival. I'd need my makeup bag, medications and my laptop, little else. I threw a few paperbacks in my bag, along with a new lingerie set Brant hadn't seen. I texted Jillian to make sure Brant was around and ready, then I headed for the shower.

Chapter 34

At forty-thousand feet, I feasted on Brant with an urgency that surprised us both, his mouth dropping when I yanked at his zipper and pulled out his cock. "Here?" he whispered, the question morphing into a groan when I took him soft in my mouth. He began to harden almost instantly. Against my tongue, he thickened, and I had to pull off and readjust my angle to accommodate all of him. He stood in the aisle and gripped my head, his fingers digging into my hair. I gripped his suited thighs and sucked him harder, needier than I ever had. God, I loved this man. God, I wanted him. All of him. I wanted him to look at me and see no other woman. I wanted to be his wife and have his babies, and for none of them, or us, or him to be broken. I wanted the impossible, and I took this instant instead.

There was only a thin curtain between us and the service cabin, and he whispered my name as his legs shuddered beneath my hands. "Don't stop," he begged. "Yes, baby." I knew that scrape of his voice, the huff of his breath, the tightening of his thighs... all the signs that he was close.

And then, the breakdown.

His hand tangling in my hair, the hard thrust of his pelvis up into my throat as he moaned my name and shot his hot release into my throat. My mouth kept working, sucking the cum from him, bobbing up and down, up and down, then he pulled away.

He collapsed into the closest chair and pulled me into his lap, his cock still twitching, still wet from me. He held me in his arms, kissed me hard, and whispered a string of sweet promises and gratitude against the top of my head.

I loved this man with my whole heart.

I needed him.

He completed me.

I closed my eyes, curled into his chest, and felt the wrap of his arms around me.

* * *

I lay in our bed, the whip of the fan above me, and stared at the engagement ring. It was nestled in a dark blue box, the glint of its diamond brilliant, even in the dark. Brant had pulled it out hours before. We had dinner on our home's rooftop deck, the glitter of the ocean our backdrop, expensive wines paired with delicious courses. After dessert, he did the whole thing again, getting down on one knee and presenting the ring.

"You won't give up," I had scolded him with a sad smile.

"I'll never give up on us."

"Me neither," I'd promised him, leaning forward and pressing my lips against his forehead. "But I can't say yes. Not right now."

I wanted the ring. Wanted to be his wife. Wanted forever. I gently worked the ring free and placed the box on the nightstand. Rolling the platinum setting in my fingers, the unique diamond stone glinted at me. It was blue, a color I had never seen on a diamond. Not too large. Between two and three perfect, unmarred carats. It would be the only thing in our union unflawed and honest, with nothing to hide. The stone didn't match us. It deserved an innocent bride marrying a man with nothing in his eyes but love. But maybe those were the couples who got the imperfect, thousand-dollar Zales specials. Maybe the flawless, priceless diamonds were reserved for trophy wives and cheating husbands. Trust fund babies with mistresses on the side. People like Brant and me. Maybe this diamond evened out our deficiencies with a few carats of retaliating perfection. I slid the diamond on, the fit perfect, and it shone in the darkness. I rolled onto my side beside Brant and ran my hand along his back, his tan skin the perfect backdrop to the diamond I would never be able to wear. I leaned forward, kissed his skin, and curled up against his warmth, the weight of the ring comforting. I closed my eyes and dreamt of perfection.

I woke up just before dawn and pulled off the ring. I carefully returned it to its box and back in his suitcase, nestled between sunscreen and rolled socks. Then I returned to bed. I wondered, for a brief moment, if Molly had called Marcus. It was a black thought in a perfect day, but Lee wouldn't leave my head. He stalked my dreams. Dominated my imagination. Pulled on me with insistent hands whenever my mind had an uncontrolled moment. I should have forgotten him. I should have left him and Molly to their life of apparent bliss. But I couldn't. Instead, I was falling for him. Intertwining my life with his until I couldn't tell when mine with Brant ended, and mine with his began.

It was a dangerous game and one that was fixing to get worse. Much worse.

I ran across the sand, my stride used to the give, my speed consistent as I dug through deep places and pounded through the receding surf. At this time of morning, I was alone. There were a few towel boys, setting up chairs in front of the adjacent hotel, but no one else. The solitude, paired with the soothing sound of waves helped to cleanse my thoughts.

I was morally lost. It was official. I'd gotten turned around to the point where I didn't know if I was climbing uphill or down. My obsession, my game with Lee? It was a losing, impossible battle. I knew that. I knew that the smartest thing to do, the safest thing, would be to ignore him and let him live his life. To stay on my side of town with Brant.

I didn't love Lee. I barely even liked Lee. I loved Brant. But Lee was ... a necessity, one that fucked me as if he was created to do it. He was a key that opened another side of my life, away from the finery, a side of life that could be filled with impulse and fun.

I ran faster, my breath ragged as I took out my frustration. I stumbled in the sand and my calves screamed in surrender.

I ignored the pain, going faster. Faster. I ran until my heart ached and my lungs broke, then I sank onto the sand, my knees disappearing into the wet suction, my chest heaving as I flopped on my back. I closed my eyes and stayed in place until my heart rate calmed.

When the sun grew hot and the first tourists started to make their way down to the beach, I rolled over and tried my best to brush the sand from my back. Then I stood up and headed back to the house, and to Brant and the life I should be living.

Chapter 36: Hawaii

"What do you think about moving here?"

I paused, mid-chew, my mouth filled with a spinach and cottage cheese crepe and shot Brant a quizzical look.

He shrugged from his place at the teak outdoor table. We were on the second story deck, just off the kitchen and overlooking the impressive cliffs and rocky beach. "I was just thinking, we could stay a few months, maybe half the year. We could spend the winters here."

I took a sip of fresh squeezed orange juice. "What about the company?"

"I could work from here. Convert the garage into a workshop. Maybe hire a few locals to help during project times."

I grinned. "A few locals? It took you five years to find Frank." Frank, the only BSX tech who had survived Brant's temperamental blowups long enough to learn how to not piss him off. Brant was a sweetheart with me, but an exacting perfectionist with everyone else, and easily set off when others couldn't keep up with his pace and mental calculations.

"Okay, then we bring Frank." He reached across the table and grabbed my hand. "I like vacation Layana."

I rolled my eyes and let him pull my hand to his lips. "What is vacation Layana like?"

He pursed his lips and tilted his head as if to consider the question. "Carefree. Less uptight."

Less uptight because on vacation, Brant was with me all the time. I didn't have to wonder where his mind was, or if I'd be eating alone at dinner. Without the stress and schedule of work, he was 100% mine. I swallowed that truth and stuck out my tongue at him in jest. "Everyone's less uptight on an island. Or maybe it's the fact that I'm a thousand miles from Jillian."

"Oooh ... easy now. She's probably got this place wired." He glanced around, but even though he was kidding, the truth was, she probably did. She was probably listening to us right now.

I wiped my hands on a napkin and tossed it down. Pushing to my feet, I sauntered over to his side of the table and straddled his chair. Lowering myself onto his lap, I ran my hands through his hair. "In that case," I whispered, nipping his ear playfully, "we should put on a show."

"I'm in," he growled. He pulled at the sash of my red satin robe, then peeled it off my shoulders, exposing my black lace bra.

And right there at the breakfast table, under the warm glow of the morning sun, and in earshot of any hidden microphones, we did just that.

Chapter 37

The jet takeoff was smooth, a thousand parts of machinery working in perfect synchronization to bring Brant and me back to San Francisco. Once we were at altitude, I unbuckled and moved to the bedroom in the rear of the plane. I pulled back the dark navy sheets and fluffed the pillows. "Brant," I called out. "What do you want to watch?"

I picked up the remote, flipping through the options on the touch screen. Brant entered the small room and wrapped his arm around my waist, pulling me toward the bed. I shrieked in protest and managed to slide the door closed before falling on the bed.

"I want to watch you come." He grabbed the tablet and tossed it aside, then gave me that intense look, the one that told me he was about to give his full concentration to a task. Putting one knee on the bed, he started to work my pants off.

"Oh, fine," I conceded, his breath hot against the top of my knees as he pulled off my sandals and then the pants. My head dropped back when his hot mouth kissed his way up my thighs and then settled between my legs. "Do what you do best."

A half-hour later, I could barely move, my body lazy and limp from pleasure. Brant rolled me over until his body was cupped around mine, and we watched a movie with Gene Hackman and

John Cusack. By the time the end credits rolled, Brant was asleep, his heavy breaths regular and deep against my neck.

I closed my eyes and tried to fall asleep. In a few hours, we'd be back in California. I could drop Brant off at home, then swing by the printer, review the newspaper proof and make sure it was perfect. Then, I could return home and catch up on my jet lag. I would need my rest. Tomorrow could be a big day. A relationship-ending one.

Chapter 38

I was a person of plans. Like Brant, I liked order. Research. Intellectual thought that put trajectories into motion and controlled their paths and outcomes.

Molly had been my problem.

This newspaper, this setup: my solution.

Carefully crafted steps to ensure a positive outcome.

Lose Molly. Gain Lee. Carry on.

Winning would give me a sense of accomplishment, a righting of one wrong. But still, a bigger problem loomed. Once I had Brant and Lee, then what? How would this story end?

The best-laid plans still deserved a purpose, and I needed to find mine.

For now, this one seemed foolproof. I ran my hand over the colorful print of the newspaper's front page. The false cover was wrapped around thirty-two pages of legitimacy, and I couldn't tell the difference. They floated seamlessly. Our articles matched the inside pages, the paper weight, color, and consistency the same, the phone numbers and emails listed all sending any inquiries from Molly directly to Don. It was a work of art. I grinned at the glaring photos, which screamed of sex. They made the perfect impression, and now... one final touch.

I took out a red Sharpie and wrote WHORE in big red angry letters across the front. There was no way he would miss that. I grabbed my cell and called Don. "It's ready."

"You approve?" he asked.

"It looks great. You got a guy to sit at her place?"

"Yep. And I'm tailing your boy. As soon as he heads to her place, I'll have him put the paper in place."

"I don't know when he'll go there. It might take a few days, or even weeks. The printer is ready and can print a fresh paper each day. Just mimic what I do on this one."

"I know, you told me. We'll stay on top of it."

"And call me as soon as it looks like it's going to happen. I want to be there."

"You're the boss."

"I'll leave this one at the print shop. Have your guy pick it up soon." I slid the paper back into the manila envelope and carefully closed it. Staring at the parcel, I gave myself one final chance to back out.

***

It took two days, and then I was there, parked outside her Mediterranean-style apartment, watching them scream and fight and destroy the chance for whatever love had existed between them.

I didn't care. I was happy that it happened. They didn't have a future anyway, not really. I was the one he belonged with, whether he knew it or not.

I drove out of her complex and headed to the spa for a celebratory massage.

Chapter 39

After three hours of seaweed wraps, a facial, and a vigorous deep-tissue massage, I picked up a sandwich for Brant and headed to his office. He wasn't there, an unsurprising fact. I stuck his sandwich in the office fridge and scribbled a love note for him. Then I got in my car and left Palo Alto, taking the winding highway that took me home. I ran a few errands along the way, detouring through Lee's part of the world in the hopes that fate might put us together. *Nothing*. I got back on the interstate.

When I pulled into my driveway, my mouth curved into a grin at the sight of Lee's Jeep, parked on the right side of my drive, his tall build leaning against the hood. His head lifted and he stepped away from the vehicle as I parked in the circular drive. *That didn't take long*. I got out and turned to him. His hands were tucked into the front pockets of his shorts, his shoulders hunched but his eyes steady, the cool afternoon wind whipping through us both.

"You lost?" I called out.

"Figured I had to leave the slums every once in a while." He waved the crumpled-up receipt from on our first meeting - the one where I had scribbled down my phone number and address, over five months ago. He glanced toward the house and raised an appreciative brow. "Nice digs."

"You look dirty," I said. His hair was wild and dusted with sand, like he'd driven top down through the desert. "Sure you aren't just using me for a hot shower?"

He stepped closer and rested his forearms on my convertible's hardtop. "You trying to get me naked?"

I met his cocky smile. "I don't need hot water for that." I shut the car door and headed to the porch, and he followed me up the steps. "Where's the girlfriend?" The words rolled out perfectly, call casual innocence.

"She's gone." He shrugged, but I caught the way his eyes lowered, and I heard the scratch in his throat, the attempt to hide the catch with a short cough.

I unlocked the door and held it open, waiting as he passed inside. I took my time closing it behind me, knowing that—as soon as it shut—the dynamic in this situation would change.

I clicked it into place and flipped the deadbolt. I turned and Lee was standing there. Close. So close that when he took a step forward, it put my back flat against the door, my keys falling to the floor, my breath catching somewhere in the space between us. He moved forward, the warmth of his body fully against me, one leg sliding in between mine, the hard press of him teasing the ache in my core. He let out a hard breath against my neck, his hands tracking down the side of my body and cupping the curve of my ass. Pulling me even tighter, he ground his hips against mine.

"I don't want to be your rebound," I whispered.

"And I don't want to be your side piece." He bit out the words against my neck. "But tonight, I need a fucking rebound. I need to bury myself inside of you. Tonight, I am your side piece. So both of us can fuck like adults and both of us can lose our minds for a night and not feel like shit about it." He squeezed my ass so hard it hurt, the hitch in my breath bringing his head up until his mouth was even with mine, his breath hot in the moment before he pressed his lips against mine. His kiss was rough and possessive and he rutted against me, pining me against the door. "You feel that, Lucky?" He grabbed my hand and put it on his zipper. Held it there until my fingers moved, gripping the stiff outline of his cock. "That's my level of need right now. Now, be a good slut, and get it out."

I fumbled with the button of his shorts. I got it free and then yanked at his zipper. Pulled it down and pushed my hand in. Let out a shudder when my fingers wrapped around and pulled him free. He was so hard in my hand. So ready. I squeezed it. Worked my hand up and down its thick length as he ravaged my mouth, the hiss against my lips telling me the tempo he liked. He grabbed between my legs, his thumb pressing my clit through my yoga pants, but the stimulation wasn't enough, not compared with the steel organ in my hand. The one that was pulsing beneath my palm. The one whose tip was wet with arousal; his shaft warm with need. I dropped his cock and put both hands on his chest, pushing him away. He fought it, his kiss fighting for my mouth, one of his hands catching my wrist and putting my hand back on his cock, my name a beg on his lips.

Fuck, I lusted for this man. I needed him. I needed him to be completely mine. I didn't want second best. I didn't want rebound sex. My desire for him trumped anything with Brant. I couldn't help that. I couldn't help the different way I felt about each man. I only knew that right now, I needed more than my hand on his cock. I needed to feel, for at least a moment, a full connection with him.

"The bedroom," I gasped out. I pulled away, past him and headed up the stairs that would take us to my bed.

"No." The resolution in his voice stopped me on the second step. I looked back. He stood in the middle of my foyer, his legs spread, shorts low on his hips, his cock heavy in his fist. "I need you right now. Lay down."

"Here?" I looked down at the Persian rug that was over a hundred years old.

"Christ, Lucky. Now. Strip."

I yanked my sports tank over my head and tugged at my yoga pants, unable to take my gaze off him. One hand pressed at the base of his cock, the other moved in slow strokes. His handsome face was hard with desire, his gaze intense as he watched me fumble out of the pants.

"Come here," he rasped, and dropped to his knees. He reached for me and pulled me down before him, the rough kiss of the carpet on my bare back. He spread my knees apart, held onto my waist and pulled me forward onto his stiff cock.

There were so many things wrong with this situation. But damn, I loved it. I stared deep into his eyes, scraped my nail across his chest, and wrapped my legs around his waist. For the next fifteen delicious minutes, I forgot about Brant, about Gymnast Barbie, about anything but him and me and that moment of time.

I was his rebound.

He was my sidepiece.

And both of us wanted more.

At least I did. Maybe anything else was a lie I was telling myself.

<h1 style="text-align:center">Chapter 40 — Jillian</h1>

It's safe to say I never liked Layana. There is something about a woman, when you look into her eyes and see calculation that I don't like. I prefer the open books, the women who pass through this office full of smiles and sunshine and optimism. I don't look in their eyes and wonder what they are thinking. I don't listen to them speak and search for hidden meanings. I don't wonder, when they leave, where they are going. But that, from day one, is how it has been with Layana. I had hoped she was a temporary fling. Surely another woman would catch Brant's fancy, that he wouldn't go for her long legs and mess of dark curls. But, alas, none did, and she stayed. And now, here we are. Both of us battling over this man. I only want to protect him. She "loves" him. We have differing views on what loving him entails. I don't want to think about what she does to keep him. Whatever it is, it's working. The man won't take his eyes off her.

There are things I could do to poison their relationship. Expose her lies, put a quiver of death into the perfect existence that he thinks they live. The problem is that she knows the secret. The one that I hug, with the tight grip of a mother bear, to my chest. The one that I have spent years protecting. If I destroyed their relationship and his trust in her? The destruction might set that secret free, expose it in the open air for whoever wanted to grab its papery truth and run wild. In that secret lies nothing but destruction. And so I sit here and continue paying the men who keep tabs on Brant. I smile when she enters the room. I help to hide her lies and deceit from him. I pretend to love her with the same vigor that I love him. And hope that one day she fades out of his life or dies.

I can take care of him. She can only—and will only—break him in two.

Excerpt, The Journal of Jillian Sharp.

Chapter 41

"Stay here. Spend the night."

His hands slowed in their rub of the towel through his wet hair. He wiped his face before dropping the white terrycloth on the floor and stepping over it, a second towel wrapped around his lower half as he strolled over to the messy pile of his discarded clothing. "I can't. Stay too long in this place, I'll start thinking I belong here."

"It's only one night." One I desperately needed. How different would a night with Lee be? Would he stay the whole night or leave me in the middle of it as Brant so often did? Would he wrap me in his arms or would he sprawl out on the other side of the bed?

He loosened and dropped the towel around his waist, and my eyes plummeted down. I savored the careless movement as he skipped his underwear and pulled on his shorts, uncaring of my gaze, his mouth curving into a confident grin as he tugged the cargo shorts over his hips.

"I have plenty of clothes here," I offered. "If you want clean ones."

He scowled. "Brant's?"

I didn't respond and he moved toward my place on the bed and pulled at the sheet until it was gone, and my naked body was fully exposed. "I fuck his woman; I don't want his life." He palmed my right breast roughly, the nipple hardening under his touch, the dark look in his eyes turning into a gleam of satisfaction. I sighed, reaching out and caressing his cock through the open fly of his shorts. It was still hot from the shower and his hand moved from my breast to my hair, gathering the long strands and pulling me upright. He lifted me off the bed and onto the soft fur rug, where I knelt in front of his cock.

"Tell me," he breathed as my I licked up the length of his shaft, the organ stiffening beneath my tongue. "Tell me which one you like better."

I looked up at him as I opened my mouth and took him in. His eyes closed as he let out a groan and gripped my head with both hands, pulling himself deeper in my mouth. Then he yanked me off his cock and tilted my head back. He stared down, his gaze studying, searching mine. I couldn't read the emotion in his eyes, but the energy between us felt like anger. Hurt anger—and I understood that. He felt it toward Molly, and I felt it toward him. The difference was, I was about to get what I wanted, while he was just chasing off the grief. "Tell me," he ground out. "Whose dick do you like more?"

"Yours is better," I whispered, our gaze locked as one, pure truth in the statement. He needed to stop thinking about Brant and about Molly and focus on us. He needed to want me and forget her. Then, everything else would fall into place. It had to.

He shoved back into my mouth. It was too hard, and I struggled to open my jaw wider, to move my tongue out of the way, my eyes watering at the rough intrusion. He thrust against me, his hands and hips working together, his open zipper scraping against my chin, his words falling down like tears.

"Look in my eyes, Lucky. Look in my eyes while you suck my cock." He slowed his motion and watched with rapt attention as he drug his wet shaft out, rubbing the tip of it against my lips. "You like this don't you? Being my whore while he pays your bills? Letting me use every inch of your body and sending you back to him ruined?" He let out a growl and pushed back into my mouth, my hands pushing at his thighs as my eyes held his. I could feel, under my palms, through the khaki material, the tremble of his thighs. He was close to coming. I increased my efforts and his legs buckled as he leaned forward, fully in my mouth, gripping my footboard for support as he came down my throat.

We stayed there for a moment, him immediately softening in my mouth, and when I pulled away, he stayed in place, both of his hands on the wooden footboard, his knees dropping to the rug as if his legs didn't have the strength to stand. I liked that, that proof of my impact, and now we were at the same level, me caged between him and the bed. He tucked himself back in his shorts and gave an awkward laugh. "Sorry about that. Next time I'll do a better job of taking care of you."

Next time. I said nothing as he pushed to his feet and looked around, finding his shirt and tugging it over his head. He buttoned his shorts and ran a hand through his hair, then patted his pockets as if looking for his keys. I wondered, randomly, where he kept them. If they stayed in his truck, how they didn't get lost to the wind. He didn't find them in his pockets and that didn't seem to worry him. He headed toward the door, almost out of the bedroom before he paused and turned back to me. It was almost comical, as if he had suddenly remembered that I was here and that a goodbye was expected.

"I'll see you later."

Not what I was expecting, nor what I wanted. He and Molly were over. Now was the opportunity for *us*. He shouldn't be screwing me and taking off, with some flippant reference to seeing me again. I wanted dates. Attention. Adoration. At the *very* least some gratitude for the back-to-back orgasms. I hadn't given Brant two orgasms in one night ... probably ever.

But Lee simply turned away, slapping his hand on the doorframe, and walked out. I heard him fumbling with his shoes and then the front door opened and banged shut.

I pulled on the footboard and stood, then crawled onto the

mattress and underneath the covers. Laying there, I tried to figure out what I did wrong.

Maybe it was too soon.

Maybe he needed time to heal.

Maybe he would come back.

Maybe he wouldn't.

Chapter 42

"What's your current temperature on kids?" Brant's voice was almost inaudible over the wind.

I glanced over, not sure if I'd heard him right. "What?" I held onto the seatbelt, my hair whipping across my face. A minivan passed us on the right, a boy's face pressed against the window, his eyes wide as he stared at Brant's convertible.

"Kids," he repeated, glancing over at me and raising his voice over the wind. "You used to talk about having a family. You haven't mentioned it in a long time."

I looked past the minivan, watching as the setting sun cast a romantic glow over a city skyline with way too many people crammed in its depths. Hundreds of thousands of them, yet I'd be willing to bet that none were in my predicament.

I trapped a loose piece of hair and pinned it behind my ear and searched for the words to translate all of the things I couldn't say. It was an impossible task, and I finally swallowed, aware that Brant had infinite patience and would simply wait me out. "I don't really think about a family anymore."

"Why not? You're born to be a mother."

I turned to him, surprised at the statement. "Why do you say that?"

"You come to life with the kids at HYA. They love you." He glanced away from the road for a moment and met my gaze long enough to communicate his sincerity.

I wrinkled my nose. "They're desperate. My own children might feel differently."

"Shut the hell up." The irritation in his voice was so out of character that I blinked, suddenly aware that the car was slowing and that his blinker was on, the vehicle moving to the right lane. He turned the wheel further and the tires vibrated against the change in asphalt as moved into the emergency lane. He pushed the car into park and turned to me.

"Layana. I've never seen someone like you—a woman who is perfectly made for every situation. You could stand by my side at the company. Lie in my bed and shatter every fantasy in my head. Raise children with me who are incredible as you. You challenge me. You fascinate me. I want to spend the rest of my life growing old beside you and discovering every facet of what a perfect creation you are. Look at me."

I couldn't. I couldn't deal with those words, that loving tone, but also couldn't evade it—and a discussion about having kids just wasn't something I was equipped to handle, not right now, even if it was blanketed in words that made my heart swoon.

"If you aren't ready to get married yet, I can understand that. I won't rush you into that." He looked so handsome there, his white button-up shirt undone at the top, the sleeves rolled up on his forearms, his dark hair messy from the wind. He fit perfectly into the setting—the billionaire, behind the seat of his luxury car. So poised, so in control. So understanding. "I'm not trying to get you pregnant; I'm just asking the question. I like to think about our future, to imagine being your husband, and I'm wondering if I should include kids in that vision."

Oh, Brant. I brought his hand to my mouth and kissed his knuckles, then turned his hand over and gently bit the flesh of his palm.

"I love you so much," he said, his fingers brushing over my cheek.

"I love you too." I leaned forward and he met me halfway, his kiss tender, then deep. Maybe, he'd let it go. Maybe, if I gave him something small, this could be pushed off for another day. He stopped the kiss. "Is it us, Layana? Is that why you no longer want kids?"

Yes, of course it was us.

I tried to kiss him, but he held me back as his gaze searched my face, looking for an answer. I met his eyes and said what I had to. "No, Brant. No. I promise."

He let out a rough breath, his hand stealing into my hair and tugging me forward, his relief clear in the desperate return to my mouth. And, in that moment, with the wind and the cars and the hum of the city around us, I let myself believe the lie.

It wasn't him. It wasn't us. *We* were perfect.

Chapter 43

"Molly came back." Lee's voice was grim when he said the words.

I looked up from my spot on the couch, a flash of alarm shooting through me. "When?"

"She showed up at Toasty's the other night. A few minutes after I got there. Wanted me back." He rubbed a fresh callus on his palm and glanced at me, his expression guarded.

Molly wanted him back. Not a surprise. I thought of the way she'd rejected my plant, her almost steadfast loyalty to Lee. She had loved him, or at least thought she did. I tried to keep my voice level. "What did you do?"

"You mean, did I fuck her?" He stood from his spot by the living room's front window. Moving closer, he stopped beside me, his body towering over mine. His eyes belied the dark look on his face. They were more cocky than angry and turning more sexual by the second.

I pressed my lips together and shrugged as if I didn't care. His mouth curved. The asshole knew I was affected, saw the insecurities and fear that I was trying to mask. He saw the jealousy and fed on it. Loved it.

He reached a rough hand out and cupped my neck. Pulled it toward his pelvis. "Suck my cock."

"What? No." I pushed on his stomach, and he caught my wrist. Shoved it down, until my fingers were at his jeans.

"Suck it and see if you earn the right for me to tell her no."

I said nothing and, for a long moment, we battled with our eyes. I wanted to suck his dick. God, my mouth watered for the feel of his hard cock against my tongue. But I'd be damned if I was made to do anything.

Holding his gaze, I pushed against his jeans and he pulled me harder, keeping me in place.

"Suck it and remind me of why I said no."

"You said no?" I looked into his eyes and damn if they weren't as tortured as my own.

"Yes." He hissed in appreciation as I undid the button of his jeans and pulled his zipper down. "I don't know why. Her beautiful face just begging for me to bend her over and fuck"— the rest of his sentence was lost in the groan that came when I took him down my throat. He fisted my hair, stared at my face, and rocked against my mouth, letting out a string of curses.

"You fuck him," he swore. "You fuck him all the time and then expect me to be a saint."

My eyes flooded with tears, and I told myself that the reaction was from the sucking efforts and nothing else. I needed to refocus his attention and the soft moan he gave told me I was on the right track. "Why?" he mumbled. "Why shouldn't I go back to her?"

I never answered his question, only his need. And when his orgasm was over and he pulled me on top of him on the couch, his arms enveloped me into his chest, and he kissed me, and the answer didn't seem to matter anymore.

Chapter 44

ONE YEAR AGO

My house was unaccustomed to a man's presence. Brant had visited twice, early in our relationship, then never returned. Now, after more than a month of Lee, it had adjusted to the weight of a man on its couch pillows. The sprawl of dirty boots kicked off in its foyer. Lee's scent invaded its hallways, competing with the scent of wood polish and fresh flowers, masculinity meeting delicacy and crushing it into dirt. For the first time, Brant's shirts and workout shorts—items I had worn home after early hookups, before I had a closet at his mansion—were finally being used.

I'd seen Lee almost every day of the last week, sucking up the time with him while I could take it. Brant had been MIA, something that had Jillian worried. She'd only seen him a few times, darting into the office at sporadic times, and not answering calls or texts. She did concede that this sort of thing was normal, especially in times of high stress. With his Apple negotiations at a breaking point and a few billion dollars up in the air, stress was certainly on his shoulders. I don't know how Jillian handled it— the unpredictability of his behavior, but with three decades with him, she knew how to handle it, and I trusted her advice and direction.

And... I didn't mind Brant's absence. It allowed me unfettered time with Lee, an opportunity that I was embracing with both hands. Every moment I held onto with claws, unsure how many more I would have left. Like an approaching storm, I could feel the end of our future, it teetering on a thin ledge of circumstance. Lee would disappear. I knew it, could feel it in every moment. And then, this entire cycle would start over with a new man, a new someone that would be my side piece to Brant.

As I watched, he stood in front of the open fridge, a hand resting on the top, his eyes skimming the interior as the cool air drifted through the space. "You have nothing," he announced.

"It's full. That hardly constitutes as nothing."

"No beer. No junk food. No ice cream. I could eat every item in this fridge and lose weight." He shut the door and sauntered into the living room. "Let's go grab dinner."

"Now?" I glanced at my watch. "It's almost nine."

"Which is why I'm hungry. That thing we ate for dinner was weak."

I rolled my eyes. The 'thing' was foi gras that I spent three hours preparing. It was Brant's favorite dish, one I expected Lee to scarf down with appreciation. I should have known, in this complicated scenario of conflicts, that he would hate it. "Fine." I stood, tossing my book down on the dark blue sofa. "I'll go change."

"Uh uh. You're fine." He grabbed my elbow and steered me towards the door.

I glanced down at my faded boyfriend jeans. "Where are we going?"

"Let's just drive till we find something. There's got to be somewhere around here that's got the game."

I grabbed my keys off the counter and pressed the button for the garage. It was a cool night and I paused in the doorway, then opened the coat closet and reached up, grabbing a folded black cashmere sweater off the shelf. By the time I stepped out and pressed the keypad, locking the front door, Lee was facing the garage, the full range of cars revealed as the doors swept up.

I stepped down the wide brick steps just in time to hear his low whistle. "Damn, Lucky. I might start fucking this guy."

Irritation flared. "I do have my own money, you know. Not everything is from Brant." It was a ridiculous defense to say to Lee, made more so by the fact that two of the four cars parked in the enclosure were gifts from Brant. I moved toward my Mercedes, my everyday car, but he reached out and stopped my movement. "Let's take the black one."

"The black one?" I stalled.

He was referring to 1989 Land Rover Defender. I'd traded my last vehicle in for it, falling in love with the beefy luxury SUV, which had been restored to mint condition, and converted from hard top to convertible. And, as awkward as this situation now was, I'd purchased it as a gift for Brant. It had been my attempt to, in some small way, repay him for the gifts he had a tendency to lavish on me.

Unfortunately for me, Brant hadn't been a fan of the vehicle. In the brutally honest fashion I loved, he'd told me as soon as he'd opened the black velvet box and paired the set of keys inside with the gleaming two-door in front of him.

"SUVs aren't really my thing." He'd passed the key box back to me, a sheepish look stealing over his face. "I don't like the insecurity of them. And the IIHS safety rating placed them in the worst classification for risk of rollover. The—"

"It's okay." I smiled at him. "I should have asked."

"I just don't need a vehicle I won't drive." He leaned over, looped a hand around my waist and kissed the top of my head. "Do you mind?"

Did I mind? I had stared blankly at the truck. "No babe. I'm glad you told me."

And I was, sort of.

A BSX employee had driven the vehicle to my house, where it'd spent most of its life in the garage. Now, Lee was in my driveway and about to swoon over the damn thing. "You like it?" I asked, already convinced of the answer, giving the way he was circling the truck, his eyes aglow.

"It's fucking sick. Is this the V8? What year is this?" He was now on his knees, looking at the undercarriage, and when he hissed at what he saw, it was the same sound he made when he pressed his cock inside of me. I didn't know whether to take that as a compliment or an insult.

"It's an 89."

"Shit, this thing must be worth a fortune. You got the keys?"

I guess there was no reason not to take it. What difference did it make? Still, it felt odd. I nodded to the lockbox on the wall. "The keys are in there. Code is 029."

He stood and strode over the box, punching in the combination and then turning to grin at me when it popped open. "Damn, Lucky. Shouldn't give strangers the keys to your castle so easily. What if I come back and steal all of these?"

It was such a ridiculous statement that I laughed, then reached for the passenger door handle. "I'd know where to find you at. You gonna drive?"

He jumped into the front seat, his hands running over the leather-wrapped steering wheel in appreciation before cranking the engine. The rumble of the diesel engine was loud in the garage and I buckled the canvas seat belt, then tied back my hair with an elastic band.

I had always been intimidated by the three-thousand-pound hunk of steel, but Lee seemed made for it, his frame relaxed as he shifted into reverse and gunned the engine with a comfortable ease.

This was exactly what I'd imagined when I bought the truck, and maybe that's why I bought it. Maybe I was trying to take my clean-cut genius and dump him into a tub of masculinity, to roughen up his smooth edges. I hung my arm out the window and swallowed my side of guilt. With the squeal of tires, Lee pulled out through my gates.

Ten minutes later, the blare of the radio competing with the whip of wind, I hit Lee's arm and pointed. "There." In the adjacent shopping center, there was a wings bar tucked between a discount hair salon and a pharmacy. An OPEN sign in red neon was lit, and Lee turned into the center. There were a cluster of cars in front, and he pulled into a spot three rows back, with empty spaces on both sides. He climbed out and waited for me at the rear bumper, his hand resting on the side of the Defender a little longer than necessary, longing in his eyes.

I fell into step beside him, our hips bumping as we walked toward the restaurant, his arm looping around my shoulder, the gesture casual yet familiar. All it had taken was a few weeks of sex and we were at ease in each other's presence. Impulsively, I leaned over and pressed a kiss against his cheek. He squeezed me tighter, extending the contact as if in approval of the action.

Maybe I was telling myself lies, but this didn't feel like a rebound. It felt like it fit, and for a moment, I let myself believe that it would all work. He would fall in love with me and only me. He would be loyal. He would—my thoughts stalled when my gaze collided with Jillian's.

Her eyes were steely and sharp, and dissected both of us, noticing everything about Lee in one long glance. A billboard of emotions shuttered across her face as she processed his arm over my shoulder, the lazy stroll of his gait, his stretched-out shirt. I couldn't look away and stumbled to a stop as her critical gaze found its way back to my eyes. There, we held each other, two women on opposite sides of a battlefield, my weapons sex and passion, hers the ties of family and history. We held an entire conversation through that stare. A heated battle of emotions, arguments discussed with tightened lips and silent looks. Then, the battle ended, the older woman closing her eyes in one, long, pained moment. I felt her disappointment. Her anger. Her frustration. I knew it because I felt it in my own heart.

I pulled away from Lee and tucked a strand of hair behind my ear, my hands dipping into my pockets.

He registered the action. "What's up? You don't want wings?" He glanced over at Jillian and dismissed her as an issue.

"This is a friend of mine. Go on in. I'll be there in a minute."

He shrugged. "Sure. Whatever." He strolled on and nodded at Jillian as he passed. "Hey there."

From the cringe on her face, I bet that he winked at her in passing.

I stayed in place, a statue of dread, and waited until he swung open the door and stepped into the bar, the music and noise sounding, then muting as the door closed behind him. Still, we stood in silence, two opposing forces separated by a half dozen feet of parking lot.

"What are you doing, Layana?" her voice was beaten, as if we'd had this argument a million times and she couldn't bear to go through it again.

"I can't..." I stopped. Tried to find my words. "You know what Brant's like." I dipped my head in the direction of Lee. "He's different. I tried ... but I can't stay away."

"You love Brant." She let out a heavy sigh. "I know you do."

I nodded. "I do."

She glanced over her shoulder, nodding to Lee. "And him? Do you love him?"

I swallowed. I felt sparks and affection, but was it love? Was it real? "I think I do."

"And does he love you?" She saw the truth immediately, before I had a chance to speak. She let out a cruel laugh. "Of course he doesn't." She said it as if I was unlovable, and I had a sudden flashback to my mother, making a similar comment about my first real boyfriend. I didn't feel as stupid now as I did then. Jillian, of all people, should understand.

Her mouth tightened. "You're playing a dangerous game."

"It's my game to play. I'm the one in the relationship." I regretted the flippant words the moment they left my mouth, because there had always been a competition between us, one that she always lost.

"You selfish, stupid girl," she spat out, and pointed a trembling finger toward the bar. "He'll leave you, Layana. One day, you'll wake up, and that boy in there will be *gone*. Brant loves you. He'll be with you forever."

I nodded, because of course she was right. What I had with Lee was fleeting, which is why I needed to hold onto it with both hands. "I know." I turned away, hiding the emotion on my face, and headed toward the bar. Her voice, quiet but firm, stopped me.

"Brant told me he proposed again."

"Yes." I turned and met her eyes. "And? Do you think I should marry him?"

She let out a huff of laughter, a cold and brittle sound that spoke of incredulity and hopelessness. "Layana, you know that I don't particularly care for you."

"I'm well aware."

She shifted the bag in her hand to the other side and I realized that it was a to-go one from the wings place. Of all places for us to pick, and for her to go—was this the universe trying to intercede?

"And you know that I don't believe he should be in any romantic relationship. You know why. You should have left him back in Belize when you found out the truth. But you didn't. You stayed with him. And I respected you for that. Five minutes ago, I would have pushed aside my concerns and said yes, you should marry him. I would have given you my blessing. But now? Seeing you with *him*?" She jerked her head toward the bar. "You are threatening *everything* you have because you want everything you don't. You don't get everything when it comes to Brant. You get what he shares with you. And you *have* to be happy with that."

She was right. Of course she was. I knew that—had known that—but what the heart wants doesn't always agree with what the head knows. And for me, in my battle of heart versus head, my heart wins every time.

She was waiting, expecting a response, and I found my voice

somewhere in my dark pit of shame. "I don't know if I can be happy with that."

And there it was. The horrible truth of my relationship. *I don't know if I can be happy with that.* With pieces of Brant. With getting what he shared. If I couldn't be happy with that—if that was indeed the bottom of it—than why was I in this relationship?

Because I loved him.

Jillian shook her head, her eyes filled with disappointment. "Love isn't about being happy. Be single and be happy. Love is about putting him, his sanity, his happiness, first. If you aren't willing to do that, then you aren't really in love."

With that blow, she turned away, her heels clipping through the parking lot, toward her white Lexus sedan, one I had walked past without noticing. There was a part of me that loved that woman and her fight for Brant. There was another part of me that hated her guts.

I headed for the bar, my path to hell lined with neon signs and temptation, all in the form of Lee.

Chapter 45

The following day I hovered in the doorway to Jillian's office and rapped my knuckles on the wall.

"Layana." Jillian looked up from the reports on her dark wooden desk and raised her eyebrows above the gold rim of her reading glasses. "What a... surprise."

I glanced at her administrative assistant, who was in the corner of her office, a clipboard in hand, his pen in frantic motion. "Sorry for the interruption. I'd like to speak to you about something."

She rolled away from the desk and sat back in her tufted leather chair, removing her glasses and folding them closed. "Absolutely. Chad, please return to your desk and hold any interruptions."

I stepped inside and perched on the arm of the closest chair. Her assistant moved by, smiling faintly of Old Spice, and quietly murmured a hello.

Jillian's wary gaze swung to me. "What is it?"

"Thanks for not making a scene last night."

Her dark red lips pursed together, pinching the delicate skin around her lips into a hundred spiderwebs. "Well, I didn't really have an option."

"I do a lot for Brant. For you. For BSX."

She rolled her eyes. "You keep a secret. Don't blow it into a monumental feat, dear."

"I need something in return. From you."

"And that is?" She stood up from her chair and moved to the coffee station built into the left side of the room. The pot was full, and she lifted two dark green coffee mugs from hooks on the underside of the cabinet.

"I need to know how many men..." I glanced at the closed door and lowered my voice, just in case Chad was in the hall. "How many men Brant is or has..."—I tried to find the right word to use in case someone was listening—"been in contact with. If there's only one. What the possibilities are for more."

She returned the pot to the machine and added cream and sweetener to both cups. It was funny that our coffee preferences were the same, given all the ways we differed. As my question hung in the air, she took her time, stirring each, then tapping the stick and dropping it into the small trash bin.

By the time she turned to me, both mugs in hand, her forehead was creased in thought. She nodded for me to close the door, then took the soft chair beside me. "Do you plan on justifying more affairs, Layana? Going to cheat on Brant with a handful of men?" She passed me a cup, then blew gently on hers. "You're not talented or sane enough for that. Trust me on that. No one is."

"Just answer the question. Please." I couldn't shed my manners; they lay on my skin like grease that only smeared when attempts were made to wash it off.

She sighed. "There's just one right now. There were some others in the past, but they have all left or died, who knows. That's why I tried to warn you before. This part of Brant's life... you need to forget it. Ignore it. Focus on building, on strengthening your relationship with him, and forget about anything or anyone else."

"How long did the others last? The other boys?" I was terrified of the answer and moved off the arm and into the chair, sinking into the soft cushioned seat.

She lifted one thin shoulder in a shrug. "It's hard to say. They don't exactly speak to me. I would guess two to three years on average, some as long as five. And Layana?"

I met her eyes.

"A couple of them have been... ugly. Violent. You can't save them all. You snagged one, congratulations. Don't get cocky and think that the next boy will be the same. The next boy is just as likely to bend you over and rape your ass."

"The boy from last night—Lee?" She cleared her throat. "You should probably know that I'm having him followed. We'll step in if he gets out of line or into any trouble."

At this point, nothing surprised me. I couldn't imagine the circus that Jillian orchestrated behind the scenes of our lives.

I felt sick, the crude words rolling off her tongue as jarring as the image that accompanied them. I imagined all of the possibilities, all of the unthinkable things I had never considered, my life too clean to know true depravity.

"It'd probably be best, at this time, for you to either walk away or put your big girl panties on. You need to make a decision. You either love Brant despite this, or you don't. How much do you love him?"

The room refocused on her words, her challenge. I closed my eyes and pictured Brant's face. The man behind the brilliance. The man who I loved in a way I didn't think was possible. The man who I would fight for, would lie and cheat and steal for. The man, who, in some way, shape, or form was savable. I knew he was. He had to be. I opened my eyes and met Jillian's. *How much do you love him?* "Enough. More than enough."

She sighed and set down her coffee cup. "I certainly hope so."

Chapter 46

Lee was drunk. When he stepped, he stumbled. When he leaned on the bar, his arm slid to one side. I glared at the bartender, the same asshole from a year and a half ago and asked for a bottled water. I got a dirty glass that he filled from the drink gun. I slid the glass back and second-guessed my decision to drive out to this part of town, this late at night. On my prior visit here, it had been the middle of the day. The bar had seemed harmless and cozy then, but at night it was filled with a different crowd that was jittery with stimuli and itching to cause trouble.

I sat on the stool beside him, in arm's reach in case he fell over. "What happened?" I pulled at his chin, trying to get a better look at his busted lip and swelling jaw. He'd called me from the bar's phone—drunk and needing a ride, but I hadn't expected blood.

"Asshole homeowner. Said I left last week with only half the grass cut."

"Did you?" The sharp look he gave me answered the question. I raised my hands. "Sorry." I glanced over for the bartender and tried to get his attention over the loud din of the bar. "Some ice!" I yelled as soon as he looked my way.

I got a few handfuls, dumped in the bottom of a plastic bag.

Twisting the top, I pressed the makeshift icepack gently against his lip. "How did that lead to this?"

"The dickhead threatened not to pay." He shrugged. "So I punched him."

Wow, the immaturity level behind the decision. "What? Why didn't you just walk away?"

He pushed my hand away and worked his jaw from side to side. He glared at me as if I was the stupid one. "I need work. Need cash." He tried to reach for a beer that was no longer there and barked out an order for another. "From someone who's never worked a day in her life, I wouldn't expect you to understand."

Never worked a day in her life. It was true, but I didn't like the way he sneered it, as if my lack of a day job made me less of a person. It was something Brant had never referenced, and I suddenly wondered if it was something he thought. Emotions and feelings often got hidden. Pushed down until they found another outlet to creep back up into.

I shifted the ice to a better position on his lip and his eyes flared as the cold compress hit the open cut.

"Shut up," I whispered. "Take it like a man."

He conceded and leaned into my hand. He still smelled of the job, of grass and sweat, but there was a new scent—alcohol. He must have marinated in it. How much did it take to make him swing at a client? What else would he do, under the influence.

"Hey princess, mind giving up that seat?"

Lee's eyes flicked back open as I glanced over my shoulder. A man stood at the bar; his tattooed arm wrapped around a woman I'd politely describe as hard. His free hand gripped the edge of my stool, as if he was contemplating giving it one firm yank that would knock me onto the filthy floor. I glanced quickly around the skinny bar; the landscape uninterrupted by the rough couple. I was the only outlier in my starched white blouse, pale yellow pants, beaded flats, a YSL bag hanging off my elbow. I'd been in pajamas when Lee had called and had gotten dressed in the same outfit I'd worn to have lunch with the HYA board members. It had fit in well at the upper crust French restaurant. Here, I might as well be wearing a giant PRISSY LADY WALKING sign.

My survival instincts, which had fallen dormant from lack of use, slowly raised their head. I did not belong here at midnight on a Friday night. It was stupid of me to walk into this pressure cooker of alcohol and rough men and expect not to be noticed, pushed around, and put in my place.

I slid off the stool with a gracious smile. "Sure."

The man's face didn't change, any delight at getting a seat disguised by a thick beard.

"Sit back down." The order was a growl from Lee, who lifted his head high enough to glare at me.

"I—We should be leaving anyway." I said, my voice low. God, I didn't need this. Lee was already bloody from one stupid fight, now defending my honor in a place packed with idiots.

He lurched to his feet, swaying slightly as he turned to face the man. The guy hadn't budged, his girlfriend still suction-cupped to his side. "What the fuck's your problem?"

I pulled on his arm. "Lee." The plea earned me a moment, a glance in which everything paused, and he looked at me and I saw everything he couldn't say in that one moment.

He couldn't buy me cars. Couldn't drown me in diamonds and buildings and trips around the world. He couldn't even pay for the beer tab from tonight's drinking. But this, this was one thing he could do. He could stand, fight, bleed for me. This was something Brant would never do, a situation my alternative relationship would never encounter. This was Lee's world.

Here he was king.

Here he would slay the tattooed dragon and be my hero.

His eyes burned the air between us, and I let out a shaky breath. Releasing his arm, I sank back onto the highly contested stool.

"You guys ain't drinking. Make room for someone who is," the man barked.

Lee rose, his entire body tight, and I saw his punch

telegraphed a million ways from Sunday. I had a moment of admiration at the flex of his arm muscles when he lunged forward, his right hook missing my insulter as the man leaned back and easily avoided the punch.

I closed my eyes, afraid to see any more. The smack of fist against flesh sounded and the bar suddenly fell silent as everyone's attention shifted. I opened my eyes in time to see Lee stagger forward and land a punch, the man's head snapping back in an unnatural fashion. I surged off my stool and worked my way in between the two, my gaze catching sight of the other woman in this equation. She snapped a wad of gum and beelined for my open stool, her concern nonexistent as long as her seat was secured.

"Stop, Stop!" I screamed the words into Lee's face, and he hesitated long enough for me to shove him back into the crowd, the sea of bodies swallowing us whole, the bar not big enough to accommodate a crowd shift without a relocation of the population. I linked my arm through his and dragged him to the door and out to the street.

I expected curses, a fight to return inside, but he only staggered in the outside air. Stumbled forward, then backward, then sat, his knees buckling in such a fashion that his descent to the ground was almost graceful, a plié that planted him on the dirty curb. His arms folded on the top of his knees, and he dropped his head to his forearms.

I took a seat next to him, as carefully as I could. The minute my butt hit the concrete, my linen pants were condemned to an early death.

It was quiet out here, the roar from the bar muted, giving us a reprieve from the bedlam. I hung my head. I should be at home, neck-deep in a bubble bath, a book in hand. Or curled in a blanket, on the porch hammock, listening to the ocean until I fell asleep.

"You'll never do it." His words were a slur of depression and desperation.

"Do what?" I kept my head down, eyes closed. I didn't want to see his face and didn't really want to know the answer to my question.

"Leave him." Somewhere in the darkness of the parking lot, there was the crunch of glass and a curse. "You won't, will you?" I felt his gaze on me, forcing myself to lift my head and meet his eyes.

A destroyed man sat beside me, his arms around his knees, and the image sent a shiver along my soul. I had seen this man in so many different lights, but this was the weakest. This is the one that touched me deepest and hurt me the most. The one that I, in some ways, loved the most.

And this is the destruction that I caused. Why didn't I anticipate this scenario? Never did I think of Lee getting hurt—of Lee caring to that extent. I wanted him to want me—I just didn't see the risk in that until now.

I told him the truth. "No, I won't. I won't ever leave him."

He broke the eye contact, resting his head on his hands, and silence fell between us.

Then, with a forward heave and strangled cry, he tipped forward and vomited onto the gritty asphalt.

* * *

A cab took us to my house. I hated leaving my car in the lot but didn't want to try and deal with Lee while I was driving. I needed both hands and full attention, in case of an incident during the twenty-minute drive.

There was no hiccup. He laid down across the back seat, his head in my lap, a loose hand resting on my thigh, as if to reassure him of my presence, and fell asleep.

I needed the break and spent the drive wondering if these emotions from him would go away as soon as he sobered up. He certainly hadn't shown anything other than competitiveness with

Brant before—and had never discussed even caring about me, much less expecting me to leave Brant for him.

"This the one?" The cabbie slowed by my gates, and I scrambled in my purse for my phone.

"Yes, that's it. Just a moment, I'll open the gate."

I used the app on my phone to engage the gate, and then returned the device to my purse, pulling gently on Lee's shoulder.

He didn't respond, and I offered the driver an extra twenty bucks to help me carry him to my bed. Once the man left, I pulled his clothes off and covered him with the duvet, dimming the lights in the bedroom and changing into my pajamas. I laid on my side next to him and stared at his beautiful face. Stared and thought and tried to sort out the mess of feelings in my head.

Chapter 47

When I woke up in the morning, he was gone, along with the cash from my wallet.

Truly gone.

Like the first time I parted from him, he was lost in the wind. His cell phone was dead. His Jeep and trailer, which was left in the Toasty's parking lot, was never moved, and finally towed away. I called Jillian and asked if her people had seen him, but they had nothing.

He was gone, with no trace of the man who held a large piece of my heart.

I didn't see him again for five months.

I tried to forget him.

Tried to accept his disappearance as a blessing, as my world with Brant carried on. The iTunes deal closed, Brant doubled his wealth, and life continued, smooth as silk. But every time I was away from Brant, I thought of Lee. Wondered about him. Missed him. Turned down another proposal from Brant, this one with candlelight and lobster on the upper deck of his new yacht.

I almost accepted. With Lee gone, I had to fight from saying yes. But I didn't.

I had to know if Lee was out still there.

Had to dig back into the darkness, verify his existence, find out more.

I just wasn't cut any other way.

Chapter 48 – Brant

I kept the ring in my office, in the main drawer of my desk. Its box was worn, my hands turning the velvet over too many times to count, and much more than it was built for.

I bought the ring months before Belize. It was on a whim, my head clearing enough to realize that I was downtown, for a reason I didn't know, a swarm of people in the daily grudgefuck that was San Francisco. I hated this city, its shove of too many people in too tight a space, the fight for air claustrophobic in its necessity. I stood on that crowded street, dirty cracks underfoot, and saw the jeweler's silver sign of black and white calm against the madness that was the crowded street. I worked my way through the crowd and stepped inside.

Earrings maybe. Something to glint among the dark curls of her hair. The store was spacious, blanketed by the calm and quiet of expense and I breathed easier. Smiled at the man who greeted me. Stepped forward, not to the display of necklaces and earrings, but to the left, my steps pulling me toward the glittering expanse of engagement rings.

I didn't know what I was thinking. I couldn't propose without coming clean. Without telling her about the black in my soul. I was damaged goods. She deserved to know that, to understand what she was stepping into. The pain that I would drag her through, should the medication ever stop working. But all of those variables left my mind when I stepped up to the glass. My gaze scrolled over the lineup of rings, and I stabbed the glass above one cluster of settings. "Let me see those."

I walked out without a ring. There hadn't been anything worthy of her. But the jeweler had worked with me and tracked down a stone that fit her. A natural blue diamond. It took them three weeks to find one large enough. 2.41 carats, in the shape of a shield. A unique shape and a unique stone. They put it in a simple setting, then delivered it by Brink trunk. It sat in my desk for another month before I felt secure, felt right. It was the biggest decision of my life, more important than any deal, any product. I carefully weighed the decision, analyzed pros and cons, and examined every facet of my relationship with Layana. Looked at it as a business decision, even though marriage should be anything but. But I already knew what my heart felt. No point in holding it underwater to drown in an unwinnable situation. I needed to go through an analytical process to ensure success.

Before proposing, I completed the analysis for me (positive result), and then for her. Tried to determine if this was a smart decision for Layana. Tried to anticipate the probability of a fallout that would occur if or when she discovered my secrets. Maybe she would be fine. Maybe she'd understand. Maybe she would never know.

Or maybe she'd run for the hills.

I had worked through scenarios, turned that ring over a thousand times ... then I had gone for it. Made a decision, let my accountants and family know, and said goodbye to all logical reason.

Love. It makes us do crazy things.

Now, I rolled the ring against the pad of my thumb, watching the unclaimed diamond flash in the light from my desk lamp.

Then I set it back in its box, closed the lid, and returned it to its semi-permanent home. I turned off the lamp and sat there for a long moment, my office and my heart empty and silent.

Chapter 49

In the game room at the HYA house, I studied a chess board, then reached for my horse piece. The bespectacled Black eight-year-old across from me cleared her throat in warning. I dropped my hand. Looked at one of my front pawns. Took a safe path and moved one of them instead.

Presley sighed in disappointment. "You aren't even trying."

"I am," I groaned. "That's the sad part about it. I can't think that many moves ahead. This is why I suck at checkers."

"Checkers is for idiots," she informed me.

I stared at the board, not sure what she had just moved. "I didn't see your move."

"E4."

Like that meant anything. I studied the bottom of the board to see if the rows were labeled.

"Oh my gosh, Miss F. It's this one." She pressed a blue sparkly fingernail on the top of a castle.

"It looks like someone needs a rescue." Brant's voice came from behind me, and I turned quickly in my chair, surprised.

"What are you doing here?" I tilted back my chin and he leaned forward, pressing his lips to mine.

Presley groaned and covered her eyes. "No kissing. It's a RULE, Miss F."

Brant broke the rules again, with a quick peck on my lips, then straightened. "Sorry. I'm a rebel. It's…" He studied her. "Presley, right?"

Man forgets where he left his car or his own first name, but he remembers a girl he met four months ago. Go figure. She straightened with glee. "That's right! Presley Andrews. And you're Miss F's *boyfriend*." She delivered the last word in a hushed tone, as if it was a secret.

"That I am." He gave a courtly bow. "I'm also much, much better than her at chess. If you're bored, I could step in. Liven up the game a bit."

She beamed and waved both hands at me as if shooing away an insect.

"She's eight," I warned Brant, pushing back the chair and standing up. "And I thought you had that meeting at—"

"Moved it up and cleared my calendar for the rest of today. Thought I'd play some hooky." He settled into my seat and hunched forward, studying the board in a moment, then reached along the back row for one of the tall things. Moving it to the middle of the board, he looked back up at me. "Thought I'd finish your shift with you, then we'd go to that sushi place you like."

I swooned a little at the idea, but paused, because he picked, of all days during the month, the absolute worst to volunteer for. "It's bathroom cleaning day," I said.

"So?" He moved something on the board. "Check." Presley hunched forward, alert. "I love bathrooms. In fact, I used one earlier this morning." He grinned at the girl, and she covered her mouth and giggled, then refocused on the board.

Yeah. I tried to remember the last time—any time—I had seen Brant clean anything, or even plunge a toilet. The HYA bathrooms were communal by gender, one big counter with sinks and then a row of private showers and toilet stalls. They were cleaned weekly, by the volunteers, and really should be cleaned every day. They were always, by the time Tuesday came around, a disaster.

"Okay," I said. "Once you finish up that game, we'll head to the—"

"Checkmate," Presley said, moving one of the bigger pieces with a flourish.

* * *

Brant looked ridiculously sexy in the grey coveralls, a mop in hand, his brow furrowed in concentration as he bent forward and scrubbed the floor. His biceps peeked through the short sleeves of the getup and while he had lost some muscle tone in the last few months, he was still impressively built for a computer nerd.

I sprayed solution on the mirror and wiped it down, admiring him in the reflection as he worked. He was quiet and quick, and surprisingly good—though I wasn't surprised that he was thorough. Brant's life was about thoroughness. Steadfast focus on a job, and its details, until it was done. The details, he always told me, are where the problems always hide.

"Your meeting went well?" I went over the glass with a dry towel, removing the wipe marks.

"Yeah."

"Everything transitioned over to Apple smoothly?" I asked.

"It did."

"Am I going to get any other details out of you?"

He paused and looked up. "Probably not." His gorgeous mouth wrinkled in a grimace. "I'm sorry. Am I being anti-social? I just want to make sure that I do this right."

"It's cleaning," I laughed and tossed the paper towels toward the trash can. "You can't mess it up." I grabbed the mop and leaned forward to get a kiss.

He turned away, avoiding the contact. "We're not allowed to kiss."

I growled and grabbed his face with both hands, forcing it to mine and deepening the peck into a full experience.

He pushed away, and a bad boy, he was not. I went for him, and he blocked me with the handle of the mop. I zigged to the right and he did the same, a boyish grin blooming on his face.

Not an ounce of genuine bad boy in his system, but he was still undeniably lovable.

Chapter 50

6 MONTHS AGO

Five months after Lee disappeared, he showed up at my house. His frame rested against the beach wall, the warm morning light casting golden shadows on his bare torso. His board shorts clung to him, his feet and legs caked with sand, his hair slicked back and still wet from the ocean.

I came to a stop, my sports bra sticking to me, a line of sweat running down my face. I wiped my forearm across my cheek and met his eyes, my breath coming out hard from my final sprint. "Hey."

"Hey."

"You're back."

He stepped forward and came to a stop in front of me, then reached out and tugged on the ends of my ponytail. "Yep."

"I missed you." I couldn't hold the confession back. It was true, no matter how much I hated it.

His grin broke, as he looked down, trying to hide the reaction. His dimple winked at me, and the combination made my legs weak.

"Don't leave me again." The strain in my voice showed and he looked back up, somber.

"Okay." He nodded.

* * *

I came down from my orgasm, his cock deep inside, his sandy body draped over mine, two shapes, both bent forward against the bedroom window, his mouth at my neck, the heave of his chest against my back as he thrust, groaned, moaned my name as he marked me as his own. He shuddered inside me before pulling out, whispering my name with a salty kiss against the back of my neck.

My legs gave out and he caught me before I fully dropped, dragging me backward until we were both flat on my bed.

"God, I love fucking you." His breath was heavy, and the bed shifted when he rolled, pulling me closer.

"Same here." I closed my eyes, appreciating the drift of air across my damp skin, and needing a moment to recover.

"I need a shower."

I grinned. "Me too. Give me a minute. I can't move right now."

"I don't have a thing to do today. Take as long as you need."

My eyes were still closed, but I felt him lift my hand. There was the delicate trace of one of his fingers over the lines on my palm. His soft lips pressed against the spot, and my fingers closed around his mouth.

"I love you like this." His voice was muffled slightly by my hand and I released it, my mouth curving into a smile.

"Like what?"

"Naked and satisfied. Nothing on, nothing to make me feel inferior."

That opened my eyes. I turned my head and tilted it up to him. "Inferior? Why would you feel that way?"

"We live in different worlds, Lucky. Don't insult me by ignoring that fact."

I kept quiet and the soft trail of his hand over my back apologized for the tone of his voice. "But you're here now."

"Yeah. I couldn't even tell you where I've been. Everything..." He grew quiet. "Everything fades unless I'm with you."

It should have been a compliment. Instead, it felt more like a prison sentence. A statement of fact. I didn't respond.

"I wish my mom could have met you."

I forgot, for a moment, to breathe. I stayed quiet and waited to see what would follow, which path this conversation would take.

"She was so beautiful. Hair like yours—curly. Never in control. She used to chase me around the house, and it would bounce, like a third person in the room." His voice dropped, as if he had fallen asleep, and I strained for more. When he spoke again, I could barely hear him.

"I can't really remember my father. I was eight when they were killed. A drunk driver, some country-club asshole on a Sunday afternoon who ran headfirst into their car. He lived, they didn't." His touch on my back had grown hard.

"I'm so sorry, Lee." I didn't know what else to say, how to react to a story that I knew the truth about.

He ignored the sentiment and continued forward, like his words were bottled up and needed an escape, his voice tight and quick, each syllable dipped in anxiety. "I didn't have any other family, at least none that would take me, so I ended up in the foster care system. I had eight different homes by the time I turned eighteen. Three of the homes were okay, but the other five..." He pulled away and I rolled over, following him. I rested my head on his shoulder and wrapped my arm around his chest. Trapped him against me by winding a leg through his, until every part of my body was linked with his. It was the only way I knew to give him comfort, to make him feel safe.

He cleared his thought. "Five ... were bad. I disappeared when I turned eighteen. Got a few thousand bucks from the state and took off." His hand returned to my back, and he drew a line down my spine. "You and I ... we've lived different lives. I've never been taken care of. Have never had enough to take care of myself, much less spoil a woman like you. My entire life has been about survival. Fighting to get where I am, to get to the point where I will be good enough for someone."

I said nothing. I just laid there, wrapped in his arms, the overhead fan putting a cool breeze of air across our naked bodies. I felt the moment when he stopped waiting for a response and fell asleep, his hands going still and heavy against my body.

It was a wonderful story. Poetic in its portrayal of his life. Endearing. A perfect explanation for the creation of this tortured, confused man. It explained his desperation for love, mixed with a side of insecurity.

Too bad it was all a lie.

I laid in his arms and wondered how many women he had told it to.

Chapter 52 - Brant

In some ways we are so close to everything, to a life in which one starts and the other finishes, a joining so complete that we are one. In other ways...

We are a world apart.

Lies. Lies are what are keeping us at arms. I started this relationship with one lie, a part of my past that I had locked away and hoped she would never find out about. She started this relationship clean and innocent and has piled on the lies ever since.

I want to rid us of all of the lies, to wipe our slate clean with one confession session. But I am terrified to tell her my secret. And I am terrified to hear her tell me hers. I know them, but I don't want them spoken, don't want it to be proven true.

More than hearing the confession, I just want to know why.

Why does she cheat on me?

What do I not provide for her?

What part of me is not good enough?

If her love for me seems fierce enough to singe, why does she sneak around with a stranger?

My biggest fear is that she loves him. My biggest fear is that he has wormed his way into her heart.

I love her too much to share her and I hate him with a vengeance that turns my blood white.

I've had her followed. I met with a private investigator and had him spend a month tailing her. But she was too smart, his report revealing that she had only spent time with me. Now, I have Jillian watching her. She is relentless and will find out anything and everything about the man who holds the love of my life in his hands.

I have been called calculating but I am not cold; I am not unfeeling. My love burns as bright as hers, as does my possession. But my anger, my emotion, doesn't simmer on the surface. It hides in wait for the moment when it needs to erupt.

Chapter 53

3 MONTHS AGO

"You won't marry me."

"Is that a question or a statement?"

"It's the beginning of a question."

"Okay, so finish it."

"I would, if you'd stop talking long enough to let me."

I looked up from the mountain of oranges before me, pausing my quest for one soft enough to eat. I grinned at Brant. "So talk."

He placed a mango in our basket, weaving through the roadside stands until he was closer to me. "You won't marry me, but why aren't we living together?"

Yes, why Layana? I searched my brain for an acceptable answer, other than Lee. I was pretty sure Lee wouldn't agree to fucking my brains out on Brant's bed. Then again, I had my downtown condo, the one that Molly and Marcus didn't break in properly. It deserved a good round of fornication. "Maybe we could do that," I finally said, moving in front of the limes.

Brant pulled at the shoulder of my sweater, stretching the cashmere in a way that shouldn't be done. "Maybe?" He wrapped an arm around my stomach and nipped at the back of my neck before turning me to him. "That's your answer?"

"It's a good answer." I raised onto my tiptoes and kissed him.

"It's a horrible answer," he grumbled, pulling me back when I tried to turn away. "Do you love me?"

I stopped. Setting my basket on the ground, I wrapped my hands around his waist and looked up into his face, the one that I loved more than life itself. "Of course I love you. Don't ever doubt that."

He leaned forward and brushed my lips so softly that I closed my eyes, needing more. "Then move in with me," he whispered. "Live with me in sin."

"That wouldn't be proper," I said.

"Then marry me." He looked around the market with an exaggerated gesture. "Do you want me to do it? Kneel down right here?" He patted his pockets, pretended to fish for a ring.

"No!" I cried out. "For God's sake, no. I will move in with you." I wrapped my arms around his neck and stole one last kiss.

"You promise?"

"I promise." Then I shrieked as he swooped me up into his arms, our basket tipping over, fruit rolling in all directions. "Brant, what are you doing?"

"We're going house-hunting." He hugged me to his chest, his arm looped under my knees, and deftly moved through the crowd toward his car.

My head craned for our basket. "What about the fruit?"

"I'll buy you a house with an orchard," he promised, setting me gently down on the pavement. He opened the passenger door and held it for me.

"Now?" I asked dumbly, stepping into the Aston Martin, watching his face as he shut the door and moved around to the driver's side. It was happy and confident, and it broke my heart a little that he had wanted this so badly and I had answered with a "maybe."

"Now." He got into the driver's seat and closed the door, then pushed the button to start the engine.

"Can't I just move into your house?" House was really the

wrong word for it. It was a mansion, with fifty thousand square feet of space he barely used and a basement lab he had spent a fortune outfitting. He couldn't move, it wasn't possible.

"That is *my* house. I want *our* house. A place to build our future. A place you pick out." He shifted into gear and tossed his phone into my lap. "Call Jill and find out which realtor I should use, then get them on the phone."

Our house. I dialed Jillian and wondered how well this would go over with Lee.

* * *

I bought my first house a week after my twenty-fifth birthday. I'd had a budget of three million dollars and went crazy and spent four. I'd looked at twelve different homes, then agonized over the decision. With Brant, I expected even more of a production, but it turned out to be ridiculously simple.

In my prior price range, I'd had to make decisions. Did I want the outdoor kitchen or the sun porch? The indoor theatre or a library? An oceanfront bedroom or a guest suite over the garage?

In Brant's price range, every house had everything. And there were only three to choose from. The realtor offered a limo, but we drove Brant's car, winding toward the coast, the homes fifteen miles apart. Everything we could ever want for thirty million dollars.

It was an easy decision. The first one was a palace of ostentatious details, hand-painted ceilings, and heavy velvet drapes. It screamed old wrinkly money and came complete with maids' quarters and an entire floor dedicated to formal rooms we would never use. It did have a ballroom, a huge expanse I envisioned using in a variety of ways, the foremost being a skating rink for our future children. But the consensus, a look shot between Brant and me upon our exit, was that it was a no.

Windere was the second property, an estate high on the cliff, owned at one point in time by the Kennedys. It had four gated acres, nine bedrooms, two pools and an elevator that went the 42 stories down to the beach. At the base of the elevator was a two-bedroom beach house, a twelve hundred square foot gem with a spa and pool. The estate had privacy, needed a staff of at least five, and was a good half hour from Palo Alto, but it was comfortable and modern. It also had a six-thousand-square-foot basement, cut into the rock and already outfitted with enough electronic infrastructure to power a small city. We were sold.

"This is it." Brant clapped the realtor, a small woman with an overbite, on the back. "Good work."

"I have one more property to show you in Santa Cruz. It's a beautiful house..." Her voice faltered, and she looked to me for help.

"This one's perfect," I echoed Brant's opinion and beamed at him.

"Draw up the contract." He slid an arm around my shoulder, then leaned down and kissed my mouth. "I love you," he murmured, and the woman stepped away to give us privacy.

"I love you too."

"First steps, right?"

I grinned. "First steps. Baby steps."

He growled against my mouth. "Don't say baby. I'm already wanting to see you big and pregnant, with kids running through this house."

The light in my heart faded slightly, and I pushed myself onto my toes, stealing a kiss before the emotion hit my eyes. "Let's get one last look at our future home."

Chapter 54

I was in my office at BSX, writing an email to accounting regarding a philanthropy donation, when my door swung open. I glanced up from my computer, freezing at the sight of bare abs stepping into the room, quickly followed by a red-faced Jillian.

"Hey." Lee grinned at me, and I stared stupidly at his chest, wondering where, when and how he had lost his shirt.

"What are you doing here?" I breathed, glancing at Jillian.

"I can't believe I found you. This place," he whistled. "It's sweet, save for the assholes in suits."

Two of our security officers eased into the office and it was a good thing I had one of the larger spaces.

"We'll escort him out," Jillian said quietly. "You should go with him. Now, before anyone sees him. We can use the service elevator."

"Have you seen the weather?" Lee dropped into one of the soft chairs in front of my desk and threw one leg over the arm. "It's fucking perfect. We should go to the beach."

I saved the email as a draft and stood, locking my computer, my mind racing through how to handle this. Brant was under a stiff deadline, and had spent most of the week in his office, spending the nights working and taking catnaps on his office couch.

Jillian reached for his arm and he gave her a look that stopped her cold. "Let's move this outside, shall we?" She glanced at me. "You know that Brant is under deadline. He has specs due by the end of the week."

I ignored her and grabbed my keys from the desk. "The beach?" I moved around until I was in front of Lee, then bent forward and kissed him, right in front of her. "Let's go."

Her disapproval reeked in the room, but she said nothing.

I patted one of the security guys on the arm as I opened the door. "I got this, Tommy. It's all good. Lee's not going to cause a scene."

They clung to us, Jillian and the two suits, as we walked through the executive level and past Brant's office. The door was closed and I grabbed Lee's arm just before we passed it, getting his attention and kissing him on the neck. He grinned at me, enjoying the attention, and I let out a sigh of relief when we made it onto the service elevator without passing any other employees.

As soon as we got in my car, Lee leaned the passenger seat back and put one of his shoes up on the dash. "So, what do you think? Which beach?"

I considered the question as I backed out of my assigned space. "We could go to Linda Mar. There's a nice restaurant there that overlooks the water."

"Yeah, that's cool. I don't have my board, but I know the guys there."

I tried to process the image of Lee surfing and maybe it's because he's currently shirtless in pants, or maybe it's because I'm used to Brant, who hates the beach... but my mind is having a mental stutter at the thought. "You can surf?"

He snorted. "Of course I can surf. You know any proper Cali boy that can't?"

Yeah, Brant. I put on my turn signal. "I can't surf."

"You can't surf yet," he amended. "But I'll teach you."

There wasn't a chance in hell of that, but I still smiled at the idea and headed to my house so we could change.

* * *

I laid back on a striped red and white towel and watched as Lee tilted back a beer, his abs popping. He stood in a group of four guys, already somehow friends, and I watched as one of them laughed and shoved at Lee's arm.

"Hey." A blonde with long wavy hair dropped onto her needs in the sand beside me and smiled. "You like Karin Slaughter?" She nodded to the hardcover on the towel beside me.

I propped myself up on my elbows. "I just grabbed it from one of the shops. Too early to tell."

"I'm in the book biz," she laughed. "I mean, kind of. I work at a bookstore, on Venice Beach, in case you're ever in Los Angeles. And that one is..." she kissed her fingertips, "perfecto. You'll love it, if you can get past the gory parts."

"Oh, good to know." I followed her gaze to the group of guys that Lee was with. "You know them?"

"Oh yeah. We're all in town for the tournament this weekend."

At my blank look, she elaborate. "It's a surf tournament. My boyfriend is Paul Linx." She grinned when I didn't recognize the name. "He's a pro surfer. Really good. But uh, your boyfriend said you don't surf?"

"No." I winced. "Barely swim. And he's um... not really my boyfriend. Not yet."

She rolled onto her butt, and she was staggeringly pretty, wearing a turquoise blue bikini that showed off her toned body and golden tan. "Ha. Well. Paul is my second boyfriend, so if you ever need one to borrow, I've got two."

"Your second boyfriend?" I sat up all the way, curious. "What does that mean?"

"It means half the time I'm at the beach with Paul and the rest of the time I'm with my other half." She twisted a lock of hair around her finger as she watched Lee set down his beer and jog back a few steps, leaping into the air to catch something that one of the men threw his way. "Paul is the one in the yellow shorts."

I could have guessed that. Paul was gorgeous and so was she. One day, they'd make beautiful babies, assuming her second… boyfriend… didn't have an issue with that. "So, uh—do you worry about getting caught?"

She turned to look at me. "Oh, no. They know about each other. They're good with that."

"Oh, really." My skepticism must have shown in my voice because her grin widened.

"No, they are," she insisted. "What, you don't think Lee would be cool with you dating someone else?"

I knew the answer to that. I had a bruise on my hip from him fucking me against my dining room table, his voice raspy with jealousy and anger as he claimed me as his. "No," I said slowly. "I don't think he would be."

"Well, you might be surprised." She stood and stretched. "We're going down to the boardwalk to get some food. You guys want to come?"

"It's up to him." I nodded to Lee, who had never shied away from a meal. "I'm sure he'd be interested." I extended my hand to her. "I'm Layana."

"Madison." She shook it, then helped to pull me to my feet. "You guys should come to the tournament this weekend."

The chance of Lee staying for the weekend was slim, but her smile and friendliness were infectious. "Yeah. Maybe we'll do that."

We didn't. We spent four hours with them, drinking and talking and shooting darts in a dive bar on the boardwalk. Then Lee got too drunk and I drove him home and he kissed me in the darkness of my bedroom and held me like he loved me.

And then, in the morning, he was gone. Four days later, I stood in line at a coffee shop and watched a local television broadcast, showing Paul standing on the beach, a big trophy in his hand, and I thought about what she said.

Maybe some men were okay with sharing a woman but Brant would not be. And Lee was not.

This... all of this... could only end in disaster.

Chapter 55

"What's going on?"

I looked up from my place on my living room floor, mid-wrap of a picture frame. Lee stood in the front doorway, hands out in confusion. He looked around the empty space, half the furniture removed last week and sent out for consignment. I held up my finger in a "wait one moment" gesture and leaned back, calling out to the back of the house. "Frank?"

A moment later, the lead mover stuck his head through the doorway. "Yes ma'am?"

"Can you round up the guys and take them to lunch? I need some privacy."

"Sure." He nodded a hello to Lee and left.

I hopped up, setting down the frame and brushed off myself. "Hey babe."

"What's going on?" he repeated.

"I'm moving. I tried to call you. Been trying to call you. You should get voicemail or read your texts.

He looked around like he didn't understand the concept, taking a few steps into the kitchen before returning. "Almost everything's gone. When are you leaving?"

"Friday."

"So, where's your new place?"

"Not far." I stepped forward and wrapped my arms around his body, my body flush with his, his reaction immediate.

He looked down and pressed a kiss on my mouth as he grabbed a handful of my ass and squeezed it tightly. "Show it to me."

"Now?"

He shrugged. "Sure. You look like you could use a break."

I looked around. Everything was half-packed, but that was what I had Frank and his team for. "Okay. Let me grab my keys."

We took the Defender, Lee's hands familiar on the wheel. I was tempted to give him the vehicle, his love of it apparent every time he sat behind the wheel. Maybe later. Now it would only cause a fight and too many questions from Brant, too much rocking of the boat. Now, he pulled around his old Jeep, which he'd been reunited with upon his return.

The drive was a quiet one, the silence interrupted only when I'd point out turns, or give directions. I snuck glances at Lee as we drove down the expensive streets, a world away from his part of town. His eyes moved constantly, notating the details, his expression broody.

I knew this Lee. This was the insecure Lee, the one who grew hostile and irritable at my life of luxury. The one who hated Brant with a fervor that scared me.

Maybe today was the wrong day to show him Windere.

"I'm starving." I reached over and looped my hand through his. "Want to grab lunch first?"

"I'm not hungry." He pulled his hand free and down shifted. "Doesn't your new place have food?"

I looked out the window and swallowed my response. This was going to be a disaster.

* * *

I saw the hesitation in Lee as soon as I pointed toward the new house's entrance. He brought the Defender to a slow stop at the gates, and one of our new guards—Roy—stepped from the small hut, saw the two of us and waved. The twin concrete and iron gates began their slow parting, unveiling the beauty that was Windere.

His press on the gas pedal was delayed, his crawl down the driveway slow, the crunch of dead leaves audible in the absence of wind. When he rolled to a stop before the six-car garage, he jerked the SUV into park, turned off the key, and just sat there, the engine dead, his hands on the wheel.

"You're moving in with him." His words were dead and wooden. Defeated.

"Yes." I unbuckled my seat belt. "It's okay, Lee. You can come in. I want you to be comfortable here."

He dropped his hands from the steering wheel and looked at me as if I was crazy, and maybe I was. "I'm not coming in, Lucky. I didn't know... you should have told me. I look like an idiot being here."

"It's just a place to live. It doesn't change anything with us."

"Uh yeah, it does. Your house, I was okay there. This place..." He tilted his head up and looked over the four-story structure. "This place has its own guard shack for fuck's sake. You think they're going to let your side piece in?"

"It's fine, Lee. You can come and go any time you want."

"Yeah, Anytime he's not here. Fuck that." A heavy sigh whistled through his lips, and he turned to face me. "You know, I'm never gonna be able to give you this. Shit, I'm never gonna be able to give you anything."

"I don't need you to." I shook my head, and tears pricked at the corners of my eyes. "I only need you to love me." The word was scary, our relationship focused on the physical, and while he had used the word before—I love fucking you, I love you like this, I love the feel of your mouth on my dick—he had never said that he loved *me*. Or that he was in love *with* me. It was a different, deeper concept.

"Love you?" He looked away, toward the peek of ocean that was visible through the bougainvillea gardens and laughed softly—wistfully—before pulling his gaze back to me. "Lucky, loving you is not my problem. Right now, it feels like the only reason I'm alive."

I lost a heartbeat, crawled over the center console, sat in his lap and wrapped my arms around his neck. I kissed him in full view of the guard shack and a threesome of movers whom I'd never see past next week. His hands slid down my body and squeezed my ass while his mouth roughly claimed my own. I pulled off, panting, and stared into his eyes. "I love you too."

"All the good that does us."

"Come inside," I begged. "You can christen the house, fuck me in every room. Make it yours."

His chest muscles tightened underneath my hands. "Hasn't he already done that?"

I smiled against his mouth and took a final kiss. "Not in any way," I whispered.

"I take back any time I ever called him smart." He wrapped his arms around me and shouldered open the door, then carried me out of the truck. Setting me gently on the pavers, he closed the heavy vehicle door and looked warily at Windere's massive main structure. "Rich prick," he muttered, resisting when I pulled him forward, his movement reluctant as he climbed the wide entrance steps. A female mover passed us on the way and flashed a professional smile at each of us. "Ms. Fairmont. Mr. Sharp."

I felt the stumble in Lee's step and pulled him through the open front door.

"She thought I was Brant," he said, glancing over his shoulder at the woman.

"You're with me and he hasn't been here. The movers will probably assume it." I stopped in the four-story entrance hall and surveyed the great room to the left, where four movers moved in quick concert, moving items into place and unwrapping the giant pieces of art that our designer had promised would be perfect for the space. Interior decorating was one thing I actually enjoyed, and I had big plans for the house—but the space was overwhelming, so we had agreed that she would handle the main house initially, and I would do the master bedroom and the beach house. Once those were complete, I could add my touches and changes to the rest of Windere, one room at a time.

"You're saying I can fuck you right here and none of them will be the wiser?" He pushed me against the closest column, his body flush and hard against mine.

I giggled and pulled away. "Behave," I mouthed, stepping into the great room and tapping the arm of the closest mover.

"Good afternoon, Ms. Fairmont." The man looked up with a wide smile, his mustache accentuating the gesture. "How are you?"

"I'm good, thank you. We'd like some privacy. Can you find Ann and have her clear the house of staff?"

"Of course, of course." The man turned to the others and barked out a string of directions. They all scurried into action.

Lee's eyebrows rose. "Does everyone do everything you tell them to do?"

I leaned back against the closest wall and pulled him back before me. "Kiss me."

His eyes darkened and he obeyed, his body slamming against mine, his mouth hard and possessive as he groped me through the thin cotton of my sundress. "I guess that's a yes," he muttered against my mouth.

"Yes," I agreed. "Now, take me eight ways to Sunday."

"Yes, Ms. Fairmont," he drawled, lifting up my sundress and yanking down my panties in one confident motion. "With pleasure."

Chapter 56

I know you don't understand.

I know you hate me.

You'll soon find out Brant's secret. I can't keep it hidden. It won't stay quiet; it's screaming silently until the plug is pulled and its howl will fill the air.

Once you find out, you'll understand. You would have done the same thing.

* * *

I'd spent almost two years on Lee. Breaking into his life, removing any obstacles, forcing love and affection to squeeze from his pores and envelop me.

I had succeeded. I had him fully in my hands. The problem was, I had no idea where to go from there.

You could only control and manipulate a man so far before your leash of control broke. Especially a man like Lee, one who grabbed at every straw he could and wanted more. I could feel the twinge of his leash. The crackle of weakening threads as he pulled hard against my grip, straining in the direction of Brant. His hatred for him grew stronger the more Lee felt for me.

Jillian was right. I was playing a dangerous game and risking everything for my own selfish goal.

Chapter 57

TWO MONTHS AGO

The ocean-level guesthouse became our sexual den and was far enough from the main house to be our own private oasis. Sometimes Lee visited twice a week, sometimes twice a month, his appearance as sporadic as a warm day in San Francisco. Lee's concern at getting through the guards waned with each trip through our gates. They didn't hesitate to let him in and always gave him a respectful nod and friendly wave. I'd told him not to speak to them, to just approach the gates, windows up, and they would let him through.

"Your guards suck."

"What do you mean?" I craned my neck back, my head in his lap, and met his perturbed gaze.

"I could be killing you in here." Lee gestured to the open space, the beach house living room finally put together after weeks of hand-picking materials and pieces.

I laughed. "Then I'd have been dead months ago." I flipped the channel, switching back to ESPN. I'd watched more sports in the last year than I had my entire life. Brant read manuals and brainstormed product improvements in his free time, while Lee watched mindless athletic games that had no impact on anyone's life.

"I'm serious. What's the point of having guards if they just smile and wave at anyone who pulls in?"

"I told you, they know who you are."

"Which is what, your fuck buddy?" His tone was bitter enough to give me pause.

I muted the TV and turned to look up into his face. "I told them to always let you in. Just stop worrying about it."

"I don't understand. Why aren't they loyal to Brant? He's the one who pays their salary. Pays everyone's bills in this place. And where the fuck *IS* he?"

This was my least favorite version of him—when his passion turned angry. When he got like this, he was so moody, and would get pissed off at anything.

Lee continued, his voice rising. "I've been over here ten times, and he's never been home. Does he even live here?"

"You know he does." I dropped my head back on the cushion and stared at the vaulted ceiling, wondering how I got myself in these situations. More impossible questions from Lee. Would they ever end? "Remember? We had a huge fight about it." Lately, fighting seemed to be all that we were doing. Fighting and fucking.

"Rich dick." He shoved me off his lap as he stood up, knocking me from the couch onto the floor. My elbow caught on the coffee table, and I yelped in pain. I glared at him, but he was oblivious.

He paced to the window, hands on his hips, the pose accentuating every cut of his bare upper half. "I swear, Lay, you better hope I don't ever run into him. You send me down here like some fucking pool boy while he fucks you up there in that mansion—"

"You hate the main house. That's why we come down here," I said quietly.

"Has he fucked you down here?" He turned abruptly and stared at me with eyes full of hatred and hurt.

"Please stop saying fuck," I whispered.

"Has he *fucked* your sweet little *pussy* in this place?" He moved closer, emphasizing every word, his voice a snarl as he pulled me to my feet and lifted me by my waist, his grip so hard it hurt. He carried me to the granite kitchen counter and sat me on it, then pushed open my legs and took his place between them.

"No."

His hand gripped my jaw and his mouth followed suit, crashing down on my lips with a neediness that ached.

"Promise me?" He dragged me to the edge of the counter until I was fully against him, the soft material of his shorts doing nothing to disguise his arousal.

It wasn't fair, the way he could turn me into a raw cavern of want with just the awareness of his need. Why did I care so much? How was I so easily manipulated by his desire?

"I promise," I gasped. "Please, I need..." I wrapped my legs around him, and yanked at his shirt, desperate to bring his mouth back to mine.

"You need what?"

I fumbled with the top of his shorts. Reaching inside, I gripped him. "This."

"What you really need..."—he moved his hips forward and his cock thrust through my grip—"is to be bad."

"Yeah?"

"Yeah."

I swallowed. "Then make me bad."

"I'll make you worse."

Then he fucked me, right there on the kitchen counter. When I came, I screamed my orgasm against the waves and the gulls and the wind. And forty-two stories above us, the colossal mansion on the cliff was silent and empty.

Chapter 58

Living together changes a relationship. Brant and I didn't have the normal relationship issues. There were no dirty dishes to argue over. No laundry left on unswept floors. No, the traditional sources of strife were handled by our over-attentive staff of seven. Instead, our relationship only improved as a result of our addresses merging.

If I had any doubt of my love, it faded every time I woke up next to him. His focus was best in the morning, and he woke me up before dawn each morning with gentle swipes of his fingers through my hair, and soft kisses placed on the neck, forehead, and cheeks. I'd roll into his arms, and there we'd spend an extra hour in bed, drifting in and out of sleep as the sun peeked, then rose over the silver ocean. There was a coffee bar by the bedroom's fireplace, and it was set to brew at six, filling the room with the scent of ground coffee beans. I would lose him for a few minutes as he fixed both of us a large mug—his black, mine with cream and sweetener. Then he'd crawl back into the massive California king bed, his body warm against my ice-cold hands and feet. Sometimes he read, my body curling into his as I fell back asleep on his chest. Sometimes we fucked, his hard-on impossible to ignore against my leg, our playful kisses turning deeper and more heated. But mostly, we talked. About his day or mine. About HYA events or BSX projects. About our future and whether we would have two kids or four. Private or public schooling. Whether they would go to Stanford or join the Peace Corps.

In the evenings, on the nights he came home, we cooked. Christine, the chef, acted as our instructor, and our skills grew with each dinner. My forte was implementation, Brant's prep. We put on music, Christine kicked us off with general instruction, and then sat back and let us struggle our way through the process.

Sometimes he'd get home too late. I'd save him a plate of her creation and sit with him on the upper porch. With the crash of the ocean in the background, we'd talk while I sipped wine and he ate like a teenager. His appetite was huge. I never knew that before we lived together. I had no idea that he snacked constantly then ate large meals, as if he was burning a thousand calories a day, his taste in cuisine as varied as my own.

I had known, and quickly verified, that he worked way too much. Had horrible tastes in clothes, music, and whiskey. Couldn't recall half of his days when we sat down to talk. Lost track of time when steaks were on the grill. Loved, above all else, the sound of my orgasm. Wanted, more than anything, to spend the rest of his life with me.

The closer we grew, the more I was tempted to bring up the secrets that lay between us. To talk through things until we discovered a way to have a real future. I knew there was some path there, despite all of Jillian's warnings to the contrary.

Our love could carry us through. It could be the glue that held him together when his world fell apart.

I wanted to kick at the support beams of all that he knew.

Expose the truth behind all of it.

Tell him everything and see if he survived.

See if he stayed.

But damn, it was such a risk.

I risked losing him, destroying his life.

I risked saving our love, our future.

Chapter 59 – Brant

I am not a simple man. I know that. We all discovered that the summer of my eleventh year. The summer it snowed in San Francisco. The summer the three girls disappeared. The summer my parents bought a computer, and I stopped playing outside. That summer, everything as I knew it changed.

The simple Tandy processor, set up in my father's office, unlocked an entire world for me. The introduction to advanced technology took my childhood obsession with calculators and small appliances to an entirely new level. A switch turned on in my mind and I opened the door wider, letting a pent-up sea of 'what if' thought processes loose.

I dismantled the expensive new purchase, its guts stretching out across my father's desk and learned its language in days. My parents were furious, then confused, then saw the genius, and moved me and the computer down to the basement. They gave me a workspace, tools, and freedom.

I worked at a furious pace. The library became my second home, and I checked out and read every book on technology they had. My interest became an obsession, my passion a madness. The more I learned, the more I opened different parts of my mind and learned of their potential, the further my intellectual capacity grew. Chaos began to reign in my mind, a complicated race of intellectual competition, as one thought process competed with another, all in an attempt to fight to the front of my subconscious.

I worked harder. Didn't eat. Barely slept. Ignored my parents and became the typical irritable preteen. I moved my bed into the basement and spent every spare moment there. It was as if technology spoke the only language that my newfound madness understood. Inside those cement walls the chaos—for one brief moment—stopped. Focus came to my life. Everything else disappeared. As I worked a furious schedule in my new home, my parents grew worried, consulted shrinks, and discussed me in hushed tones as if I was sick.

They started to take me to doctors, a slew of them. Dr. F was the face that stuck. A constant presence in the carousel of different tests and meds. He was a psychologist, one who asked questions and examined my experiences. He tried to sort through the kaleidoscope of my mind and understand its structure and balance. He pulled from me dozens of stories and covered every facet of my adolescence. I answered all of his questions but never could seem to tell him what he wanted to know. His focus was always stuck on two dates: August 2nd and December 12th of my eleventh year. When asked about those dates, I remained mute.

It wasn't a conscious decision; I wasn't being stubborn or secretive. I didn't tell him because I didn't know what happened. It was as simple as that. I couldn't remember. Or maybe, my subconscious wouldn't let me remember.

Around the time that I thought the chaos would split my mind in two and reveal a brain cavity filled with wires, Dr. F solved the riddle. He found the right cocktail of drugs that quieted the madness and put a muted skin over all of the colors. He narrowed my world down to the basement, where time passed in a sea of grey. We switched from public school to homeschooling, any friends faded away, and I re-engineered my life with firewire cables and more CPUs. Dr. F and the tests eventually stopped. Jillian moved in, my parents returned to their jobs, and after a while, life took on a new reality: Jillian and I against the world. I built computers, she brokered deals, and we became successful. Any deceit we orchestrated ... it didn't seem to matter. Money was rolling in, and my parents lapped up anything we said like milk.

I lied for almost a decade, Jillian covering my sins with a smile and words so smooth that I almost believed them myself. Then, she brought me a new medication and I didn't have to lie anymore.

It'd been 27 years since that eleventh year of my life.

I was in control. I was in love. I would convince her to be my wife, and we would work through her issues together.

I had never been better, and the future was mine.

Chapter 60

ONE WEEK AGO

The crash of a plate cut to my core as Lee's arms swept everything off the entry table in one angry sweep. He was drunk, his eyes bleary, and had announced his arrival with a steady press on the doorbell between the guest house and main home. At the loud sound, I'd pulled on a robe and taken the elevator down to the beach level, the incessant buzz of the bell ringing through the elevator, a long foreshadow of the train wreck that greeted me. He had managed, through his drunk stupor, to take the outside stairs all the way down, and initially, I wasn't sure if the heave of his chest was from exertion or fury.

"I never wanted this! You wormed your way in my fucking life and now that you have me, you don't want me!" Lee gasped out the words, his eyes wide, hurt twisting his features.

"Of course I want you. I love you." I tried to pull him into my arms, but he shoved me away, knocking over a waist-high statue in the process. The jade obelisk tipped away from me and I reached for it but failed, the heavy piece slamming into the marble floor with a loud crack.

"You say that, but you're still with him! What kind of sick twisted girl are you? I swear to God, I can't—I can't take this. You leave me and go and fuck him and it's killing me. I can't think about him touching you." He stared at me, and his eyes were dark and heavy with emotion. He exhaled hard, his hands trembling as he reached out and pulled me to him. "Tell me you love me."

"I love you." I held his stare and wished that he understood, my own eyes filling with tears.

"Tell me again."

"I love you."

He pulled me into the dark bedroom with frantic strides and stopped me in the doorway, ripping at my blue and white striped pajama pants, pulling the cotton material down with one hand while the other gripped my neck so hard that it hurt. When he pushed me onto the bed and shoved his cock inside of me, I wasn't ready and he was so hard, and I gasped from the pain but ohmygod did I love him.

"I can't lose you," he swore, lowering his body on top of mine. His hips started to move, and his cargo shorts rubbed against the back of my thighs as I wrapped my legs around his waist. "You're my everything." His mouth, surrounded by unshaven stubble scraped against my collarbone as he softly touched his lips to my skin. It was different than every other piece of this equation and I arched underneath him, pushing against his cock and pulling his head tighter to my neck, my arousal spiking as he kissed and bit the skin, creating a possessive trail. He pulled and pushed and branded me with his cock, the rhythm increasing in speed, and I moaned, the muscles under my fingers flexing as he fucked me with his frustration and feelings.

Then his lips opened against my neck, and he moaned my name, his thrusts slowing as his orgasm came. Our bodies slowed, his final thrusts hard and deep, and then he stilled. Staying inside of me, his cheek brushed mine as he brought his mouth to my ear. "Tell me."

"I love you," I said weakly.

Then he laid down beside me and rolled me over until my back was against his chest, his arm wrapped tightly around me, his hand tenderly cupping my breast. He was so much larger than me, and the tuck of our bodies put his mouth against the top of my head.

"I don't know what to do." His voice was blurry and soft in the dark room, his words almost lost in the hum of the fan. "I love you too much to leave you. But I can't do this. It is killing me." Then he said the words I dreaded, the ones I never wanted to hear but had stalked me in my dreams. "You have to choose. You have to."

Ten minutes later, his breath evened out as he fell asleep. I stayed in place, his arms relaxing around me, and began to cry. Sometimes getting everything you ever wanted sucked.

It had been long enough. Any love there would have to be strong enough. It was time. I needed to rip the roof off all of our lies.

Part Three

It was time to pull the roof off all of our lies.

Chapter 61 – Belize

TWO YEARS, FOUR MONTHS AGO

The moment Brant turned, in that Belize hotel bar, at 1:43 AM, I knew something was wrong. I just couldn't place what. I couldn't figure out why the hairs on my arm stood up. I couldn't figure out why the noise of the bar suddenly seemed to fade. I stood there, stared at him, and tried to place the problem.

"Hey." He grinned. A wide grin that showed his dimple and white teeth and spoke of carefree games of football on Saturday nights. When he smiled, his eyes carried the gesture, crinkling at the edges, creating the effect of a man who knew his charm and carried it easily. "You look lost, sweetheart." He reached forward, cupped the edge of my elbow and tugged me closer. Reflexively, I held up my hand, touching his shirt, pushing on it without any force. I was just trying to stop my forward motion while allowing my mind to sort what about this situation felt wrong. My gaze flicked right, to a polo-wearing blonde perched on the closest stool, whose outfit screamed resort employee, her hand gripped around the neck of a beer that I'm pretty sure she wasn't old enough to drink. His other hand, the one not dragging me into his space, was resting on her bare thigh. I stared at that hand and wondered why he didn't move it.

"Honey." He raised his voice, trying to get my attention and my attention snapped up to his face, that wide smile still there, his eyes on me. He'd called me honey. *Honey*. That was a word I'd never heard roll off his lips. I looked back at his hand and watched as his fingers moved, caressing her thigh. As I *fucking* watched.

I ripped my gaze from the sight, taking it back to him, my eyes raking every surface of his face, looking for clues. Was he high? Pupils normal. Drunk? Didn't really look it. He looked normal. If normal had a face that looked nothing like Brant. If normal looked flirtatious and easy-going, like a man who had friends and watched sports. Like a man whose hand was moving further up blonde tennis chick's leg.

I pushed hard against his chest and snapped my fingers at the girl. "You. Get out of here before I have you fired." She blinked and looked at Brant, then back at me. I didn't wait for a response, I turned to Brant and prepared to give him a full helping of every pissed off emotion in my body.

His face tripped my tyrannical plans. It was irritated, and he reached out and grabbed the shoulder of the blonde, pushing her back down on the stool when she went to stand. "Stay, Summer," he said under his breath, and I reached a level of pissed off that I had never experienced. *Summer?* He rose to his feet, towering above my height in the hotel slippers. "Miss, you should probably be the one to leave."

Miss? I gawked at him. If Honey had thrown me off, Miss kicked me into next week. I avoided looking to my right, hating the feel of the blonde's eyes as my boyfriend made a complete ass of me.

"Miss?" I sputtered. "What the fuck's wrong with you?"

He shook his head, and glanced around at the people beside him, as if I was the crazy one in this situation. He stepped closer to me and lowered his voice as he tilted his head down and stared directly into my furious glare. "Did I miss something? Did I do something to you without realizing it?" His eyes dropped, and I flushed for a quick moment when I realized he was staring at the sheer fabric of my top, the robe gaping open enough for him to see cleavage. I stepped back, wrapping the robe tighter, my mouth working, my hand thrusting his cell phone out, incoherent thought manifesting itself into speech, anger in the form of words, spilling out.

"I don't know what kind of sick game you're playing, Brant, but we are through. Take your cell and get your own fucking room."

"Brant?" His eyebrows met in a way that I'd never seen but was incredibly hot. The image almost distracted me from the next line of bullshit out of his mouth. "My name isn't Brant."

My name isn't Brant. The most idiotic sentence that, I could guarantee, had ever come out of that man's brilliant mouth. I laughed. "Your name isn't Brant?"

"No." He said it with such certainty that, for a minute, I thought I might be the crazy one after all. "You have me mistaken for someone else." He held out a hand as if I would have any interest in shaking it. "Who are *you*?"

The night had left Crazytown behind. I blinked at him and understood nothing except that everything was broken.

* * *

"You know my name," I whispered.

He tilted his head in a gesture of recollection, then shook his head. "No. Sorry. Have we met?"

I glanced from his innocent face to the blonde, her brows raised in an expression that indicated her impression of my sanity. Then my gaze traveled over the crowd, everyone's perplexed pity fixed on one common source: me. Not Brant, who appeared to be in the middle of a nervous breakdown.

I crossed my arms and pinched my skin, just north of my ribs, just to make sure I wasn't dreaming. I wasn't.

Brant's cell was still in my hand and, without a word, I slipped it into my pocket, turned, and fled the bar.

Hot tears slipped down my face. I veered at the sight of a stairwell door and pushed it open, then sat on the first step of the flight. My composure lasted until the door shut and then I broke down in the privacy of the stairwell.

Was *this* the end of us? Not Jillian, not an affair, or a fight ... instead this insane middle of the night confrontation with a man who didn't know my name?

I stopped rocking and tried to think, logically, through this. I analyzed his face, his reactions. The words, my instincts. I had believed the words that came out of his mouth—or rather, believed that he believed them. It was what had made the entire scene maddening. But if he believed the words he had spoken, if he believed that he didn't know me, believed that he wasn't Brant....

Was this the secret? If so, it meant it was real. That this wasn't a blip of abnormality but a ... lifestyle. A forever. I pulled out my phone, dialed Jillian's number, and damned the consequences.

She answered on the last ring before I lost my nerve to voicemail.

"Hello?" Her voice had aged, or maybe it was just the fact that it was almost three in the morning.

I cleared my throat. "It's Layana Fairmont."

"I have caller ID. I'm well aware of who you are."

"I just ... Brant ... he was downstairs in the hotel bar. And he didn't recognize me." I closed my eyes and hoped that those sentences made sense. This was the test. She would either know exactly what I was saying or jump to the conclusion that I had driven my boyfriend insane. Which, from where I was sitting, was still a fairly good possibility.

Her sigh told me everything I needed to know. It wasn't surprised or irritated. It was resigned. Expectant.

"Who was he?"

Of all of the possible responses, that one caught me off guard. "What do you mean?" "He said he wasn't Brant."

Another sigh. "I had hoped this wouldn't happen."

"Excuse me?"

She was silent for a long moment. When she finally spoke, it was the voice of an old woman. "There was a reason I didn't want you to go away together. You think I hate you. You think I'm trying to fight your relationship. But you were wrong. I was just trying to keep this moment at bay. Trying to salvage any chance of Brant having some normality."

"I don't understand." It was the understatement of my century.

"Brant has dissociative identity disorder, DID. He's had about five different personalities over the last three decades. I wish you'd gotten the name of the side you met tonight. I thought he had improved..." She stopped for a moment, the line going so quiet I worried I had lost her. I glanced at the screen and checked the connection. "I don't know as much as I'd like. He's very good at hiding; his personalities are even better. They are still, to this day, hiding from Brant."

"Hiding from Brant?" I stood up and squeezed my hands into fists, trying to slow the racing of my mind. "He doesn't know?"

"No." Her voice sharpened to a fine point. "And he can't find out. His doctors have been very clear on that. His conscience walks an emotional tightrope. Finding out ... it would be akin to pushing him off the edge of that rope and having him crash. Everything would collapse. His gifts, his personalities ... the doctors don't even know if Brant would be the one to stay in control, in the forefront. We risk, at that moment, losing the Brant that we know—the Brant that you love—possibly forever."

My legs felt like they were going to give out and I leaned against the concrete wall, unable to hold up anything other than my sanity. Pressing my fingers into the lines of my forehead, I closed my eyes and wished I could roll back the last half hour.

The secret. It had finally arrived. I had met it. And my heart felt like it had shattered from the impact.

"It won't last long," Jillian added. "Normally he'll switch back within a few hours."

"I've got to go," I mumbled into the phone.

I expected Jillian to offer some compassion, to extend some sort of olive branch in this horrible moment, but she delivered just one terse command.

"Keep the secret."

***

"Layana?" Brant's voice came from behind me. I ended the call and turned, my shoulder scraping against the painted concrete, and faced him.

He stood on the stairwell landing, his hands in his pockets, concern in his eyes. *Layana.* He had said my name, had remembered my name. A feat I wouldn't have previously considered a victory.

I stared at him, accessing the situation. The wide smile from the bar was gone, as was the girl. *Summer.* I tested his name on my tongue. "Brant?"

"What are you doing in here?" He stepped forward, his hands running over the sides of my arms as if to warm me up. "Are you okay?" He peered forward, studying my face. "Have you been crying?"

"I'm okay." That was a lie, deeper than any I'd ever told him. I searched his face, finding everything there that I knew. Responsibility. Gravity. Somberness. I reached out and wrapped my arms around his neck, breathing in his scent, the hang of smoke still on his clothes. I tightened my grip as his arms wrapped around my body. I pressed my lips against his neck as I wondered if he had kissed her.

"Come on." He lifted me off the stairs and carried me, like a child, to our room. I curled against his chest and, when he laid me on the bed, I pretended to be asleep. I didn't want questions, had too many inside my own head that might burst to the surface. I laid on the soft pillowtop and let him drag the blankets over me. A half hour passed, and then I felt the sink of the bed when he got in beside me, his skin smelling of soap. He wrapped his arm around me and pulled my body back against his.

He whispered in the quiet room. "I love you."

I love you too. I kept my body still, my breath even, the words only in my mind. I waited for him to fall asleep and tried not to think about the ring in his suitcase.

Chapter 62

The next morning, I stayed in bed. The room was full of light when Brant's lips brushed the back of my neck.

"Come on, baby." His voice was sweet against my skin. "Big plans for today."

I curled my knees to my chest and thought of the ring box. *Big Plans.* Talk about terrifying. I pulled the blanket tighter and let out a groan.

"What's wrong?" His hand softly brushed across the top of my head, smoothing down my hair. It was probably the same hand that had slid up that woman's leg. The one that had caressed her thigh like he wanted to fuck her.

"I don't feel well." It was half true. I wanted to vomit at the thought of what he had done last night. If he hadn't come to— would he have left with her? Or invited her up to his—our —room?

"Really?" His voice held concern, but also disappointment. What were his plans for that ring? A beachside proposal? When? Today? Tonight? Yesterday, I was ecstatic at the idea. Now, I wondered if I could sneak away and catch a flight home before he caught wind of it.

"Call the front desk. See if they have a nurse or doctor on

staff." I didn't lift my head, and the pillow muffled the words, but I was certain he could understand them.

"A nurse? You're that bad?" He gently touched my forehead, but fever wasn't a symptom of heartbreak.

"Hurry," I whispered. There was the rustle of sheets and the bed lightened as he moved to the desk that was set against the wall. He picked up the phone and pressed a button, then spoke with hushed words that I couldn't hear.

"Someone will be here in a few minutes. What can I get you? Water? Aspirin?" He was moving into problem-solving mode, and maybe feigning an illness was a bad idea. Then again, at least he wasn't dropping to one knee.

I groaned in response and pulled the blanket tighter.

I'll give the expensive resort credit. Within a few minutes, there was a polite knock on our door, and two nurses and our butler arrived. They swept into the bedroom, all efficiency and concern, and beelined for my side. Gingerly propping myself up, I grimaced in faux pain and asked Brant to give me some privacy with the nurses.

As soon as the door closed, I quickly whipped away the blanket and stood up, pressing one finger to my lips. I moved to the closet and opened my suitcase, unzipping one of the interior pockets and withdrawing six crisp hundred-dollar bills from the cash that I'd tucked inside. I handed each of them three hundred dollars and whispered a quick explanation of my needs.

A few minutes later, they opened the bedroom door, their faces grave, and informed Brant and our butler that I needed to return home immediately. From my spot back in the bed, I heard the butler offer to arrange transportation. Brant accepted, more tips changed hands, the duo of nurses getting double-compensated, then they left. The butler started the business of packing our items while Brant knelt at the side of my bed, his face at eye-level, his hand gripping mine. I winced for good measure and tightened the curl of my body.

"I'm so sorry, love. I wish there was something I could do."

I closed my eyes, hoping he would stop. Surely the butler needed help with packing, or the plane needed to be paid for—something that could pull him away from me.

"I love you so much. If anything happens to you..." There was a break in his voice, a desperation that filled me with guilt.

I opened my eyes and saw him patting his pockets, then looking around wildly. *Oh no.* I pulled on his hand, drawing his attention to me. "I just want to sleep right now," I mumbled. "The nurses gave me something for the pain..."

I closed my eyes and let my hand slacken in his grip, feigning sleep. His palm shifted in mine, slipping away as he stood. His lips pressed against my forehead and then he was moving away.

The return trip was made by private jet, with no lines for security, no baggage claim. The hotel's limo pulled into the private airport, and we were airborne fifteen minutes later. The flight attendant offered me a tan leather couch that was made up with pillows and a blanket, and I laid on my side. Brant sat at the end and pulled off my ballet flats and set my feet in his lap, his hands gentle as they rubbed my soles.

I tucked my hands under the pillow and avoided looking his way. I fought not to recoil at the touch of his hands, but I was terrified of doing anything to encourage him to pull out that ring box and ask the question I had spent months pining for. I pinched my eyes shut to avoid conversation and counted down the hours until landing.

As I pretended to sleep, I tried to remember exactly what Jillian had said. *Dissociative personality disorder.* That's what she had called it, right? Or maybe it was dissociative identity disorder. *Given the time and different stages of his life, he's had as many as five different personalities ...* His hand on the girl's thigh. Her smudged lip-gloss. How many women had he flirted with? How many had he slept with? All while dating me? Falling in love with me? Preparing to propose to me?

He's very good at hiding; his personalities are even better. All of the missed dates. The things I'd blamed on forgetfulness. So many times he'd left during the night... to go where? To do what?

We risk ... losing the Brant that you love ... forever.

All I wanted was to be back home. I needed my house and my solitude and the chance to figure this mess out, and to decide if there was any chance of keeping my heart together from splitting in two.

Three months later, Lee stepped up to me in that gas station store and flashed his smile. What would you have done? I had loved one side of Brant. Was it really that strange that I fell in love with another?

Chapter 63

PRESENT DAY

I don't care what Jillian says, I have to tell Brant the truth. He's an intelligent man, the smartest I've ever known. He loves me, and Lee loves me. There should be a path, somewhere, with that intersection of emotion, that will work.

Maybe I should talk to Jillian about this, but I can't. I'm too worried about what she would say. The orders she will shove down my throat. Orders I have no intention of following. Orders that will probably be logical and just, but I'm pressed against an electric fence, and I just can't take the sensation a moment longer.

I know what the right thing to do is: to allow Brant to live his separate lives without interference. I understand that. But it's too late for that. I fucked up this entire situation two years ago. When I saw Lee and stepped closer. Fucked him in a parking lot and fell in love with his smile. Chased him down and wrestled his heart into submission.

I only have two options. Lose Lee or tell Brant. The first I'm too selfish to consider. The second puts Brant's psychological well-being in danger. Again, I know what I should do. What path Jillian would scream at me, her hatred compounding with every word, and it would be completely justified.

Am I really this horrible? I think the answer is yes. I know it's wrong, but my love is too strong to feel anything but right. I can't lose Lee. And I did—I've been doing all of this—out of love for Brant.

Yes, this is selfish.

Yes, I am putting Brant in danger.

Yes, I am possibly saving my relationships in the process.

Yes, I am taking the biggest gamble of my life.

I love them both too much to do anything else.

I pour two glasses of wine slowly, watching the dark burgundy liquid as it sloshes into the crystal. Through the open glass sliders, the wave of ocean wind is crisp in the dark evening, and out there, on the wide balcony, Brant waits for me. On a normal evening, we would discuss our future plans, the events of the day, memories from our past.

Now, as I walked through the open doors and took my place on the outdoor couch next to Brant, I wondered if those nights were gone from our relationship forever. Handing him his glass, I try to figure out where to begin.

* * *

Out above the water, the moon sits, half full, its reflection stretched over the rippling water. Small birds have made their nests in the rafters of this porch, and they coo and trill at odd intervals in the night. I watch as he settles back against the dark navy cushions of the outdoor couch, the tips of his fingers resting on the top of the wine glass. Every few moments, he takes a sip, and this is his favorite—an expensive merlot that we discovered at a charity tasting and now had a case delivered twice yearly, the bottles placed in the climate-controlled wine cellar below the kitchen.

His wine is half gone by the time I finally speak. "I've been keeping something from you." I set my glass on the table and twist on the cushion to face him.

He follows suit, setting down his wine, his attention on me, the clench of his jaw the only sign of his tension. I stare at that tightening muscle and wonder about it, the tic one that I rarely see in Brant.

I swallow and try to find the next sentence, my hands knotting together nervously as I attempt to pull together a path of intelligent thought. All of my preparation, the hours I contemplated this moment, and yet every thought had left my mind.

"Is this about the other man?" His voice is deadly calm. A calm I have never heard from him but would have expected if I'd ever envisioned an angry version of Brant. Calculated, controlled, and angry.

I tried to follow the path of his question. "What do you mean? What other man?"

"The other man you've been seeing." He says the words casually, but I see the tightness in his face, the stiff line of his mouth.

"What are you talking about?" I stall, but of course he knows —he must have known. I was stupid to think otherwise. The man is brilliant. He can spot minute changes in a hundred pages of code. I haven't exactly hidden my behavior. I was naive to assume that an absent man couldn't catch someone who—in his mind— didn't exist. But that was my mistake. Brant wouldn't think that Lee didn't exist, he would just not realize that Lee was him.

"We're both intelligent adults, Layana. Don't play stupid." His voice is harder than I've ever heard it, yet still quiet in volume.

I swallow. "Okay. Yes, in part this is about him. Just bear with me for a minute. I'm getting there."

"I've been waiting for you to explain what I'm not providing for you." There is a tremor in the words, and this is what hurt sounds like. Hurt that I caused, in trying to maintain our future. The hint of the anguish is small, easily missed, yet in the structure of Brant's voice I hear them as loudly as if he is screaming.

"It's not what you think. I—"

"How long have you been with him? Five months or is it longer? I suspected before but didn't know for sure until we lived together." He leans forward, resting his elbows on his knees, his eyes intent on mine. Analyzing. Searching for truth among so many old lies.

"Two years."

That hurts when it hits. I see the flinch in his features. The swallow of his throat, the brim of moisture that comes to the edges of his eyes. He drops his head to his hands. "Two years." He swears under his breath. "Is he why you won't marry me?"

"Not in the way you think." I hadn't intended for my relationship with Lee to be the catalyst that started this conversation, and I itch to move on—past my betrayal.

"Do you love him?"

I move closer to him on the couch and lift his head, forcing him to meet my gaze. "I love *you*. Everything about this has been about you."

He yanks away. "Stop talking in riddles and tell me why."

"I need you to look at me. I need you to listen."

He does. He turns back to face me, looks me in the eyes, and focuses. He drops his ego, his hurt, and focuses on my words. He does what Brant was built to do. Analyze and interpret.

I give up my hunt for the perfect words and dive in.

"His name is Lee. I met him in Mission Bay. He does odd landscaping jobs out there for cash. He was dating another girl for a large part of last year. I've been sleeping with him off and on for two years. I used to do it at my house, now I do it in the guesthouse. Lee is not his real name, it's an identity that he's adopted." I swallow, then go in for the kill. "Brant, his real identity ... it's you. He's a personality that your brain created, an identity that you adopt at times, mostly during times of stress. You have a condition called dissociative identity disorder. It's what used to be called multiple personality disorder. I haven't been cheating on you. The other man ... it's you. It's just a different side of you, one who has his own personality."

His expression doesn't change when I stop talking. He just stares into my eyes.

A long moment passes, then stretches into two. He blinks a few times but holds my gaze as his mind works into overtime. "I'm thinking," he finally says. "Trying to decide if you are lying or if you sincerely believe what you just told me."

"I'm not lying."

He studies me in a way that he's never done before, as if he is assembling a different clue from every part of my face. "I believe that you mean what you're telling me," he says slowly. "That doesn't mean you aren't insane."

I smile slightly. "I'm not insane."

"One of us is. I'd much rather it be you."

My smile drops. "You're not insane."

"I'm absent-minded, I'm not living separate lives."

"I've been fucking your other personality for two years. You are."

"Do you love him?" The question, when repeated a second time, has entirely different tones. Now it is thoughtful, almost kind. He probably thinks I'm mental.

"Yes." I blink, and tears are suddenly present, blurring my vision. It isn't fair to love a man in two different ways. One way is hard enough.

"More than me?"

"No."

"You're mistaken." His lips press together and his jaw hardens, his stubbornness coming out to play. He smooths his hands down the front of his slacks and goes to stand up. The wine glass topples and shatters on the brick floor and I flinch at the harsh sound.

"Jillian is the one who told me." It's a gamble, but it gets his attention.

He is navigating around the sharp edge of the coffee table and pauses, then turns to me. *"Excuse me?"*

I move to the end of the couch, following his retreat, and grab at his pants, trying to keep him in place. "When we were in Belize

—the weekend you were going to first propose. I woke up in the middle of the night and couldn't find you. I went downstairs and saw you in the bar. But you weren't yourself. You didn't recognize me. You introduced yourself as someone else—"

I stop as he roughly pushes me aside. The action was more Lee than Brant and I choke back the rest of my sentence.

"You're wrong," he snaps. "You were confused. Probably drunk."

The dig is so unlike Brant that it takes me a moment to react. I struggle to my feet, and reach for his hand, but miss. Frustration bubbles through me. "No! I stood in the bar, and you told me *you didn't know me*. You made a fool out of me, you made me look crazy. You had your hands all over another woman. I left the bar and called Jillian. She's the one who told me." I lower my voice, and at least he isn't walking away, he's standing half inside the kitchen, his head cocked toward me, listening.

"She told me that you've suffered from DID since you were ten. Since you became a savant. She said the doctor said you can't be told the truth. That you might have a mental break and lose Brant and adopt one of the other personas. Your parents, Jillian ... they all know. They keep the secret to protect you!" My voice gives out on the last word, the hoarse rasp of the final work breaking the sentence in two.

He spins back toward me and steps closer, his hands fisting, and the calm stride of his voice is broken by the frustration in his tone. "So why then, Layana, are *you* telling me this?"

"I can't..." I lose my nerve, too scared to voice my selfish thoughts. "Lee ... he wants me to choose. What you do in your other lives, I tried but I can't ignore it. I can't be your wife and know that when you are away from me, when you are living another life, that you are touching other women. Falling in love with other women. I need you to be fully mine. I need you to love only me. Right now, I have you both. I love you both. But Lee, he wants me to choose. I can't lose him, Brant. I need to find a way to have you both, without losing either of you."

"So your plan was to tell me. To burden me with this?"

I wanted to go to him, to hold him, but it was as if there was a forcefield of hostility around him. "I don't know. A part of me thought it would be freeing." But had I? I had wanted company in my misery. I had wanted an end to the charade, to the lies, to the push and pull of unpredictability and guessing games. I had believed—still believe—that Brant could somehow solve it. He solves everything at work, with every project he tackled. Why would this be any different?

"I want to speak with Jillian. I don't believe you."

"How can you love me, want to marry me, and think that I would lie about this?" I fist my hands in my hair, wanting to pull out the long strands in frustration. I step toward him, then stop at the precipice of the house, and the warmth beckons to me, a stark contrast to the cold man who is watching me with wary distrust.

I force myself to close the distance between us and stop in front of him, my bare feet curling into the red brick, toe to toe with his grey dress socks. I lift my gaze and stare up at him, hoping, praying, that the man I love will look inside himself and find the man I can't live without.

His mouth tightens but there in his eyes... there is a hint of softness, of love. He lowers his head and touches his forehead against mine, his eyes closing as we connect. I press my hands to his chest, feeling through the soft fabric of his shirt, and inhale the clean, strong scent of him.

"It's inconceivable, Layana," he says softly, his breath ghosting over my lips. "What would you do if I told you that you had another person living inside of you?"

"But I don't." I pull back my head, hating to break the connection, but needing to see into his face. His handsome features are in the shade, and I want to suggest that we go inside, to sit down at the dining room table, but I don't want to disrupt the progress we've made. If I have to stand in the doorway all night, we can.

He snorts. "Yeah, well. That's how I feel. I'm in my head all day long. Have been for almost forty years. Trust me, there's no one else up there."

With that, he pulls away from me and strides toward the kitchen. I wait to see what he is going to do, but then he's shrugging into a brown canvas jacket and heading out of the double front doors. Less than a minute later, I hear the roar of his car.

I let him leave and wonder who will return.

Chapter 64 – Brant

It's not possible, yet she's not lying. She can't be. Everything about that interaction screamed truth.

I need Jillian. I need to look in her face and find out the truth. I press my hand to my fist, and the stress is sitting there, like a giant steel anvil, pinning my breath in place.

It's time for a pill. A blackout is coming, pushing on the edge of my sanity with greedy feelings, and my mind's source of relief is simple in its black oblivion.

But maybe I shouldn't. After a decade of the medication, I'm suddenly suspicious of the pale pill that calms my world, refocuses my anxiety, and lets me sleep. A pill a day keeps my normal life in play. That's what Jillian always said.

Is everything I've known a lie? How deep does this level of deception go?

Two decades ago, on December twelfth, I blacked out. When I came to, half of Jillian's face was beaten in, her eyes puffy slits, two teeth missing from her smile, her lip split. They said I had gone crazy. Jill had tried to pacify me and I had turned on her, windmilling punches and kicks until I knocked her onto the ground and climbed on top of her. Continued the beating until I ran out of steam, then apparently stood, took the stairs up to the living room, and watched *Judge Judy* until my parents got home. I don't remember that part. I woke up in a children's psych ward with no memory of the exchange.

That was back when I used to have blackouts. It was explained that they were my brain's way of coping with the pressures that my intellect forced on it. Spots in time where I would act in a manner that made no sense. The longest lasted five hours. Two decades ago Jillian found a doctor who solved my problem and provided a cocktail of meds that calmed my dark demons. The blackouts stopped, my only moments of dark occurring when the drowsiness side effect knocked me out. I've lived without a relapse for decades.

Blackouts. That is what I've been told, what I believe.

I push harder on the gas, my hands trembling against the steering wheel. I need to see Jillian. She is at the root of all of this. She will have the answers.

She always does.

Chapter 65 — Brant

Jillian is standing on her home's front entrance when I pull in. In a city filled with modern monstrosities, she found the scariest and ugliest of them all—a giant grey stone box, with thin strips of glass that dissected the surface in hard right angles that cut diagonally across each room. Layana had taken one look at the house and declared that it would be impossible to find curtains for it—such a strange observation but a hypothesis that was proven true when I first walked in. The interior wasn't any warmer than the exterior—all white furnishings, gold hardware and black marble accents. Voices echoed in the house, and if you left without running into a sharp edge, you were more coordinated than me.

I park in one of the empty spots off her circular drive, beside a wall of tall thin cacti that resemble twelve feet tall cucumbers. I step out of the Aston Martin and swing the door shut, then lock it with my fob.

As I take the pebbled path toward the front door, I lock eyes with my aunt. Wind buffers the long black coat around her, her hands tucked in its pockets, a resolute look on the face of a woman I love as much as my mother. As I climb the deep front steps, we hold the long look. There's fear on her face and I try to understand it, but I've never been so confused.

I reach the top of the entrance landing, and it's a stark wide platform, empty of anything but columns. Jillian steps backward, keeping distance between us, then turns and walks rapidly toward the lime green double front doors. As she approaches, the lamps on either side glow brighter, illuminating the path, and I follow her lead, as I always seem to do.

My breath fogs in the evening chill and I jog up the last few steps, anxious to get inside and out of the cold. She holds open the door, waving me in and offers me her cheek as I cross the threshold and into the brightly lit space.

Her cheek is ice cold as I kiss it, and I wonder how long she has been standing outside, waiting for me. "Jillian," I say in greeting.

"Brant," she says with a resigned sigh, removing her jacket and holding out a hand for mine. "Let's go to the parlor."

The parlor is trademark Jillian—stiff, expensive, and functional. I sit on the edge of a white divan and watch her face as she settles into an upright chair. It is even tighter than normal, her face as pale as the furniture, and the dread in the pit of my stomach grows.

"Layana called me," she says. "She told me what she told you."

I watch as she smooths the front pleats of her charcoal slacks and wait for her to dismiss the idea. Surely, she will dismiss the idea.

"I never wanted you to date that woman, Brant." She sniffs.

Not the words I am expecting. "Is she telling the truth, Jillian?"

She carefully smooths her hands over the top of her hair and pats a few windswept pieces into place. Finally, she looks at me. "You wouldn't even believe me if I told you, Brant. She has you so twisted around her finger. Multiple personalities?" she scoffs. "It's her delusional attempt to explain an affair."

She stands and paces before me, her pointy-toed shoes clicking on the floor like a metronome. "You're the one who suspected her of cheating." She points a trembling finger at me. *Trembling*. Was it from anger or fear? "You know what's going on here, Brant. She's found someone else and doesn't want to lose you over it."

My relief at her dismissal warred with my opinion of Layana. Jillian was right, I had suspected her, but I also knew that something had to have triggered the affair, there had to be an explanation paired with the betrayal.

I match Jillian's stance, rising to my feet. "So Layana invented an *identity disorder* to explain it? Do you have any idea how insane that sounds?" Something's wrong. Jillian won't meet my eyes and her gaze is skittering all over the room. "She doesn't know," I continue. "About my blackouts. She has no other ground to stand on. She looked me in the eyes and told me something she thinks to be true. Said that it was something *you told her*."

I was starting to lose control. Breath was pushing out of my chest in short bursts as the pounding in my head increased. Rage, I identified. That is this emotion. It's a foreign emotion that I haven't felt in a long time and don't understand. I can feel my psyche shuddering, as I lose a layer of my control. This is inappropriate, especially with Jillian, and I blink, focusing on her, but can still hear the snarl in my voice as I step closer. "Don't lie to me, Jillian."

"Brant... you don't understand." She falters. "Your medicine stopped all that."

"All of *what*? The blackouts? Or my stepping into another persona altogether?"

She holds up her hands, and I stop, realizing how close I am to her. Her eyes are wide with fear. But of what? Of me? It's a ridiculous thought. But still, just to be safe, I force my fists to relax.

"I don't know anything about another persona. All I know is

that you've been doing perfectly well. Your work has never been better, your focus more crisp, your creative insight more in tune."

"Fuck the work. I'm talking about my life, the person I am when I lay my head down to sleep."

"You don't mean that." She turns toward the large black fireplace—its flame the only source of color and life in the room and moves closer to its warmth. "Your work is everything, Brant. You and I... we're changing the world."

"We're building computers, Jill." I follow her and grab her thin shoulder, pulling on it until she is facing me, her gaze jerking erratically around the room before settling on mine. "What's going on with me? Is she right?" I am begging her, my fingers biting into her soft sweater, and in her eyes, there's a swarm of indecision that gives her deception away.

Fury boils through me at the tell, ripping apart the veins of my composure, and I grip her other shoulder with my free hand. I shake her, and I can feel the rattle of her small bones—the bones of a woman I thought I knew. "Tell me!" I scream, the sound echoing around the tall room. "Is there someone else inside of me? Tell me!"

It feels like there is, like a monster is taking control of me— because this violence, this eruption of control is not like me. I watch, in slow motion, the snap of her chin, its wild jerk as I shake her shoulders and I should stop, should release her, should step away, but I don't. This feeling, an overwhelming hatred of the unknown, shatters every tie of self-control that I had in place, and I notice, for the first time in decades, the fracturing of my world into pieces. A dark sweep of oblivion takes my anger and dissolves it into a sea of black.

Black.

Nothing.

Maybe it is another personality taking over. Or maybe it's the injection stabbed into my back, Jillian's eyes leaving mine for a brief second to look over my shoulder and nod her approval.

Chapter 66 – Brant

I wake up restrained. Testing my movement, my wrists and ankles have only a few inches of give. I jerk hard but the action is useless. I lift my head and can see a man in my peripheral, moving toward me. His features come into view, and despite the muddy waters of my mind, recognition immediately dawns.

"Dr. F." I let my head fall back on the pillow as he reaches forward, resting his hand on my chest, his face pinched with concern. "Where am I?"

"You're at Jillian's home. She thought this would be a better place to keep you, away from the press or public eye."

"Untie me." I try to ask with as much civility as possible but am certain he hears the anger behind my tone.

"Not yet. Jillian told me what happened... and for our safety we need to keep you restrained a little longer." He pats my arm as if he is turning down a request for a popsicle, not my right to freedom.

"Let me the fuck up. I'm not going to hurt you. I've done nothing to allow you to restrain me like an animal." I yank with all my might at the restraints, and a wave of claustrophobia swells through me.

"Brant, forget the restraints for a moment. We need to talk."

He pulls up a chair and sits, withdrawing a small notepad and a pen.

I close my eyes and will my muscles to relax, to ease the friction against the restraints. I envision the motherboard of Laya, the components that connect to make it run. The pieces of nonsense that communicate to breathe life into an inanimate object. *Peace.* With my claustrophobia under control, I open my eyes. "What do you want to know?"

"What happened when you blacked out?"

"When?"

"Yesterday. You blacked out in Jillian's den."

That was yesterday? I realize there is sunlight streaming through the windows and wonder how long I was out for. "I didn't blackout. I was drugged. "Where's Layana? I want to see her." *I need to see her. I owe her an explanation, though I don't have one yet.*

"We don't think you should have any visitors until we figure this out."

"Excuse me?" I glare at him but it's hard to be imposing when you're tied to a bed and can only move your head.

"We don't think—"

"I heard you. I just can't believe you would speak to me as if I'm a child. I'm an adult. I don't care what you *think.*"

"Mr. Brant, you've been declared incompetent. For the moment, I am your personal physician, unless Jillian appoints another one. And Jillian is your personal representative."

Oh my God. I'm going to break again. I can feel the creep, can see dots in my vision, and I struggle to stay grounded. "I can't have been declared incompetent. There is a process involved. Probate court. A psychological examination by a medical practitioner." I know because decades ago, when I was just a teenager, the conversation was had. I'd listened, my ear to the door of my room, as Jillian and my parents had discussed what would happen to my fortune if I ever lost my mind or melted down.

"Well, as you know, I'm a medical practitioner. And Jillian got some strings pulled. We have a provisional application in process, which has been approved by a local judge. It will stand until the courts open on Monday. Look, Brant. All you have to do is relax and let us help you to get back on your feet."

My brain tries to grab at straws it can't reach, and I don't know if the issue is what they injected me with or if this is what a mental breakdown feels like. I just want my normality back, the righting of this topsy-turvy ship. "I need my medicine," I gasp. "Please."

"We're going to hold off on any medication until we see the frequency of your switches."

We. The word grates on me and as frustrating as it is to have one person controlling my life, the idea of a *we* is even more infuriating.

"My switches?" My chest hurts, and the weight of the stress feels like it will break right through my sternum.

"Your switches into other personalities. We can't understand them until we observe them. This controlled environment is my first opportunity to do a proper job of that."

"Other personalities?" Dammit, I need Layana. If this is true, which Dr. F seems to be implying, then I need to talk this through with—

BLACK.

<h1 style="text-align:center">Chapter 67 – Lee</h1>

I wake up in an old lady's bed, complete with floral sheets and a canopy top. Shifting against the stiff mattress, I stare at a fancy gold-print wallpaper and try to place where I am. I had to have been shit-faced drunk to go home with a senior citizen and end up in her bed. Moving my head slowly to the left, I come face to face with an old bald man. I flinch, and the dude is staring at me like he's about to cut me open for surgery. Shit. I try to sit up but my hands won't move, my wrists pinned to the sides of the bed with handcuffs. Double shit. I jerk hard at the restraints and my arms feel like I spent the whole day doing curls.

I twist to look at the old man. "Who the fuck are you?" I spit out.

The man smiles as if he has all the time in the fucking world. "Let's get your name first. Then I'll tell you mine."

Screw that. I press my lips together, not wanting to yield the power of answering first. Then again, I'm handcuffed to a fucking bed, so maybe the power struggle is already lost. "Lee."

"Lee what?"

I frown, not sure what he's getting at. "Lee Let-Me-The-Fuck-Up-Before-I-Kick-Your-Ass."

Baldy has the guts to laugh. "Oh, *that* Lee. Nice to meet you. I'm Dr. Finzlesk."

"Am I under arrest?" Wouldn't be the first time I've woken up in a jail cell, but it would be the first cell with hardwood floors, twelve-foot ceilings, and framed art.

"No. I'd just like to ask you some questions."

"How'd I get here?" I'm used to waking up in odd locations, but this shit takes the fucking cake.

"Is that something you often ask yourself?"

"Just answer the fucking question."

"You grew violent; you were sedated. We restrained you so that you wouldn't hurt anyone else."

"I hurt someone?"

"Not too badly." The man smiles, and it's an odd response, like there's a joke he's keeping from me.

Not too badly. What the fuck's that mean? Irritation blooms, but my head fucking hurts, like someone's clamped a vice to my temples. I close my eyes against the pain and that asshole's smile. "Whose house is this?" he grits out.

"A woman named Jillian Sharp. Do you recognize that name?"

"No." I straighten at the familiar last name. "Is she related to Brant Sharp?"

"Yes."

It's like a puzzle that is missing the pieces. I hate puzzles. So I'd hurt someone related to Brant Sharp. Maybe I'd finally snapped and tracked down that rich fuck himself and kicked his ass. Gotten a chance to fight for the woman that I don't really deserve.

"What's the last thing you remember?"

I stare at the ceiling, which has a grid of beams. Screw this asshole and his questions. They need to let me the fuck up, then maybe I'll answer some questions.

"Lee? What's the last thing you remember?"

"Fuck you. Give me my phone call."

After that, I keep my mouth shut and don't say a damn word. Hours come and go, and Baldy doesn't give up—his skinny butt pinned to that velvet throne-looking chair, his creaky voice asking questions over and over, not giving up.

Finally, with the windows dark, dozens of questions unanswered, the doctor stands up with a sigh. His bladder is probably busting at this point. Setting down the blank notepad, he opens his bag, removes an item, and approaches the bed.

I jerk at the hot prick of metal and whip my head toward the doctor. "What was that you—"

BLACK.

Chapter 68

Two days have passed, and I can't get Brant or Lee to answer their cell.

It was the last thing I wanted to do, but I broke down and drove to Jillian's house. She answered the door in a lavender suit, every bit of her buttoned into place, but I could see the strain on her face. Her eyes were as bloodshot as my own. We both love him; I know that. I understand that she's dealt with this for decades longer than I have. I know she's mad at me for breaking the balance, for shoving the truth into his face despite the consequences. That decision, that action—I might be the one responsible for tipping the scale and causing his psyche to crash. Right now, he was out there somewhere, and potentially falling to a depth that he might not ever rise from.

In my moment of confession, I might have lost the man I love.

Had I? The unanswered question is killing me.

Jillian doesn't know where he is either. He hasn't called her or responded to her texts. She didn't verbalize it, but I could feel the weight of her blame. This was exactly what she warned me of and, for the first time, I deserve every bit of her scorn.

Together, we agreed not to call the police. To just wait and hope for him to surface. She's monitoring his credit cards and bank accounts, and sooner or later, he'll use one.

He has to.

Chapter 69

At four in the morning, I wake with an idea. Rolling onto my back, I stare at the coffered ceiling as the pieces of a plan slowly click into place. As soon as a hint of light coats the walls, I sit up and reach for my phone. I consider calling Don, then decide on Marcus instead.

I dial his number and stand, moving to the large glass doors at the edge of the room and look out over the morning view. At this time in the morning, the water begins to glow amber and pink, with fog hanging over the water like a blanket of cotton balls. The view is incredible and one that I typically sleep through, and Brant always enjoys a cup of coffee in hand.

"Hello?"

I pull open the door and inhale the crisp cool air. "This is Layana. Are you busy?"

"I'm sleeping." He doesn't sound asleep. He sounds annoyed, but I don't care. Right now, Brant's safety trumps his sleep.

"I'm coming to you. Text me your address."

"Is this about Molly?"

Molly? I hadn't thought about her in months. "Text me your address." I hang up the phone and shove my feet into a pair of wool-lined boots. I move quickly through the halls to my office, where I steal a piece of paper from my printer, grab a gold Le Blanc pen from the desk, and pull open the second drawer of the left cabinet. Withdrawing the appropriate folders, I sit down at the desk and write down a list of details in my neat block font—a carryover from my prep school days. Folding the paper into quarters, I stand and push it into the pocket of my cashmere drawstring sleeping pants.

Taking the elevator down, I step into the cavernous garage. Lights automatically warm the space, highlighting the glossy hoods in rapid succession. Vintages beside luxuries beside exotics. My phone chimes with Marcus's address at the same time that I press the button and open the third garage bay.

Marcus had been the one who'd gotten rid of Molly. Hopefully, he could help me find Brant.

* * *

Marcus answers the door wearing only paid blue pajama bottoms, and the view of chiseled abs does absolutely nothing for me. I move into his ranch-style home, beeline for the tiny kitchen and slap a piece of paper on the counter.

"This is what I need." I explain the plan, then dial a number on my cell phone and hold it out toward him. "Call them."

He studies the page, then looks at me. "A phone call? That's it? For a thousand bucks?"

I shrug. "It's five am. I figure I owe you graveyard rates. But you have to sell it. Otherwise..."

"Yeah, yeah. I got it." He sighs and starts the call.

"Put it on speaker," I whisper.

He obliges but glares at me while he does it.

"Eurowatch Assistance, how may I help you?" Of course, the female voice carries the haughty British accent I'd come to expect when dealing with the English car brand.

Marcus clears his throat. "Hello. My name is Brant Sharp, and I'm afraid I need help in locating my car."

"Certainly, Mr. Sharp. May I ask, is this a theft?"

I hadn't prepped him for that question and shake my head, but he is already ahead of me, his mouth curving into a smile as he delivers a wry chuckle that sounds very convincing. "No, nothing like that. I'm afraid I've just lost track of it."

"I understand. To begin, I will need to ask you a series of security questions to verify your identity. It's for your own protection."

"Go ahead." Marcus leans back against his kitchen counter and holds the paper in front of him, his attention on the details I've written there.

"What is the VIN of the car you would like to track?"

"J2R43L2KS14JD799F," he recites.

"Please hold while I pull up your profile." A series of keystrokes clicks through the speaker.

I exhale, hoping I have enough information. I had copied all of the details on the car's purchase from the file, as well as his personal identification items. I can't imagine that Aston Martin knows much more than what was presented at the time of purchase.

"Mr. Sharp, may I have your address please?"

"My current address is 23 Ocean's Bluff Drive."

"And your driver's license number?"

There are three more questions and Marcus passes each of them with flying colors. We both let out a breath when the woman moves on.

"Please hold while we locate the vehicle."

I give Marcus a thumbs up and he rubs his fingers together. Reaching into my pocket, I pull out his cash and toss it onto the counter. Knotting my hands together, I close my eyes and wait for the voice to give me a hint to my soulmate's location.

"Mr. Sharp, if you have a pen, I have the location."

I open my eyes and move closer, and my stomach heaves. I feel like throwing up, but I haven't eaten anything in almost a day.

"Go ahead." Marcus pushes the page toward me, along with a pen.

"8912 Evergreen Trail, San Francisco, California. Please know that, if you wish, we can remotely disable the engine."

Marcus glances at me, and I shake my head in response. "That won't be necessary. Thank you for your help."

"Thank you for calling Eurowatch, Mr. Sharp. And thank you for being a member of the Aston Martin family."

Marcus reaches out and ends the call. "That help?"

"It does, thanks." I key the address into my phone and grab the paper, my mind mentally walking through the next steps. I should call Jillian. Get her involved, or at least in the loop before I head wherever Brant is.

I come to a sudden stop before the door, and he bumps into me from behind.

"What?" He steps back. "Everything okay?"

I stare at my phone screen. The first search engine result is the property appraiser site for San Francisco County. 8912 Evergreen Trail is a home, purchased for seven million dollars a decade ago by Jillian Sharp.

I yank at the front door, my fury propelling me forward.

"What's wrong?" Marcus calls after me, and I glance back to see him in the door, his hands braced on either side of the frame.

I pause and swivel back toward him. I thrust the paper at him. "Call them back. Find out how long his car has been there. Then text me and let me know."

"That's going to cost you another—" His hands raise when he sees the fire in my glare. "Okay. Just joking. I'll call them."

"Now!" I bark out, my steps increasing to a jog as I head toward my car.

* * *

My suspicions are confirmed when the text from Marcus comes through, the message displaying on my windshield's heads up display.

SINCE FRIDAY NIGHT

My fury, which had been building in my chest since the moment I identified her address, whipped through me like a snapped wire. That bitch had stood on her front porch and lied to me; his car probably hidden away in one of the adjacent garages. She'd let me stand there guilt-stricken and led me to believe that Brant was wandering around lost, unsure of who he was, in the middle of a *psychological break* because of my actions. That smug, judgmental glare, while he had been inside her house the whole time. Had he stood at one of the large upper windows and watched me? Is he mad at me? Is she using this time to turn him against me? I need to know what is being said and where his mind is. If he's in a strong place or a weak one.

Early traffic is beginning to clog the 101 as I head toward Jillian's neighborhood. I should have recognized the address the moment it had been announced by the Aston Martin representative. Granted, Brant and I have driven to her home so often that I knew it by sight, not address. Still ... I bite my lip and try to organize my thoughts. I roll my shoulders, trying to relieve the tight bundle of muscles that was cramping along my upper back.

Okay, I told myself. It's okay. Soon, I will see him. He's safe. He's not lost. His mind must be intact if he is at Jillian's.

I just need to talk to him. To bring him back, because without him, I'm lost.

Chapter 70

Jillian lives in Nobb Hill, one of the snootier areas of San Francisco, if I have any right whatsoever to call anything snooty. I pull into her drive and park in the circular drive, shutting off the engine and staring at the ultra-modern house. There is a white late model BMW parked on the black pavers beside me. I look at it with new interest, trying to remember if it had been there yesterday. Coming up blank, I take the steps toward the front door. On the entry level, I pause and consider the fact that it's barely seven a.m.

I try the level handle, unsurprised to find it locked. I glance at my phone, double-checking the time, then press the doorbell. Repeatedly.

My trepidation over the early hour disappears the moment Jillian swings open the large door. She's already dressed, her hair in place, full makeup on. Her curious look turns to an impressive show of faux alarm upon seeing me. "What's wrong? Is it Brant? Did you find him?"

An incredulous laugh bubbles up my throat at the questions, delivered so convincingly, and I can't believe that she's continuing this façade. So much for expecting her to be contrite and honest.

I force the laugh down. If she wants to play that game, so can I. "No." I tuck an unwashed strand of my hair behind my ear, aware that hers looked salon-fresh. "I haven't. I'm really worried. May I come in?" I'm not an actress, but the words came out pretty well, my rage disguised as concern.

Her dark red lips pin together. "It's awfully early, Layana. The staff isn't even up yet."

I call bullshit on that. Jillian demands secretaries at BSX arrive by 6:30 AM. Her house staff probably starts their day before the sun rises. I shove the door open and squeeze by her, ignoring her huff of annoyance. "I just need a minute, Jillian. I'm going crazy with worry."

"Well, please keep your voice down," she says stiffly. "This needs to be a short visit."

Short visit, my ass. I pause in the entry foyer and wait for her to shut the door. She turns to me and gestures toward the parlor.

* * *

It's time for me to admit that I have underestimated this woman. I've stood opposite of her for three years but haven't appreciated the extent of her deception. Now, I know the truth—that Brant is here, or has been here—yet I'm almost persuaded by her acting. I sit in her formal sitting room, listen to her smooth lies, and start to feed her rope, curious where she plans to take this. I feed her foot after foot and watch as she sits in a plush red upright chair, ties a complicated noose around her neck and hangs herself.

It's a masterful act. One that goes through irritation, then sympathy, then a full breakdown of tears over 'where our boy could be'. She's *so* worried for him. Terrified. And such the perfect portrayal of a loving aunt. I watch her performance with dead eyes, horrified by the ability of this woman who has orchestrated Brant's life for two decades. She's run BSX during that time. Protected his secrets while spinning lies of her own. I sit beside her, grip the velvet arm of a chair, and wonder where in the home Brant is.

Once the noose is tied, once I know her selfish loyalties, once I fully understand my enemy ...

I push to my feet and scream Brant's name as loud as humanly possible.

Chapter 71

Jillian shoots to her feet, confused, and her gaze darts to the upper right. I take off in that direction, sprinting up the geometric staircase, moving faster than a high-heeled senior citizen can even think about going. I scream his name over and over as I tear down a marble hallway, my steps echoing through the halls, and skid to a halt when I hear my name. It was from a few doorways back, and I retraced my steps, pushing open a bedroom doorway right as Jillian appears at the top of the stairs.

She's breathing hard, gripping the metal railing as if she needs it to stay upright, and I'm not certain, if she had a heart attack right here, that I'd even care. I hear my name again and I turn back to the bedroom and try to understand what I'm seeing.

There's a bald man I've never seen, standing at the edge of a bed, in front of a thrashing figure entangled in sheets. The stranger and I stare at each other for a brief moment, then my eyes drop to Brant and he smiles and it feels as if my heart will explode. "Help," he gasps. "Get me out of here." Then he jerks his hands up and I see the restraints and my vision goes red.

"WHAT THE FUCK IS WRONG WITH YOU?!" I whirl as Jillian enters the doorway, skirted by two female employees. They stood there in a line between me and the door, three soldiers shoulder to shoulder as if preparing for battle.

"Layana," Jillian starts, her hands patting the air in a calming fashion. She's still out of breath from the chase, and I'm reassured by the heave of her silk-covered chest.

"WHO THE FUCK HAS THE KEYS TO GET HIM OUT OF THOSE?" I point to the shackles that have Brant tied down like an animal. As if he is dangerous, or insane, or anything other the gorgeously brilliant man that he is.

"We had to restrain him. He was violent."

"No, I wasn't," Brant argues from behind me.

"You don't know what you were!" Jillian snaps.

"You," I snarl, pointing a sharp finger in her face. "You don't have the right to fucking talk to him anymore. I'm taking him with me right now."

"Now, now. Watch your language," Jillian clicks her tongue. "How nice to see the trash that lies beneath that blue-blood smile, Layana."

I look at her in disbelief. "My *language*? That's what you want to discuss right now? While you have Brant *tied down*?" I look around at the other strangers in the room, all who look unsure. "Who the *FUCK* has the keys to unlock him," I hissed through gritted teeth, my body rigid with anger.

"I do." The man by the bed pulls a key from his front shirt pocket and looks to Jillian.

I move in between them, blocking his view, and point to Brant. "Untie him." I use the sternest voice in my arsenal, the one I use with the kids at HYA.

"Don't move, George," Jillian's voice rings out.

I snatch the key from the man before he has a chance to think. I meet Brant's eyes while freeing his right hand. "I love you," I whisper.

"I'm sorry," he responded.

"Shut up, baby." I move to his leg strap and come chest to

chest with Jillian, her fingers wrapping around my wrist with an iron grip.

"Please call Duane and Jim," she says crisply to the women behind her. "I need them to get over here immediately."

Duane and Jim. Her hoodlums, though she had always described them as "security personnel" for BSX. I twist my wrist until her fingers lose their grip and shove Jillian back. She lets out a cry as her legs give out and she falls backward to the floor.

"Wait!" I cry at the two women, anxious to catch them before they leave. "Right now,"—I gasp—"you have a decision to make. You are both BSX employees. If you have any interest in your job security, I'd suggest you get over here and help me free the owner of your company."

Chapter 72

My car burns rubber on its Nobb Hill exit, Brant's groan from the passenger side causing my foot to ease slightly, my eyes leaving the road for a moment to assess his condition. "What's wrong?"

"Nothing. Just get us away from her."

I press a button on my steering wheel and speak when the tone sounds. "Call Home." I reach over and grip Brant's hand, my fingers looping through his, an interlocking squeeze I don't want to ever lose.

The ringing through the speakers ends, replaced by the efficient voice of one of our security personnel. "Sharp residence, this is Len Rincon. Good morning, Ms. Fairmont."

"Len, I'm with Brant. We'll be arriving home in about ten minutes. I want the house on lockdown. No one coming in or out unless you talk to me. Especially not Jillian Sharp."

"Is Mr. Sharp also available, Ms. Fairmont?"

"I'm here, Len. And I agree with everything Layana just said." Brant leans forward to make sure the microphone catches his voice.

"I'll need you both to provide your security passcodes." Any camaraderie I've shared with this man over the last few months is gone. Suddenly, I recognize the ex-Special Forces asset we'd hired.

It was a welcome transition, and the panic in my gut eased a little. It would be okay. We were in good hands. At least we would be as soon as we got home.

"4497," Brant says.

"1552." I glance at him, considered at the pale pallor of his cheeks. Had they been feeding him? What drugs had they had him on?

"Thank you. We'll be ready when you arrive. Is there anything else we can do?"

I glance at Brant, speaking when he shakes his head. "Please connect me to Anna."

"Connecting you now."

Our house manager answers with an efficient perkiness, and I'd be willing to bet that she'd been up ever since I left the house.

"Hi Anna. Can you have Christine prepare breakfast? A full spread of everything Brant likes. Also, please prepare the bedroom and the spa. I also need you to bring a physician in. Brant needs a full tox screen done, so have them bring whatever they need for that." I had a sudden idea. "Actually, call Dr. Susan Renhart. She's at Homeless Youths of America. Tell her it is urgent, and that discretion is important. Mention my name."

She doesn't ask questions, just repeats the instructions back to me, and I have never been more grateful for the ex-headmistress who now ran our household with a rigid effectiveness. I end the call and glance over at Brant, his eyes closed, his features tense. "Stay with me, babe," I say softly.

"I'll never leave you," he says. "Not willingly." He turns his head and meets my gaze. "I'm so sorry for everything I must have put you through."

"We have the rest of our lives to talk about it." I squeeze his hand and glance back to the road. "Right now I'm more concerned with Jillian. Brant, she's—"

"Crazy," he finishes with a growl. "Crazier than me," he amends with a wry laugh.

"I can't—" I couldn't even put the confused rage I was feeling into words. "How long has she had you there? How did she even get you tied down to that bed? And who was that guy?"

"She injected me with something. I went straight there after I got in the fight with you so what—how long has it been? Twelve hours? A day?"

"Three days."

He is silent at the news, but I can see in the tight flex of his jaw, the subtle fist of his hands, how much the timeframe angers him. This is what I am more accustomed to. Not the wild fight in the bed, but the small battle restrained inside of him.

I press harder on the gas, and zip through an intersection before the yellow light turns red. The car's windshield is fogging in the chilly morning air, and I hit the defrost button on my steering wheel and try to think through Jillian's next steps. "Should you call your parents? It might be best for you to speak to them before Jillian does."

I reluctantly pull my hand from his, putting both on the steering wheel before he feels the shake in my palms. I am literally *shaking* with anger, at myself, at Brant, at the manipulation this woman has had in our lives. "Brant, what kind of sick person ties someone down? We have to think about what else she's capable of."

"Maybe it was for the best."

I let out a strangled laugh. "What? Are you kidding me?"

"What if I'm dangerous?" His voice is quiet but walks the steps of giants.

I slow the car down as we approach our private drive and jerk my gaze to him. "You're not dangerous, Brant."

"Brant isn't dangerous. But you said yourself I have other personalities, what if one of them..." He suddenly leans forward and grips the sides of his head. "Oh my God."

"What?" I pull the wheel hard and make the turn through our gates. They are open, Len standing by the guard shack and waving us through. I gun the Mercedes's engine and careen down the long driveway and then brake hard by the front doors. Shifting into park, I undo my seat belt and twist to face him, alarmed at the grief on his face. He was breaking down on me, right there in his seat, and while I had seen him shift personalities before—this was something different. This was a cascade into a dark, negative emotion. I pull at his arm, grip his shirt, try to pull his attention to me, but his eyes are vacant, his hands still clawing at his head as he shakes it from side to side.

"December twelfth," he whispers. "Oh my God. December twelfth."

The date means nothing to me, and I turn off the car and reach for the handle, about to get out and go around to his side when suddenly he stills. I turn back to see him drop his hands into his lap, a calm settling over him as he raises his head and finally meets my eyes.

"I remember." He says softly. "I remember December twelfth."

TWENTY-SEVEN YEARS AGO

There is not a moment when I feel the switch, when it bubbles through me and replaces one person with another. There is nothing to fight. Nothing to struggle against. I simply open my eyes to a place I don't recognize. I stare around, take in my surroundings, and then continue.

Our minds are unique in that they are like infants in their acceptance of what is shown. I don't wonder that I don't remember yesterday, because I have always had no yesterday. To me, that's normal. That personality has never lived another way. I don't find it strange to be suddenly awake and at a restaurant and midway through a meal because that is what I know. How I know life to be. The regular world, as a species, doesn't question the fact that they close our eyes each night and eight hours passes in a millisecond. A person doesn't question the fact that they may have said things in our sleep or they shrug over a conversation they had in the middle of the night with a spouse—a conversation they don't remember occurring. And just as they don't question that, I never questioned the last two decades where things didn't always make sense. I blamed any gaps in memory or sudden changes in location on my medication's side effects or my knowledge that that is how the world works.

But now, suddenly, I remember something. One glimpse into a day I have wondered about for twenty years.

I didn't know much about my world when I opened my eyes on December twelfth, other than a few simple facts. My name was Jenner. I was eleven. There was a girl down the street named Trish who had a pet mouse and wouldn't let me play with it. She'd shown me the tiny, trembling figure a few weeks earlier and I had touched it. Pale white with red eyes, I had poked it too roughly and she had pushed me away. Pulled it close to her chest and screamed that I'd never touch it again.

I was Jenner. I was in a room with a strange woman who I didn't know and I had no interest in her brand of authority. I wanted my mom. I wanted my blue house with the broken porch rail and the iced tea pitcher that collected condensation in the fridge. I didn't want to be in a basement with a woman whose mouth was tight and whose eyes were black, who smelled of vinegar and coffee and whose finger wouldn't stop jabbing the paper before me.

"Focus, Brant. Multiply the fractions. We don't have all day."

I'd never seen this pile of crap before. Numbers above and below lines. The crooked cross, which I knew *meant* to multiply but I didn't know *how* to multiply. I pushed the paper away and looked at her. Said the only truth that didn't make me sound stupid. "I'm not Brant."

"You certainly are Brant. And you did three pages of these yesterday in the time it took me to use the restroom. So don't tell me you don't know how to do it."

I don't know how to do it. I said nothing, only stared in her face. "I want my mom." It wasn't so much as wanting my mother as wanting to get away from this woman.

She looked at me. "Your mother is at work, Brant. You know that. She'll be home at six. Until then, you're stuck with me."

She was a liar. This ugly woman opened her mouth and all

that spewed was a lie. My mother didn't even have a job. She stayed home all day. Spent time with me. Let me watch TV and slipped me Oreo cookies with glasses of milk during commercial breaks. I pinned my lips together and stared at the paper. Hated this stranger.

"Do you want to work on your computer for a bit, and then return to this?"

"I want to watch TV." The clock above the shelves showed that it was almost four. Mom let me watch TV after three.

The stranger frowned. "You don't like TV anymore, Brant. It hurts your head, remember? Why don't you work on your computer?" She pulled at my arm and I snatched away, her grip slipping off. She grabbed me again and her nails dug into my skin in a way that *hurt*.

I didn't know what she expected me to do with the "computer" which was really just a pile of junk on the desk, a computer screen hooked to a bunch of plastic and metal. The only computer I'd ever used was my father's, which was simple, the first step being the large and easy-to-find power button. This thing didn't even have a power button, and that made me feel stupid. I shook my head.

"Then we're back to fractions," she sighed. "Do these four pages now, no excuses, Brant."

I looked up, away from the worn page that had been pushed and pulled between us until it had a small rip in the right corner. "I'm not BRANT!" I screamed and the anger pushed out of my throat like it had legs and arms.

The woman's head jerked back, and her eyes changed, like they didn't know what to do. I liked it. I pushed away from the desk and stood, and I was almost as tall as her, a growth spurt already putting me a head taller than my classmates. It made me stronger than the others. I was definitely stronger than her.

"Shush, Brant!" she got a hand on my shoulder, digging in her nails and trying to push me down into the chair, but it was easy to stay up.

"I'M NOT BRANT!" I shoved both hands into her chest, and it's the first time I've ever touched someone's boobs. It was cool, even though they were old lady boobs. She fell back, her hands waving through the air on her way down.

I ran over and sat on her stomach, like how Rowdy Roddy Piper had done to Ric Flair on TV on the video my dad showed me. It worked, she pushed and yelled but went nowhere. Ric Flair had done a spring jump that had thrown Roddy off and across the ring, but she only moved like a worm under me.

"Brant!" she yelled, hitting my chest and using the voice that my mother did when she was really serious about something.

"I'M NOT BRANT!" I swung with a stiff fist, the way my dad showed me. Her head snapped back, and she finally stopped yelling as she tried to protect her face. She couldn't. I kept swinging, like a windmill, and her hands grew weaker and weaker, like little bird wings fluttering and then dying. She was making little sounds but by the time my arms grew tired she was quiet.

My dad had always been really clear. You let someone push you to a certain point, but then you had to stand up for yourself. First with your words, then your fists if the words didn't work. I had tried to use words. They hadn't worked, so I tried fists.

I had liked using the fists. I looked at the woman beneath me and almost hoped she called me Brant again. Pushing off of her, I looked at my hands, ignoring her when she made a small sound. There was blood all over my knuckles. That was a first for me, but I felt like an MMA fighter. I started to wipe my hands clean on my pants, then stopped. Mom would be pissed if I got blood all over them.

I looked at the clock and cheered up at the realization that I had almost two hours to watch TV before my mom showed up.

I climbed over her body and headed up the stairs with a smile. Wait until Dad heard about this.

Chapter 74

Brant finishes telling the story, his voice tight with torment. There's a moment I think he's going to cry, when he's describing how the skin on her face tore under his knuckles, but he makes it through, then inhales deeply and looks at me as if he's afraid of what I might say.

We're still in the car, my door open, the morning chill frosting my neck and I grip his hand in mine and bring it to my mouth, kissing his knuckles. "Brant, it wasn't you. You know that."

"What I just remembered ... that was me. Me peering into another world that makes no rhyme or reason. *I did that*. I hit her over and over, like she was a punching bag. It had been like a game, one that I played until I was bored of it. My mother..." His voice drops and he reaches up and pinches the skin between his eyes. "My mother came home and found me on the couch, watching television, eating popcorn, with Jillian's fuckin' blood on my hands." He lets out a hiss. "I remember it like it was me, even though it wasn't. Why am I suddenly remembering that? After twenty-seven years of nothing."

"Do you know Lee? Remember any memories of his?" I am almost scared of the answer, of watching his reaction to Lee's memories.

He shakes his head. "I don't know anyone named Lee. No. I have ... nothing, Layana. One memory, that's it. But fuck, that's enough. After that, I don't want any more."

I squeeze his hand and release it. "Let's go inside. Stop thinking for a bit and let me baby you."

* * *

Anna has earned every bit of her generous salary. We walk into a house that smells of food and home, the staff ducking out of the rooms upon our arrival. Brant sits down at the kitchen table and doesn't say a word. His fork starts moving, and there is no sound but the scrape of his fork against the china and the quiet sounds of him chewing. His eyes are on the plate, his chair pulled close to the table, and within five minutes, a lobster and spinach omelette and two waffles are gone. When he finishes, he stands with a quiet cough and wipes his mouth with a linen napkin. "Please tell Christine thank you for the food."

"I will. Anna prepared the spa, if you want to soak in the hot tub."

"I'll just take a shower."

I nod and smile. "Of course."

Suddenly we feel like strangers, two lovers awkward in their own home. I don't know what to say to him and he seems embarrassed, all over a situation I have known about for years. I want to hug him. I want to pull out his fears and lay them to rest. Kiss him and tell him I will always love him. But he has a cloud around him, one that screams 'don't touch!' So I stay in place and watch him head for the bedroom.

I reach for his plate and Anna scurries around the corner. "Let me get those, Ms. Fairmont."

"Thanks." I drop my hand and sigh. "Did you reach the doctor?"

"Yes, she'll be here within the hour."

"Good. Please show her to our room when she arrives."

"Certainly."

Having no more purpose in the kitchen, I walk to our bedroom, easing open the door quietly before stepping inside. The lights are off and the black-out shades are down, the only illumination coming from the glow in the hearth and a flickering candle beside the bed. There's the crackle of the fire and the comforting smell of vanilla and coconut. I pass through and enter the bathroom, checking to see that towels are heating. Then I sit on the teak bench beside the tub and stare at the fogged glass of the steam shower.

I stare at the blurry movement behind the glass and try to guess at what this man wants. I have no idea what his thought process must be. I've tried to put myself in his shoes, but the situation is so foreign. I can't connect with the idea of not knowing what I've done or how long I will be present in this psyche. I know how much unknown I have to accept as his girlfriend and how hard that is. How much trust I have to put in the Brant I know, but what about the versions I don't? The one he described in the car... that explains a little of Jillian's trepidation, her continual warnings.

I stand up and pull off my clothes, leaving them in a pile on the marble floors. I slide the door open and step into the thick white steam of the shower.

The large rectangle enclosure is a cloud of fog, and I can't even see my hand before me. I stumble through the steam, my bare soles feeling their way across the pebbled stone floor until I reach Brant. His skin is hot and flinches at my touch. I don't say anything, only step closer into the hot spray of the body jets. I wrap my arms around his waist and rest my head on his strong chest.

"I'm not very good company right now," he mutters.

"You're always good company." I stand on my tiptoes and press a wet kiss on his lips. It's too brief and I try to press closer to him, but he tilts his head up and looks toward the tiled ceiling.

"I'm so lost right now," he whispers.

"You have me. Together, we'll never be lost."

"I have you, but for how long? You aren't going to want to put up with this."

I rub the length of his arms and massage along the top of his shoulders, then craw my fingers up the cords of his neck and cup his face. "I'm here with you forever. I've been telling you that for years, Brant. Years when I knew about your condition. Years I've loved you through it. I don't love you *despite* this. I love you *including* this. Every part of you, even parts you don't know."

He groans and his chest vibrates against me. "You mean the people I don't know."

"Well, yes. Just one." I look up into his face and we are in a break in the steam, the spray of water keeping him into view.

"And you fucked him."

"Yes." I wiped away the water from my face, pushing my wet hair out of my eyes.

"That pisses me off." There's a look I've never seen on Brant's face before, one of possession, and in it, I see pieces of Lee. I smile and rise on my toes, trying to kiss him.

He starts to turn his head away but then his palms close on my ass, and he pulls me tightly to him and presses his mouth against mine, his kiss hard and deep and then rips away from me. "I'm jealous of him, you know that? How ridiculous is that?"

"Jealous of Lee?"

"Yes, *Lee*." He says the name like it is dirty and grabs the bar of soap, rubbing it roughly across his chest.

"It's a mutual dislike. He's extremely jealous of you."

"He is?" The shock in Brant's voice makes me chuckle.

"Are you kidding? The brilliant billionaire who I'm madly in love with? Of course he's jealous. He knows exactly how much I love you, even if you are blind to it."

He rubs the soap slowly over my cleavage, then gently across and around one nipple. I feel our connection return, a righting of the balance between our souls. "So... this is why you won't marry me? Because of how I am?"

I swallow and move closer till our soapy chests are flush against each other. I lower my mouth to his wet skin and kiss the hard line of his collarbone. "It was why I *wouldn't* marry you. Because of my lies, the secrets I kept from you because of it. I didn't think you deserved a wife with such a huge secret."

He pulls away and studies my face intently, like I'm an equation he can't figure out. "And now?"

I hold his gaze. "And now ... there are no more lies. Not from me."

His body stills, his muscles growing rigid, and when he speaks, it's only his lips that move. "Are you saying that now..." He pauses, water dripping off his nose, and his eyes are thick with vulnerability, "that you'll marry me? With me like this?"

I step forward, pressing every piece of me against him, wanting to crawl into and hug his broken, terrified heart. "I'm saying that nothing would make me happier."

He groans and presses his lips against mine so hard, so strong, that it almost hurts, his hands grabbing at my skin and pulling me against him as if he will never have the chance to touch me again. "That's a yes?" he asks abruptly, pulling off my mouth, as if the last-minute verification is needed.

I smile, finding his eyes. "That's a yes, Brant Sharp. I will marry you and be your wife whenever you want to have me."

"Yesterday," he blurts, returning his attention to my mouth. "Now." He presses forward and pulls me tighter, making me aware of the size of his need. "Forever."

Then my future husband makes love to me in the shower of our home. And I make sure, for the next fifteen minutes, that no one else crosses his mind. Literally or figuratively.

Chapter 75

"When will the doctor be here?" Brant pulls on a T-shirt, then reaches for a pair of jeans when I'd rather him be in pajamas, in bed, behaving as my patient.

"Soon." I looked around for my watch, but I'd forgotten to put it on.

He opens his sock drawer and reaches inside the segmented space, moving aside a pair of silk socks. Tucked behind them was a small black bottle, one he tossed to me. "Ask her what these are, and what they do."

I examine the bottle, twisting open the lid to see it stocked with white tablets. "Label says it's Aciphex. I thought this was for stomach acid. You think it's something else?"

"It's not Aciphex." He gives me a sheepish look. "Jillian gives them to me each month, says they're to control my blackouts. Given her recent behavior, I'd like to double check."

"Your—what?" I hold up a hand. "Wait. We have so much to discuss. The majority of it concerning Jillian. Let's compare notes, before the doctor gets here."

He winces. "I'll tell you as much as I know."

I pocket the bottle of pills. "Come on. Let's sit on the deck and talk."

* * *

"When I was eleven, everything in my life started to change. It came with the onset of puberty, hormones affecting more than just my temperament and body. It was as if my brain turned on full force, in a hundred ways at once. I could do dozens of calculations in a minute, but I also was bombarded with colors, images, thoughts ... more than I could handle at one time. I'd want to do three things at once. Or I'd have two different opinions on the same subject, at the same time. For instance, on the topic of God. I'd argue with myself, present both sides of an argument, understand the nuances and opinions of either side and feel strongly on both points." He collected his thoughts, then continued.

"Everything became, in a series of months, maddening. My brain worked in overtime, and I was exhausted over it. That was when the blackouts started. My brain would go sixty miles an hour then ... nothing. There would be hours of time where I would blackout and do things I had no recollection of."

We were on the corner balcony off the bedroom, looking over the shimmering ocean, and the sunny view didn't compute with the dread in his voice. I stayed quiet and waited for him to continue.

"Then, on December twelfth, I woke up from a blackout in a children's ward. Jillian was in the hospital and that was when the doctors and medical tests started. I don't remember a lot of that time, but when I got out, Jillian moved into our house. I never went back to school, didn't see my friends anymore. Everything had changed, everything was focused on keeping me home, on keeping my brain busy. Jillian was the one who directed that attention on computers. We discovered I did better if I had a problem and focused on it. Complex math problems, or unraveling code to debug a virus—anything that involved complex thought quieted the madness. This was in the early days, back when computers were input output computation tools.

Data processors. That was about it. I learned to build a computer in fifteen minutes. Then I began the focus of improving the machine, its performance, then—once that was solved—its capabilities." He took a sip of ice water and then placed the glass down and glanced at me.

"But the blackouts continued. My parents were worried. Worried I would have another occurrence of whatever had happened in December. So I was put on a sedative, something to keep me calm. It stopped the blackouts, but I couldn't think on it. It dulled everything, including my ability to process intelligent thought—at least not on the same level as before. I grew increasingly quiet, lost interest in computers, in everything. So..." He shifts, pressing his palms together and staring out onto the water. "Jillian and I made a deal."

I sit up a little in my chair. "A deal?"

"I stopped taking the medication, and she covered for any blackouts I had. At that point in time, close to the completion of Sheila, I was in the basement 90% of the time, with her for the majority of that. I was only seeing my parents at meals and before bed. Any blackouts I had, Jillian concealed. In exchange, I focused on getting Sheila finished and ready for our meetings with investors."

"You were, what? Twelve at this point?"

"Eleven."

"Not old enough to make that deal."

"I wasn't a typical eleven-year-old. I was intelligent enough to make a quantified calculation of risk versus reward. And since Jillian was the one most at risk, and since she was the one spending time with me, I made the decision."

"No. *She* made the decision. How much did she make in your initial sale?"

"A few million dollars. Ten percent of the deal."

I bite my tongue because if he's anything at all, it's intelligent enough to see the twisted motivations that would have spurned Jillian's actions. After a moment, he resumes.

"When I was around twenty, we started BSX. With BSX we could stop selling off my projects and instead develop them in-house. Our income increased ten-fold, and I decided I had enough money to live the rest of my life. Enough residual income that my children wouldn't ever have to work. So I went to Jillian and told her I wanted a change. Told her I wanted to resume the medicine."

"Why?"

He sighs. "Not knowing about my blackouts ... it was a constant fear in my life. I'd have them without even knowing it. Jillian would wear a long-sleeve shirt, and I'd wonder if she was covering up bruises from my touch. We were still, for the most part, sequestered from the outside world. And I wanted to live, to have a life, to work in an environment where I could collaborate with others, have relationships, friendships. I wanted normality, and I was willing to sacrifice my career for it. I was okay with a muted intellectual life if it meant security in knowing and controlling my actions. And, more importantly, not worrying about what else I was doing."

"What'd she say?"

He snorts. "She didn't take it well. Thought it was a horrible idea. Brought up the projects we had ongoing. Printed out our ten-year plan. Cursed me for wasting my talent. But, she eventually came around and tracked down my old doctor, the man you met this morning at Jillian's. She put him on salary for BSX."

So that's who the man was, the one who had been beside the bed, while Brant was tied down to it. I growl without meaning to and he laughs and holds out his arms. "Come here." I move from my chair to his, and it's a tight fit but I curl into a ball on his lap. He wraps his arms around my back and hugs me to his chest, inhaling into my neck and nuzzling the skin with the scratchy surface of his face. I'm not used to the facial hair on him. He hasn't shaved since before he disappeared, and it reminds me of Lee and the times when I would have him for days at a time.

He continues on, his voice calm, like he isn't telling me a horror story. "Dr. F tried me on a different medication, whatever's in that bottle. It was supposed to be a downer with caffeine, something to calm me while keeping me alert, focused. It worked immediately. My brain processes were as strong as ever and my blackouts stopped."

I wait for more and the moment stretches out until my curiosity can't hold it in any longer. I push on his chest, getting enough distance between us so that I can see his face. "And?"

He shrugs. "And, that was it. I've been on that medication for almost two decades. Haven't had a blackout since." His mouth is tight, gaze jumping minutely as his mind works out the problem before him.

It's not hard to figure out. For me, it seems painfully clear. "So, you believe that? Or do you think she's been lying to you? Hiding blackouts from you?"

His gaze meets mine and it's so steady and honest that I almost believe it. "I don't know why she'd do that."

Bullshit. He knows exactly why she'd do that. Knowing him, he probably had a diagram of motivations and probabilities already completed in his head.

"There's another issue." He sighs and readjusts me on his lap. "Jillian told me that I've been declared incompetent, and that she's been appointed as my conservator."

"So, she's in control of your business and your finances?" I frown. "What about your medical decisions? Can she do that?"

Lee would have already been punching walls and vowing to rip Jillian's throat out. But Brant was the man he always was. Calm. Thoughtful. Even now, faced with Jillian's manipulation and betrayal, the only evidence of his concern was in the pinch of skin in between his eyebrows. "The question of my competency could certainly be challenged. I can see a valid argument for the possibility that another one of my personalities could make choices that negatively affect my life, and therefore permanent or important decision-making ability should be removed from my person all together."

"But you're brilliant. You've been in control of your decisions for twenty years."

"And what kind kind of risks did I take? Did you ever see me take actions as Lee that might have endangered myself or our lifestyle?" He rotates me in his lap so that we're in direct eye contact. I avoid it as I think through the last two years.

Lee: seeing multiple women. *Risking our relationship, and exposing us both to STDs.* Lee: often drunk, getting in fights, coming home bloody and bruised. *A liability nightmare as well as danger to himself and others.* Lee: prone to tempers and driving under the influence. *More liability. More risk.*

"Did I?" Brant pulls my face back to him.

"In ways," I answer carefully. "Lee is a loose cannon. He doesn't have your level of control, nor intelligence. He acts without thinking things through. But ... he isn't going to walk into your bank and withdraw your money. He has no idea that he's you, so he isn't going to mess with your business or finances. The risk he poses to you are mostly liability. I could see him doing something that Brant Sharp is then sued for. He's reckless and he acts like he doesn't have anything to lose."

Brant groans and drops his head back. "That sounds disastrous."

"And this already happened? The competency thing?"

"My memory is a little confused due to the medication. But I think got something in place temporarily, and it's being signed off on Monday. What's today?"

"It's Monday." This is good. We can stop it, if we move fast enough. My mind ticks through who we should call.

Behind us, the sliding glass door moves and Anna's head tentatively sticks out. "Mr. Sharp? Ms. Fairmont? The doctor is here whenever you're ready."

"Thank you." I smile at her, then I meet his eyes. "Let me call my family's attorney. Have him stop Jillian. I don't want to trust BSX legal—"

"I don't either," he interrupts. "I agree. Use an outside attorney. Your father's will work until we can find permanent counsel."

"You should call your parents."

He frowns. "I know. It's not a conversation I'm looking forward to having."

"Do you think they'll side with Jillian?" I untangle myself from his lap and stand.

He shakes his head. "I don't know," he says slowly. "We've all let her run things for so long, without questions. I don't know if I would have believed it myself if she hadn't chained me to a bed."

I offer him my hand and pull him to his feet. "I love you."

"I love you. Thank you for sticking with me through this."

I grin. "Thanks for not giving up when I turned down your proposals."

He turns over my hand, running his thumb over my bare ring finger. "Your ring is at the office. I'll get it for you as soon as I can."

"I know you will." Through the glass, I can see Dr. Renhart, standing by the coffee bar, speaking to Anna. "Ready to see the doc?"

He nods. "Absolutely."

Chapter 76

Dr. Susan Renhart is dark-skinned and almost as tall as Brant, and she greets us both with a tight nod, showing none of the bright smiles she showers on the HYA children. I introduce the two of them, then we sit at the leather seating cluster by the two-story fireplace in our bedroom. After Brant gives her a quick recap of his psychological history, he passes her the bottle of pills.

"I've been on these pills for almost twenty years."

Her eyebrows rise at the name on the bottle, her hands opening the lid with a practiced efficiency. She sprinkles a line of the white pills along her brown palm. "What do you think these are?"

"I was told that they were a depressant, one with caffeine in it. Something to keep me productive while keeping me calm enough to avoid a blackout. I take two each morning, and one whenever I get stressed."

The doctor rolls the pills in her hand before keeping one and dumping the rest back into the plastic vial. "When's the last time you took one?"

"I think it's been about three days? I've been drugged with something, so it's hard to tell. And ... since I haven't been taking them, I may have had blackouts when I was at Jillian's. I'm not sure."

"Blackouts?" she frowns. "I thought the issue was DID."

"It is." He pauses and sends a quick glance at me. "I'm sorry. I'm so used to thinking of them as blackouts, that's what I've always understood them to be."

"Did you take any medication at Jillian's?"

I stand and move a few steps away, aware of our need to contact the attorney. I scroll down to Damon Forsyth's cell number and press Send. I haven't spoken to the high-powered attorney in years, but I know he will answer my call. While I hate the weight of my family name, there are times when it comes in handy.

Brant's gaze follows my movement. "Not willingly. But the doctor there injected me with something. At least once, maybe twice, I'm not sure. I want to know what's in my system and have documentation of that, should we need it."

She nods and reaches down, unbuckling the leather strap of her sleek doctor bag. "Let's pull some blood and get a urine sample."

"Layana," the attorney's deep voice crackles through my cell and I step away, into the hall.

"Hey Damon. I need your help."

* * *

Jillian's brigade shows up before Dr. Renhart has finished. As Brant sits by the fire, a needle in his arm, I flip the TV channels to the security channel and watch the camera outside of the main gate. Our guards are by a trio of Black Escalades, their stance aggressive and I watch as the second vehicle's door opens and one of Jillian's security guards gets out. There is a heated conversation and I click the volume higher out of habit. There's no sound and I sigh in frustration.

"Relax," Brant says, his head back on the chair, his eyes closed.

She's taken six vials of blood so far and I watch as she twists the final test tube onto the rubber stopper. "She can't touch us, babe."

She already has. This game feels like one that we've been playing on her board, with no instructions and a pair of trick dice. I had thought that I had stolen Brant from her all of those years ago. But now I'm questioning everything. How much of her manipulation I played into.

There is movement on the cameras and I turn back to them, watching as the three SUVs do a quick U-turn through the cul-de-sac outside our gates. I need to understand the woman we're at war with.

"You know," Brant says, and now he's sitting up, the doctor undoing the tight orange band from his upper arm. "Her heart is in the right place. She's just trying to do the right thing."

"For what?" I sputter. "For you? BSX? Or to help herself?" I shake my head.

"I don't mean to interrupt, but I need to get these to the lab." Dr. Renhart stands and loops her stethoscope over her dark curls.

"Sure. How long will it take?" Brant moves to his feet and flexes his forearm, pressing on the place where she had taped a bit of gauze.

"The results of the blood tests won't be available until tomorrow. I'll call you with the findings as soon as I have them. Anything you were injected should pass through your system in the next twenty-four hours. In the meantime, take in lots of liquids and eat fairly bland foods." She fishes her cell phone out. "I'm going to drop you the contact for Dr. Henry Terra. He's the foremost authority on DID in California, if not in the country. I would suggest you call him immediately, if not for your own psychological needs, then to get his legal advice or support for trial." She turns to me and reaches out, wrapping me into a firm hug. "Once you sort this out, I expect to see you at HYA."

"You know me, I can't stay away." I smile at her, and there's a tinge of pity in her eyes that I hate. Brant and I are fine. We're strong. I broke down the wall of lies and we survived and are fighting back, any negativity focused on Jillian. We have love, the rest will get better or worse, and I would rather have worse than any more lies.

"I'll be in touch soon," she promises.

She walks away and Brant wraps his arm around me and pulls me close, his mouth soft as he presses a kiss against my neck.

It was a moment of peace and unity in the craziness, a moment of calm in the storm, a reminder that we were one and together, we could make it through anything.

I roll in Brant's arms and press my chest against his. I wait for the familiar spark of chemistry but there is nothing there. We're both exhausted—mentally and physically—and I cling to him and press my cheek to his chest, listening to the reassuring thump of his heart.

I had told myself, for two years, that I was dealing with Lee out of necessity. This doctor—Dr. Henry Terra—he might have a cure, something that might kill off the other personalities and leave only Brant.

Just Brant.

No Lee.

That will be perfect, right? I tighten my arms around his waist, and push the question away. I ignore the small voice in the back of my mind, shouting out the truth - that a part of me loves Lee. Needs Lee.

A tear ran down my cheek.

Chapter FF

On Tuesday morning, Jillian's injunction to push Brant's custodial motion through is stopped, courtesy of our new team of legal representation. Currently, we have three attorneys who are rigorously opposing any and all attacks on Brant Sharp's character, and all billing an enthusiastic eight hundred dollars an hour.

It's worth it, especially since Jillian has both the funds and the means to put up a fight. So far, she's slunk away, and I won't be surprised if she drops the incompetence battle and comes back to the table with her hat in hand, determined to make amends.

That would be the smart thing to do, and while I don't have many nice things to say about Jillian—she is an intelligent woman. Months of legal battles will only hurt the public image of BSX, throw Brant's credibility into question, and destroy any chance of a family reunion between her and Brant. Plus, there was the evidence of his blood test results—a cocktail of illegal drugs administered under her watch. Add to that the misinformation about his medication over the last two decades ... she should be arrested, along with his doctor. I feel adamantly on the point, but he is just as resistant to the idea.

He is, as he has frequently pointed out, a billionaire. CEO of one of the most powerful tech companies in America. Engaged to a gorgeous and brilliant woman (okay, I couldn't argue with that). His life, under her control and medication, had gone well, in his mind. And he believed that her heart was in the right place.

I don't understand it. I don't understand justifying any of it but I'm keeping my mouth closed and trying to support him through a time when he is barely holding everything together.

I keep waiting for Lee to make an appearance, given the stress he is under, but I've only seen Brant. That's a good thing, of course.

I swipe through the screen on Brant's car, softening the lumbar support and turning on the seat heater. The car bounces gently over a bumpy section of the highway as we head back from the office, my ring finger now heavy with the weight of my new acquisition. It's beautiful, of course, glistening from my fourth digit and I finally feel worthy of it.

Brant dropped to one knee on the rug in his office, right beside the hidden safe, his smile infectious, his lack of patience so endearing as he hurriedly pulled the box from the slim interior and immediately opened the lid.

I felt odd, standing beside his printer in loose linen pants and sandals, my hair in a messy knot at the base of my neck, with no makeup on. He had paused and taken a deep breath, composing himself, before looking up into my eyes and asking for my hand in marriage.

Will you take my hand in marriage? He'd never asked it that way in the past—so formal, but I was glad that it was different, and had dropped to my knees in front of him, putting us at eye level together, and immediately said yes.

The office had been empty, the BSX facility closed pending the outcome of the hearing. After I'd said yes, we'd lain back on the carpet beside each other and I'd held my hand up and we'd both stared at it, giddy at the step we had just committed to.

I cup my hands in my lap and twist the band, not surprised that the ring fits perfectly on my finger. "I know you don't want to press charges or speak to the police, but what are you going to do about Jillian's role at BSX?"

Brant looked away from the road for a quick moment and met my eyes. His jaw tightens and his grip on the steering wheel works the leather as he flexes his hands.

"I don't know," he says carefully. "I need to speak to the DID doctor and understand my realistic capabilities when it comes to my ability to run the company."

"Does it matter? I mean, will that affect what you—"

"No," he interrupts. "Regardless, Jillian has to be removed from any role of power."

I sigh, conflicted on the subject. "The company's her life, has been for twenty years." Brant won't be happy running BSX. Financial sheets bore him, meetings drive him insane, and I'd be shocked if he knows the names of ten of the employees.

He likes to be in a room, alone. Working, fixing, creating. Jillian does a great job in her role, even if she was psychotic in her treatment of Brant. I have no desire to reward the woman but hate the destruction of the status quo.

Brant taps at the buttons on his steering wheel and the car's screen changes as he selects and dials the number for BSX.

A perky voice answers moments later, and I guess someone is still working despite the office being closed.

Brant clears his throat. "Hank Michen in Security, please."

I blink, surprised that he knows a name in security. Maybe he *can* name ten employees without pause. In fact, it's likely he has the entire employee roster committed to memory.

The next voice is deeper and more intimidating in its greeting.

"Hank, this is Brant Sharp. I need to lock Jillian Sharp out of everything."

There is a long pause before the voice drawls back through the receiver. "At the risk of losing my job, is this a joke?"

"I assume you have caller ID. Verify it against the internal corporate directory. I can also verify my driver's license number or social security number, both of which I assume you have on file in some location."

"That won't be necessary, Mr. Sharp. It's nice to speak to you. I don't believe we've ever had the chance. When you say *everything*, do you mean— "

"Her office, her email, her remote ability. Anything that could give her an iota of access. Turn off her campus gate codes and transponder. I don't want her to step on BSX's campus without being flagged and stopped by security."

Another long pause. "Is this a temporary or permanent situation?"

"I'm not sure yet. For now, it's indefinite, unless you hear otherwise."

The man clears his throat. "You should know, Mr. Sharp, that we received a similar call from Jillian Sharp yesterday with the same instructions for you."

"And?"

"And I refused. I tried to call you, but you didn't answer your cell. I left a voicemail for you."

"You did the right thing. How long will it take to lock her out?"

There's the muffled sound of a receiver being covered, then he returns to the line. "Less than a half hour for everything. We'll have remote access cut before the end of this call, sir."

"Good. I'll call you directly if there are any changes. Don't accept orders from anyone other than me. And text me your cell phone number."

"Yes sir."

Brant glances at me, and there's a moment of hesitation where he turns something over in his mind. "Hank, if I do call, or if someone else calls pretending to be me, don't listen to my directives unless I verify my identity with a code word. I don't care if I'm standing in front of you, don't do what I say unless I verify it with the word."

"What's the code?" If the request seems odd, Hank doesn't show it.

"Sheila."

"Got it."

"Also, take instructions from Layana Fairmont, should I be incapacitated for any reason."

"I don't really feel comfortable taking orders from someone who is not a BSX employee, Mr. Sharp."

"This is a unique situation. Just until we get this sorted out."

The man sighs, and the sound is thick with his feelings on the subject. "Does she have a code word also?"

I spoke up so my voice will be caught by the microphone. "I'll use the same word, just to keep things simple."

"Okay. Anything else, Mr. Sharp?" The emphasis on the Sharp name makes his wariness of me clear. I grin at the snub and reach over, running a hand over the back of Brant's neck.

"That's it. Thanks, Hank." He ends the call and leans into my hand. He says nothing as he accelerates down the 280.

* * *

That night, we lay in bed, his body curled around mine, the heat of his skin keeping me warm against the sateen sheets. The television's volume is barely audible, and this is the fourth episode of *Big Bang Theory* that has played. I can feel his worry, it's in the rapid thump of his heartbeat and the rigid muscles of his forearms, cupping me tight to his chest. His brain is working overtime, ticking through all of the possibilities of what might have happened without his knowledge.

"Have I cheated on you?" His voice is soft against my neck, and there is a thread of hope in it that I'm asleep.

I roll in his arms and look up into his face. "Never."

"But as Lee... I never—"

I lean forward and kiss him. "You did, but it wasn't cheating."

"Don't justify it. If I kissed, touched other women, then I was unfaithful to you."

"I did some pretty despicable things to win you over," I say. "Things I'm not proud of."

An interesting mix of jealousy and regret darkens his face. "With other men?"

I glare at him. "I would never," I swore.

Relief sweeps over his face and it's his turn to steal a kiss, this one deeper, his hands pulling me atop him as he rolls us over. "You know," he says hoarsely and slides his hands down my back and cups the meat of my ass, squeezing hard. "There were so many nights I watched you sleep and wondered if you were cheating. I kept trying to figure out what you were keeping from me."

I pull back and sit up, studying his face in the flickering light from the television. "What? You never said anything to me."

He let out a wry chuckle. "What would I have said? Accused you of cheating?"

"Yes." I nod. "That's exactly what you should have done. I can't believe you didn't confront me." I cross my arms over my chest, a little hurt over the omission. We've always been so forthright and honest. Well ... my arms sag a little. I did kind of hide an entire side of my life—and his mental health—to myself for years. I had no right to be mad about him keeping his concerns to himself.

"And what would you have said to me, if I had confronted you?"

I wince. "Okay, so maybe it was good that you didn't. I mean, not that I would have lied to you but—"

"You would have lied to me."

"I—I wouldn't have lost you over it. It would have just forced the issue to the forefront sooner."

"I didn't bring it up because I didn't want to lose you." He reaches up and gently brushes a bit of hair away from my cheek. His brow furrows as he pulls me down to his chest, and his need is hard against me. "I was worried," he whispers, "that you might—"

"Never be worried."

He surges up, crushing his lips against mine as he grips my waist. My hips move underneath his urging, rocking me back and forth against the stiff ridge of his cock. My panties stick to me, and the extra friction is both maddening and delicious, all at once.

I break from his kiss long enough to speak. "You have me forever. You always have."

He rolls us over and pushes his hand roughly between our bodies. He works my panties to the side, and I claw at the top of his underwear. Gasping, I grip him and press the head of him against my core, and he thrusts his hips and pushes inside me. *Oh my God*. It's a first, Brant giving me himself bare. Even though I've had it with Lee, it's different. Everything has always been different between them. How they kiss, the places they touch, the way they fuck. Brant shoves deeper inside and I open my legs and cry out his name as he thrusts his possession in with strokes that reprint his name on my soul.

Without the lies, without the secrets ... it's better than it's ever been. I break beneath his body and sign away the last bit of my heart to this man. This complicated, layered, brilliant man. The owner of my soul. Forever.

Chapter 78

On Wednesday Dr. Terra flew in from Dallas. We had spoken to the Dissociate Identity Disorder specialist yesterday and stressed the need for an immediate meeting. Our urgency had been understood, along with the awareness of who Brant was and how deep our pockets were. The man cleared his schedule for the entire week and, if I had to guess, DID billionaires are few and far between.

At the sight of the BSX jet touching down on the private airstrip, Brant rises to his feet and approaches the large window of the lobby. He's been anxious all morning—we both have been— and I feel a wave of relief at the sight of the Citation jet, slowly rolling down the tarmac. Brant's fingers are drilling against the side of his slacks and I approach him slowly, watching as he stares out the window, his attention fixed on the plane.

"They made good time." I loop my arm around his and hug it, hoping to ground him a little. "Got here before the storm."

"I expected them to. The trajectory of the storm is south-southwest." He points to the dark cloud that is blackening the horizon. "And that's why they landed this direction, so they'd be facing into the wind. Last night I read the FAA's pilot's handbook of aeronautical knowledge. I've been thinking about getting my pilot's license. What do you think?" He turns to face me, his face intent as he waited for my opinion.

Last night, I saw the light on in the library, but assumed he was reading some of the psychology journals and textbooks there. They were all ones I'd already read, ones I'd purchased in the last couple of years. There weren't any clear answers in there, but I had still expected that he would dive into them. Instead, he'd been reading about aerodynamic theory and thinking about flying planes. I smile at the absurdity of it. "I think you'd make a great pilot."

"You do?" He seems unsure and he's different off the medication. I'm still learning his cues, his reactions to things. He talks more and smiles easily—even on a week like this one when there's not much to smile about.

I loop my hand through his and we wait by the concierge desk, watching as a short Nigerian man descends from the plane and strides down the path toward the FBO. He spots us as soon as he steps through the revolving glass door and onto the polished white marble of the lobby. I smooth down the front of my plum-colored silk blouse as he approaches.

"Good afternoon." He beams, and his teeth are impossibly white and straight. "Brant Sharp, I presume?"

"Yes. This is my fiancée, Layana Fairmont."

His palm is cool and small, his grip firm. I smile and meet his eyes. "Pleasure to meet you. Thank you for coming on such short notice."

He nods quickly, rubbing his hands together and watching as our pilot appears with his leather duffel. "Of course, of course. I'm anxious to get to know you both."

"My car's out front," Brant says and gestures to the exit. "Let's head to the house. We can dive into everything on the way."

* * *

Brant yanks his G Wagon into drive and the SUV purrs to attention. The doctor quickly reaches for his seat belt and clips it into place. The armored SUV had been a recent purchase—one that had sat, practically untouched, in one of the garage bays. Brant and I don't really have friends, we rarely have a reason to need more than the two comfortable seats in his Aston Martin. I run my hand over the quilted leather of the backseat realizing I can't hear any noise from the outside, not even the 787 that is taking off right outside the tinted window. The soundproofing is incredible. Still not worth the exorbitant price tag, but incredible all the same. Maybe it's the bulletproof panels and glass, able to block both high caliber rounds and the pesky sounds of real life.

"My primary objective is to fix this as soon as possible. I've cleared everything else off my plate to focus on this." Brant glances over at the doctor and I can't help but admire how handsome his strong profile is.

"Fix this?" Dr. Terra questions. "You mean, removal of your additional personalities?"

I bite the inside of my cheek as Brant brakes at the exit of the private lot, his fingers drumming the wheel impatiently as the gate slowly opens. Patience is Brant's weak point, in all areas of study. I can already predict his frustration at catching the doctor up on the history and details of our situation. So far, he's been annoyed at a dozen everyday inconveniences that Jillian used to handle. It's just growing pains, we'll sort and smooth everything out with money and employees, but money can't walk Dr. Terra through Brant's past. Money can't fix the fact that, right now, my man feels broken.

As soon as the gate opening is wide enough, Brant floors the gas.

* * *

"Dissociative Identity Disorder is not an easily fixed affliction. While other psychiatric disorders can be controlled by medication, DID is not a 'curable' disease. The original medication you were given as a child, I have to assume, was depressants, given to a level that would have dulled any personalities to a point where they were undistinguishable from your core personality. It makes you a bit of a—if I can use laymen's terms—a zombie. Obviously, that's not a solution worth exploring."

Brant's hand tightens around the pen in his fist, the flex of his forearm distractingly attractive. I place my hand on his arm and squeeze the muscle there.

Brant's gaze jumps from my hand to Dr. Terra's face, then to the garden view. His office's floor-to-ceiling windows do a stunning job of showcasing the three-story greenhouse that straddles the space between this wing and the next, and right now the vivid purple violets and blood-orange hibiscus are in full bloom.

"So what solution *is* worth exploring?" Brant finally asks, his pen poised over the page, ready to write notes on the response.

"Intensive therapy. It's not sexy and it takes time, but it has the highest probability of success. I'll create a plan, one with schedule sessions with a local psychiatrist. Initially, you'll need to meet with them at least three times a week. There will be a serious of hypnosis sessions in which the doctor will speak to you and Lee and counsel you both through the process."

"And that will fix it?" Brant asks.

The doctor hesitates. "Well, I believe that eventually, Lee will either fade away or that parts of his personality will merge with yours. It's not a guarantee, but it's likely, depending on how Lee responds to the therapy."

Brant responds in minute ways that would be invisible to most people. There's a slight pull of the skin around his mouth. A bulging of the veins on the back of his hand as he grips the pen tighter, then writes something down.

...depending on how Lee responds to the therapy. It's safe to say that right now, out of the three of us in this room, I am the one

that knows Lee best. My hypothesis? He's not going to respond well.

Brant carefully places the pen and the notebook on the black desk and then meets Dr. Terra's eyes. When he speaks, it is with careful and thoughtful precision. "It just doesn't feel like someone else in inside of me. Could she be wrong?"

He doesn't look at me. We're sitting right next to each other, our knees brushing underneath the conference table, yet we're a hundred miles apart. *Could she be wrong?* What he was really asking was if I was lying. A month ago, I would have been offended, but right now, I didn't have the energy to care.

The doctor doesn't react, maintaining his level of warm professionalism. "Everything you've shared so far is consistent with DID, including your inability to feel the other personalities or be aware of them. You may not know Lee yet, but you will before this process is over, assuming you participate in my suggested therapy program."

"I'll participate. I want to do whatever I can to get it out."

The bite in his voice puts me on edge, as does the word 'it' in regard to Lee.

"It'll take both of you. I'll need Layana's help to speak to Lee and to convince him to leave."

I look up. "Convince him to leave?" I have never convinced Lee, in two years, to do anything. Every interaction was a struggle and my only success in any manipulation of him had been the coordination of the Molly breakup.

"Yes. We can't force him out of Brant's life. It will only be successful if Lee is willing."

I nod, like it will be easy. "I'll do whatever I can to help." Just like when I was young, I say what's expected of me, and swallow the rest. I nod again, my features calm, and try to figure out how I feel about Lee leaving me forever.

Brant leans forward, his forearms resting on the table. "And I don't want you to refer me to a specialist. I want to work with you, here. For the next few months at least. We'll pay anything.

Handle all of your housing, transportation, food. We have a research lab that you can use as a medical office, and we can provide you a receptionist, staff, whatever you need."

I smile politely, knowing that it will happen, that Brant will convince Dr. Terra to abandon any other commitments and make himself available, just as money and influence makes everything else operate properly in our world. I sit quietly, one ankle crossed over the other, my hands in my lap, and try to unravel the tangled pile of thoughts that are infesting my brain. Somewhere, in all of that, there is how I truly feel about this, but I'm a little afraid—very afraid—to discover what that is.

Stop. I force the turn of my mental gears to skid to a halt. It doesn't matter what I want or whom I may love. My happiness is sacrificial in order to save Brant. I watch the doctor's mouth move and try to catch up to the current place in the conversation.

Chapter 79

TWO MONTHS LATER

"You're breaking up with me?" Lee stares at me, his hands tight on the metal chair's arms, his face hollowing as he bites the inside of his cheek, a nervous gesture I suddenly recognize as unique to him, and a tic that I will miss. There are so many, and this conversation has been a catalog session of ones that I will need to learn to live without ever seeing again.

I'm going to miss the way he sometimes drops his eyes when he asks a question, as if he is afraid of the answer. Miss the way his smile pours through his eyes and the sexual confidence that soaks his movements. I'll miss the way that he is the dominant, most cocky man I have ever met, yet is deeply insecure in a way that hurts. He has been terrified of rejection since the day I met him. And now, in a room he doesn't recognize, the psychiatrist's new office cold and impersonal, his fears are becoming a reality.

"Lee, try and relax," Dr. Terra says, speaking from behind us.

I wince at the sound of the doctor's voice. He needs to shut up. He shouldn't even be here. I told him that. Told him that this is a private moment, one that will go over better if there isn't a party to Lee's rejection. Especially not someone who feels the need to interject. But they—the doctor and Brant—were worried about my safety. They thought the doctor and his sedative should be present, in case it needs to be used.

In case Lee gets violent.

He won't. I *know* he won't, not with me. I told them that, screamed it at them, but they refuse to listen and here we are—Lee and me ... and the doctor.

As if on cue, Lee turns his attention to the man.

"I'm sorry, but who the *fuck* are you?" In three long steps Lee has the man's throat in his hand, the doctor on his toes and backed against the wall of the examination room. His face is close to Dr. Terra's and his entire body trembles with rage as he glances over at me, ignoring the delicate tendons pinned underneath his hand. "Are you fucking serious, Lay? You're breaking up with me? For that rich dick?"

I stare into Lee's eyes the entire time. It was a lifeline between us, as strong as a wire, held taut as the doctor fumbles a hand into his pocket. I don't move, don't breathe as Dr. Terra withdraws the syringe and stabs it through the thin green cotton of Lee's shirt.

He flinches and I stay in place, watching as betrayal seeps into his eyes and he glares at me like he hates me and loves me and needs me, all at the same time. I stare at him and watch as his eyes close and he lets go of Dr. Terra and slumps to his knees, then falls forward on his face on the dark grey carpet.

Chapter 80 – Brant

Ever since finding out my condition, I've read everything I can find on Dissociative Identity Disorder, my research hampered by the fact that there is little on the subject. What I have read is troubling, made more so by a likely omission that my mind will not reveal.

DID is typically caused by emotional trauma of some sort. Abuse, or a significant event, one the brain tries to hide, initially creates the first sub-personality as sort of a protective defense against the knowledge it doesn't want the brain to have. The rare DID exceptions are brain damage, physical impairments that cause a shorting out of the cranial lobe from which idiosyncrasies result.

I haven't had any physical damage, no hard blows to the head, no horrific accidents that would have caused multiple Brants to emerge. I also, with the exception of December 12th, haven't had any traumatic events. And December 12th happened after – and was a result of – my development of DID.

The obvious answer is that I must have had a traumatic experience and have psychologically hidden it. I called my parents and believe them when they claim ignorance of any triggering events. My curiosity isn't worth contacting Jillian. Right now, she can rot in hell.

Dr. Terra has tried, in a roundabout way, to unearth this possibility. He forgets the man he is dealing with. I'm intelligent enough to attack a problem head on. I don't need subtle pecks at the corners of my brain. I need to split my psyche open and dig at the root of my problem.

I can feel the incident. It nags at a part of me, like that errand you walked into a room to do and then forgot. It lies, just out of reach but at the corner of my mind, occasionally tapping at my brain matter when it wants to drive me bat-shit crazy. I need to unearth it. Need to open my past and find the key.

Now, for the 32nd evening in a row, I try. The chair beneath me creaks as I sit on the back veranda, my feet propped against the railing, the skies dark as a storm approaches. I can feel the air thicken, thunder clapping as lightening streaks the sky. I contemplate going inside to avoid the rain, but the overhang should keep me fairly dry. As the rain begins to tap a staccato beat on the roof above me, I close my eyes and try to remember the past. I try to remember a summer twenty-seven years ago.

And then, listening to the familiar sound of rain against a roof, it comes to me.

Chapter 81 - Brant

Sheila Anderson had been beautiful. Half Cuban, she had tan skin, dark hair and eyes that gleamed when she laughed. I had never spoken to her. I sat three seats behind and one seat over, and just stared.

I was nervous; I was awkward.

She was untouchable.

When she left school each day, I followed her. I had a valid excuse. She lived a street over and both of our paths home followed a logical route. So I followed, and I watched her hair bounce, and I stared some more. She was always with friends, she giggled, she whispered, she hummed, and I listened.

I listened to her giggle until the day that she cried, and my world broke in two.

It was a Wednesday and it rained. A big sloppy downpour, where one foot outside meant a plaster of all of your clothing to your skin, no 'quick dash' possible to keep yourself dry. I saw her standing in the front porch of the school, her steps tentative as she contemplated the initial step into the torrent. I stood beside her, offered a small smile to her friendly beam. We waited together, until the moment that she ducked her head and ran, squealing, her hands covering her head.

I followed, and it was just the two of us running across the parking lot. Through the church. Down the road with the fence. Past the house with the dog. We ran, and it just kept coming down. The rain was ice cold and unrelenting, nails against your skin.

She slowed, and I slowed and it came time for me to turn down my street. I stopped in the middle of the street and she continued past me with a smile and a wave that I could barely see through the rain.

I watched her until I could barely see her pink shirt. Then I glanced left, the sight of my mailbox barely visible through the rain, and ducked my head against the wet needles. I turned on one shoe and ran after her.

The man's arm is one I have seen in a hundred nightmares and never understood its place. Thick and dark, not from the color of his birth, but from the tattoos. A sleeve of evil, skulls and snakes, the muscles of his arm jumping with the action of his ink. I was a few steps behind her when his arm shot out, grabbing the back of her as easily as one would pluck up a cat. The rain obscuring my view as I saw a blur of arms and legs, the heavy patter of rain muffling the cries. I slowed, unsure of what was happening as he pulled her against his chest and stepped away from the sidewalk, into the heavy shade of trees, ducking into the yard he had come from.

I wiped at my face and moved closer, my chest heaving from exertion and something else – the tight feeling that something was wrong. The yard showed no sign of them, but I heard her screams, the sound muffled by something other than rain. I looked right and left, hoping to see someone. An adult. I needed an adult.

I moved closer to the house. Picked my way over its stepping stones, one slick enough to put me in the grass, my hands skittering over the ground and coming up dirty as I pushed myself to my feet. I couldn't hear her anymore and that scared me more than the screams. I hitched my backpack higher and wiped my hands on the front of my jeans.

The house in the yard had three steps, then a short porch. I climbed the steps and stepped onto the porch, leaving the rain behind. My clothes dripped everywhere, creating a puddle on the grimy brick floor.

I looked over my shoulder to the yard, then back to the house. There was the faint sound of something inside. I eased closer to the door and put my ear against the wood. It was a television playing, and a burst of canned laughter came through.

There was a loud noise from inside, and I bolted to the corner of the porch. Ducked into a ball, I hid behind a swing. I accidentally bumped it with my shoulder and it creaked into motion, giving away my position. I moved away from it, against the house, and soldier-crawled over to the window, which had a skinny opening between two blue curtains. I held my breath and then peered in.

There was the television, playing a black-and-white western. There was a rug. A few beer cans sitting on an end table. My gaze lifted to the room beyond the can, and I saw Sheila Anderson.

I won't share the horrors of what I saw, on my knees, on that porch. I know I closed my eyes too late. I know my hands fisted on either side of my head as I tried to drown out the soft sounds of her screams. I now know why I hate the sound of rain. I now know why, that afternoon in August, my mind broke into smaller pieces and locked that afternoon into a place where I was never to find it.

Now, I struggle to stand, the image of Sheila in pain imprinted on my mind. I stumble to the door, frantic to escape the sound of rain. Opening the slider, I see Layana rise from her place on the couch, her eyes on me. "Did you remember?" she asks.

I nod, unable to say more, and open my arms as she steps forward and wraps me in a hug.

Chapter 82

Today is my second attempt to break up with Lee. We've spent three weeks preparing for it, and this time the doctor has agreed to stay quiet and behind the one-way glass in the adjoining room. Brant hates that decision and is still convinced that I'm in danger. He had the Brant-equivalent of a meltdown, which involved him slamming a fist onto the table and striding out of the room. It took him a half hour to cool off and then he reluctantly agreed with the plan, and now I'm back in the room with him, reciting the lines I've been coached through, the hypnosis protocol that will trigger Lee's presence.

My initial breakup attempt had been done without clueing Lee into his condition. With the massive failure of that experiment, we regrouped and decided to share the condition in hopes for better results.

Two weeks ago, Dr. Terra told Lee about the DID diagnosis, and his role in Brant's psyche. Lee refused to believe it, wanted to talk to Brant, then lost his temper when that option was refused. As he kicked his chair over and threw the trash can against the wall, Dr. Terra stayed calm and cited facts that laid the truth out in simple clear reasoning that Lee refused to listen to. He vocalized his hatred for Brant with every four-letter word known to man. It was disastrous. I fled the watching room halfway through the outburst, unable to watch his breakdown.

Since that day, Dr. Terra has met with him four more times, and Lee has grown more hostile and uncooperative with each session. The last meeting, he just laid on the couch with his eyes closed and cherry-picked the questions he felt like answering. Today, I'm hoping my presence will help. I need him to listen, to be open to what I say, and I pray he doesn't break my heart any further.

"Lucky." His eyes open and he sits up, glancing around the room before meeting my eyes. I am tense, his emergences sometimes volatile, but he only rubs his neck and shoots me a sad grin. "So, I'm still stuck in Crazytown, huh?"

"Yeah."

He holds out his arms. "Come here. I need to hold you."

I don't hesitate, moving forward and breaking Dr. Terra's rules with every step. I don't care if it's not the right thing to do—I need it as badly as he does. I miss him. I sit sideways on his lap and sag into his chest. He inhales deeply against my neck, his chest rising underneath me. His mouth grazes across my neck and his teeth scrape and then gently bite the skin right below my ear. I lean closer, feeling every single digit as he runs his fingers down the front of my body, and he whispers my name as he kisses a line from my ear to my collarbone. "Don't do it," he whispers. "I know what you're going to say, and you can't say it."

"I have to," I breathe, and now his hand is skimming over the top of my bare knee and sliding under the hem of my skirt, in between my thighs, his fingers pushing roughly against my attempt to keep them together. I think of the doc, right on the other side of the glass, his pen and pad of paper in hand. *Within one minute, subject began to grope Ms. Fairmont.* I thought of the video filming this session for Brant to watch, after the fact. I thought of the script that we had gone over ad nauseam that I'm supposed to stick to. In it, I tell this beautiful man that I never loved him, and that I only dated him to keep tabs on Brant. I'm supposed to stress the fact that I want him to leave so that I can be with Brant. *Lies.* Filthy, dirty lies. His fingers are incessant as he pushes his hand higher up my thigh, underneath the tweed A-line skirt that is only helping his cause. This morning, I spun the racks of clothes in our massive closet and picked this one out of the hundreds on hangers. I could have selected a more restrictive style, or a dress slack, but I didn't. Did I know what he would do? Had I picked it intentionally? Am I really that cruel—to myself? To Brant? Part of me already knows the answer, but I cram that piece down into my stomach, as far from my conscious thought as possible. "Stop," I say weakly, just to prove to our audience that I am trying, sort of trying, to be good. "Please, Lee. Stop."

He ignores me, as I knew—hoped—he would.

"You don't have to say it," he continues his case as one hand travels higher and the other pries my legs apart, his mouth hot against my neck, stealing rough kisses in between his words, kisses that burn at my skin and leave emotional marks that won't wash off.

"I do, Lee." I fully abandon the script the moment my thighs lose the battle and fall open. His fingers move immediately to the silk crotch of my panties, teasing me through the fabric as his tongue flicks and sucks against my neck. "I can't keep dragging Brant through this," I gasp out. "The only way it will work is if you leave."

He tugs my panties aside and pushes two fingers inside of me, the sudden invasion causing me to stiffen, and he takes advantage of the moment to kiss me. His tongue is deep and forceful as he pushes and curves his fingers, fucking me with them right there on the couch. I try to think of the doctor, of the video camera, but I can't stop him. I don't want to—not when I have craved this for weeks. Every single night I've laid in bed next to Brant and felt nothing but a cold distance as he's tried to sort his way through this. Now, I open up my legs further and press his hand to me, urging him deeper, letting him understand the level of my need and begging him to take me further.

"I don't give a damn about that man," he growls, pulling off of my mouth and pushing to his feet, dumping me off his lap. I fall, my hands flailing out and he catches me just before I hit the floor, the rescue more out of necessity than chivalry.

"Bend over," he orders and yanks at the zipper of his jeans. "And listen to me." He pauses and waits until I turn, my knees already on the couch, my hands gripping the back of the cushion.

"I will never leave you," he swears. "I will never let you fuck him without my name on your mind." He places a hand on my back, pushing up the black sweater until his palm is against my skin and grips my waist, squeezing me. With his other hand he lifts my skirt, bunching it around my hips, pulling my soaked panties to the side. "Tell me you still love me."

There is the hard press of his cock, first at the back of my thighs and then inside of me and my back arches at the dominant, angry invasion that seems devoid of any control. I gasp out his name and claw at the back of the couch as he withdraws, then shoves back in. It's torturous, the intense pleasure of his entry and the delicious need of his withdrawal, and I cry out when he stops, just his head inside, and nudges gently in and out, the minute push so different, so teasingly short of what my body needs. "Please," I beg, reaching back for him, desperate for more.

"Tell me you still love me."

I close my eyes tightly but it's not enough, the tears seeping through and streaming down my cheeks, my feet straining on their toes as he rocks a tiny bit deeper inside and breaks every last dam around my heart. "I love you," I whisper and earn an inch or two more.

"Tell me you need me."

"I need you," I weep. "Please."

He grabs the meat of my ass, squeezing it hard as he pushes fully in, then drags out.

Over.

And over.

Over.

And over.

He fucks me as if I am dirty and his slut and his to do whatever he wishes with. He fucks me as if he can give me any order and I will greedily obey. He fucks me as if his cock is my lifeblood and every stroke of it ties me to his will. I cry out his name and close my eyes to the tears as he relentlessly takes me because all of it is true.

"I will never leave you, Lucky," he whispers as he leans forward and wraps a hand around my chest. He pulls my hair until my head is arched back and his mouth covers mine. He kisses me and swallows a bit of my soul in the process. "I will never leave you," he promises as he buries himself in me and releases his orgasm.

Chapter 83

There is silence in the observation room when I open the door and walk back in. Dr. Terra is sitting on the stool at the desk, his trusty pen in hand, his notebook page full of cramped neat writing, and I can only imagine what he's written down.

He looks at me and I look at him and I don't have the emotional fortitude to defend myself or to discuss what has just happened. He looks at the window and I look at the window, and Lee is there, on his back on the couch, his pants pulled back up but unzipped. He looks pleased with himself, and I don't want to know how far back I have set this process.

"I'm sorry," I say.

"You haven't been honest with me," he says, and it's not said in anger, but in observation. "You have a stronger connection with Lee, potentially more so than with Brant."

I shake my head. "That's not true it—" I pause. "Ever since we told Brant the truth, he's been more distant. What you have seen with me and Brant—it isn't normal. It will go back to normal once we figure out how to get Lee to go away."

"Are you sure that is what you want? For Lee to go away?"

"I'm sure that it's what Brant needs." I don't trust myself to say anything more than that.

"Today was not a good day, Ms. Fairmont."

"I know."

"I am sorry." He twists in the stool so that he is facing me and presses his palms together between his thighs. "I imagine it is very difficult for you to love two men that are inside of one body."

I am close to crying and I have already degraded myself enough in front of this man today. "I have some work to take care of. You'll finish up with Lee and give Brant an update?"

He nods. "Certainly."

"Thank you." I walk stiffly to the door and let myself out into the hall. In between my legs, some of Lee dampens my panties and I need to clean myself up, but I can't bear the idea of washing him off.

Chapter 84 — Brant

Motherfucking shit damn asshole. The expletives stream through my head like lines of code, and I don't know why Dr. Terra let this go on without stepping in and stopping this shit.

Jesus, I hate myself. If there was a way to kill myself—this part of me—I'd do it. I'd rip that motherfucker out of me and beat him to a bloody pulp.

I accelerate out the driveway and don't look back. I left Dr. Terra and went straight down to the garage, avoiding the areas in the house where Layana might be. I don't know what I will say when I see her. I can't right now. I'm too afraid of how I will look at her, given the anger and the disgust that is radiating through my chest. What's horrible about it is that the disgust is as much for me as it is toward her. That was my body doing those things to her. My voice, saying those things. Me.

It's so fucked up.

How am I going to be able to look into her face? How can I block out the image of her bent over that couch, her skirt hanging from her waist? Her thighs had *shaken* from the force of his thrusts. That look on her face when she looked back at him. When she begged him for more. When she told him she *loved* him.

I can't accurately express how it feels to watch my body, my face, my dick—fuck my fiancée. Before Dr. Terra began recording our sessions, there was a part of me that hadn't believed. That thought that maybe Layana was making it all up. The preferred scenario was that she and Jillian were both fucked in the head, and I was the only sane one. Of course, my parents had also supported the idea. For all three of them to be lying or mistaken was a highly unlikely probability, yet my brain held on to it like a lifeline. The more I thought about it, the closer I came to convincing myself that it was valid.

But then I saw the first hypnosis session.

In that twenty-four-minute video, I saw the high-definition footage of myself—and it was like watching a complete stranger. I moved in a new way. Smiled as if I didn't have a care in the world. I spoke in trash language with poor posture.

After that, I believed. How could I not? It was a gift and a curse, all at once—because once I realized that this was real, then I also realized that I've had carbon copies of myself running all over San Francisco and doing God knows what to God knows who.

There had been two decades where I could have ruined lives, screwed strangers, hurt people, or worse. Maybe I have children out there that I've fathered. Maybe I've killed someone. Maybe I met a woman and married her and then just disappeared.

My brain is running on repeat with the scenarios and even the good scenarios are bad, because they are memories and experiences lost forever.

There've been moments in the past few weeks where I've wondered if maybe Jillian was right to shelter me from this. Ignorance, as they say, is bliss.

But then I remind myself that I don't know what I have been up to. According to Layana, Jillian's henchmen always kept tabs on me and would move vehicles, provide cash, clean up my messes, and keep me out of trouble.

But what messes? Drunken stupidity or assaults?

The steering wheel vibrates and Layana's photo appears on

the navigational display. For one of the first times in our relationship, I silence the call and, as if summoned, an image of her face, eyes closed in ecstasy, worms its way into my head.

That asshole fucked my woman in a way that I haven't.

Maybe in a way that she liked.

Definitely in a way that she liked.

I already knew what arousal looks like on her skin. I could tell you within seconds how far—or close—she was to orgasm, how she sometimes liked to fight it, to hold it off as long as she could, before it wracked her body. I knew the sounds she made when she enjoyed something and the way she looked when she wanted more.

I knew all of that before I watched the video of him and her. He hadn't accomplished anything that I hadn't done before.

I'd made her crave me.

I'd made her lose all control and sanity.

But I hadn't done it like he had. He had fucked her, in every sense of the word. It had been a ravaging—like he needed her body just to breathe.

She had loved it. And loved him. Loves him.

I have to consider the fact that I am trying hard to remove a part of me that she might require.

Her name disappears from the screen, and I can't keep driving forever. Eventually, I'll have to go back and face her, and I'm terrified that I will look at her and see disappointment in her eyes that I'm not Lee.

Maybe she won't, but it's hard to know because we're so disconnected right now. We're sleeping on opposite sides of the bed and skirting around topics, and I know the emotional distance is on me but ... shit. That man—Lee—he didn't have any emotional distance from her. On that video, in that short period of time, they were closer than we've been in weeks, and I hate him even more for it.

I focus on the road and make the engine roar loud enough to drown out my thoughts.

Chapter 85

There is one piece of good news in all of the bad. Brant's hypnosis has not brought any other personalities out to play. Lee is, at the moment, the only soul between us and normality.

Now, I have to stop screwing around and do what needs to be done. The plan is for me to do a clean and stern breakup with Lee —without involving his penis this time—and then ignore him for the next five or ten sessions. We believe that will be long enough for him to give up and sulk off into a corner of Brant's mind where he may never resurface again. Dr. Terra says a DID mind creates alternative personalities to protect the primary, or to act out in a way that the primary won't allow. If the primary can fill that void by himself, the alternative personality may disappear altogether. *May.* A short word that carries so much weight. Other possibilities ... Dr. Terra won't discuss any other possibilities. He says our awareness of those possibilities increases the likelihood of Brant's mind exploring those paths, seeing them as alternative outs that will only delay things and drive us all bonkers.

So today, I'm going to end it in a way that leaves no doubt in Lee's mind. Not like last time. I'm mortified by what happened, what was caught on the camera, and watched by Dr. Terra and

Brant ... I swallow, trying to keep the cucumber roulade I'd eaten for lunch down.

I am an intelligent woman, one who is traditionally in control of her emotions, but Lord help me, I cannot look in that man's face—Brant's face—and pretend I don't love him. I can't see that level of anguish and pretend that I don't care. If he touches me, I can't stay unaffected, but I must try my best. I must hold a tight and unflinching front.

I settle into the chair and Brant gives me a tight smile. He rubs his palms together as if to warm them and he is as nervous as I am.

I take a deep breath as Brant lies down on the dark blue couch, and it's a new couch. I wonder what happened to the other one and when they moved it out of here. It feels like a question I should ask, but would he sense my desperation in it? Because I suddenly want that couch. I want to move it downstairs into our love den, and I want to lie on it naked and close my eyes and touch myself to the memory of our last time together, whenever I want to.

Instead it's gone, like it never happened, and that's probably why Brant got rid of it, because the sight of it likely reminded him of what Lee and I did on it.

"Layana?" Brant cranes his head back and looks at me. "Are we going to start?"

"Of course." I force a smile and begin the hypnosis script.

* * *

When Lee comes out this time, it is different. The fight is weaker in his eyes. He doesn't immediately reach for me, doesn't bound to his feet. He suddenly seems like an old man in Brant's body, and I am both heartbroken and hopeful at the change. This is what Dr. Terra said would happen, that Lee would grow weaker and weaker with each session.

I don't move from my spot in the chair. I sit there and feel like

I'm watching him die, and in a sense, I am. A minute passes, and it's agonizing. I'm close to speaking when he finally clears his throat and begins.

"I'm not smart. Not compared to you and Brant."

Just a sentence in and already the tears are coming, welling in the back of my throat and leaking from the corner of my eyes. I swore that I wouldn't cry, was going to pin down all emotions and keep everything professional—but I'm already unraveling, just from the gruff sound of his voice.

"I'm guessing that you two have a plan. Some way to remove me."

I look down, breaking the eye contact. A tear streams down my cheek.

"What is it? What's the plan?" He sighs as if the weight of the question is heavy.

"You already know I need to break up with you." My voice wobbles and I swallow, forcing myself to straighten up my posture and look him in the eye. Emphatic, that's what I need to be. Emphatic and confident. Damn, he's handsome.

"And then? When I fight it?" He hunches forward, gripping one fist in the other, his face tight, voice strained. "When I come out every time his mind loses control—what then?"

We are over, Lee. That's what I supposed to say. The words stick on my tongue and I inhale deeply, then force myself to deliver them.

"We are over, Lee. If you come back, I'll ignore you. What happened last time—that was the last time. We are over."

He laughs, and it's a sad chuckle that runs fingers up my inner thigh and breaks my heart, all at the same time. "You know why I kept coming back to you, Lucky?"

"What do you mean?"

"Back in the beginning. When I first met you. When you used to chase me around like a dog in heat." The words are rough, but his face isn't. "You weren't my type. Don't get me wrong, you could make my dick stand up and salute the flag in a few sections, but I like my girls rougher around the edges. I didn't want you and your fancy words and your perfect makeup and hair—but there was one thing that was different about you from every other woman."

He turns his head and looks at me, and whatever he's about to say, he means every word of it. I lean forward, desperate for the knowledge.

"It was the way you looked at me. You believed in me. You thought I was something special. You fucking cared about me and for me. Fucking loved me." He pauses, and I can't look away from his eyes, I can only nod because he's right. Of course I felt that way.

A change crosses over his face, and it's a harden of everything, a flip of a switch, from nostalgia to anger. I sit back in the chair, needing a little distance and unsure of what is setting him off.

"I thought it was love for me. Now, I know it's not. It was your feelings for him. Your love for him. Not me. And that's why you chased me. Why you wanted to be with me so badly." He runs a rough hand through his hair. "I spoke to the doc, after you and I fucked in here." I flinch at the words, tossed out so carelessly, as if the act had been nothing. As if it hadn't ripped out my heart and left it on the carpet lying between us.

He slides to the edge of the couch, resting his elbows on his knees and the slight distance closer makes my heart beat a little faster. "He explained that you were dating me, fucking me, just to keep Brant closer." He heaves to his feet and walks closer, until he is standing before me and he's definitely mad now. Not weak Lee, fading into the background. Strong, furious Lee, whose eyes are burning into me with disgust and betrayal.

And there wasn't anything I could say to argue with him. It was true. For the first year, before I fell in love with Lee for Lee—I was just keeping Brant as contained as I could. Babysitting his body until his mind returned.

"Every time you kissed me. Spread your legs for me. Got on your knees and sucked my cock, it was *for him*. That's what he said, and do you understand how that makes me feel?" He places a hand on each arm of my chair and bends over me, my back stiffening as he lowers his face to my neck and inhales my scent. Burying his face in my hair, he whispers my name. "God, I'm gonna miss your smell."

The tears flow like rivers down my cheeks and my control breaks into a thousand pieces as I clench my eyes shut and stay still, my fingers digging into my thighs so hard that the fabric of my slacks rip. I take a shaky breath and it comes out as a sob. "I'm sorry. I'm so sorry."

He places a soft kiss on my cheek, then a series of gentle imprints along my cheekbones and chin, catching each of my tears before his lips brush mine. I open my mouth, but he pushes away and I feel his absence before I open my eyes, my vision clearing to see him standing before me, his arms crossed over his chest, his features tight with anguish and anger.

He knows that I used him, but it doesn't mean that I didn't love parts of him. I loved fucking him and I loved his imperfections when Brant was so complete, grounded, and brilliant. I loved his wild side, he gave me the proof that I was *not* my mother, that I had chosen love and a lower-class life, even if it was just for long enough to eat chicken wings and fuck a stranger and ride in a vehicle that was made in America. I should say something—anything—but I have nothing but false apologies because I would do it all again in a heartbeat.

He blew out a breath in frustration. "I loved you. I *still* love you. Even when I hate you, I love you. I always will. Like I said, I'm an idiot, but I know that what I feel for you—it's not going away." He bites his lip in a way that tells me he is close to crying. My vision blurs and I rub a hard hand over my eyes, wanting to cement every last view of this man before I lose him forever.

He sags, then drops to one knee, then the other, on the carpet.

We're eye level now, and he presses his palms together in a begging motion. "Just tell me what you want. If you want it, I'll leave. Not for him. I'll never do anything for him. But for you, I'll do it. I'll fucking kill myself inside of him."

I want to tell him I love him. I want to tell him but am no longer sure that I mean it. No longer sure that I love *him* and not because he is a part of Brant. The guilt of what I've done is suddenly enormous. I know what he wants to hear, what his eyes are begging me for, and I could tell him the things I love *him* for, but it will only complicate this situation even more.

So I say the right thing, what will help Brant the most. I say the words and wonder at the effects they will cause.

"I need you to leave. Brant and I ... we want a family. A life together, without you. But I swear that I will never forget you, and I will always miss you."

He looks down and his hands clench into fists as his mouth tightens into a flat line. When he finally lifts his chin, his eyes are wet, his face red with emotion, and we stare at each other.

I *do* love him. I must. Otherwise I wouldn't be breaking right now.

He pushes to his feet and walks over to the couch, then lies down on his back and closes his eyes. "Call the doc back, Lucky. Let him take me out."

I swallow. "You're leaving?"

He shrugged his shoulders without looking up. "According to him, I can let go. Go wander in lala-land or disappear into Brant somewhere. Dissolve into fucking nothing. I'll let him walk me through the process. You don't need to be here for it."

I want desperately to hug him. I want him to wrap his strong arms around me and kiss me and give me one last moment. I want him to hold me against him like he can't get enough and a part of me doesn't care if that moment breaks him.

Instead, I stand up. "I'll look for you in Brant. He could use a little more Lee."

"Yeah. Whatever, Lucky."

I walk to the door and stand there for a moment, waiting to see if he'll look up, give me one last moment of contact, but he doesn't. He keeps his eyes closed and I never get a final look at them.

I open the door and leave a part of my heart in the room.

Chapter 86

It's been almost four hours, and I'm still waiting. I'm in the lounge area on the other side of the observation room, a solid door keeping me from knowing what is happening between the doctor and Lee—or Brant. Lee/Brant. I couldn't watch their discussion, and honestly, I really don't want to know what is said. Right now, I left things solid. I was somewhat firm with him. I didn't sleep with him, at least. One gold star on my horrible report card. Maybe not gold. A silver star. A check mark. C+.

I pace across the Persian carpet and ruin my manicure with my teeth. I sit on the loveseat and flip through channels on the television, watching a few minutes of one channel, then another, then turn off the set. There was a full bowl of red foil chocolates on the coffee table that is now half full, and I'm gnashing through one of the peanut butter ones now.

I've reached a new level of jittery. This feels a bad night in college when Dianna Forge held an Uppers and Manicures party, and it was all fun and games until everyone passed out and I was the only one awake. The uppers wore off and depression nosedived me into a black hole of despair, and I was staring at her manicure scissors and considering the effects of using them on the thin skin on my inner wrists.

This is different, the cause isn't from a pharmaceutical mix of stupidity, but the result is similar. An avalanche of all of my mistakes and the issues that are facing Brant and me.

What if the company gets taken from him?

What if Jillian decides to kamikaze this situation?

What if Brant never forgives me?

What if Lee doesn't leave?

What if he leaves and I'm not happy with the new person that Brant is?

What if another, different personality arrives instead?

The waiting is insufferable, as is the unknown variable of whether my future husband comes back as two men or one.

At four and a half hours, I can't take anymore. I go into the observation room long enough to jot a note down to Dr. Terra that I am heading to Windere and to call me when they are finished. I take Brant's car and drive straight home.

The house is like a funeral home. A brightly lit one with a million-dollar view, fresh flowers in every room, and dread hanging thick in the air. The staff smiles a hello as I walk straight to the elevator and take it up to our suite. I skip the shower and crawl into bed fully dressed. I call out a command to close the blinds and the system whirs into motion. The room darkens into pitch black, and the hum of the fan is like a lullaby. I close my eyes, my legs twitchy and aching from pacing, and wrap the soft upper blanket around myself. Willing my mind to stop moving, I say a long prayer for Brant.

Somewhere during the prayer, I fall asleep.

* * *

My cell goes off and my body jerks into consciousness. I kick off the blanket and run my hands over the covers, finding the phone. I answer it while moving off the bed and I call out for the lights as I reach for my shoes. The lamps beside the bed glow to life. "Hello."

"Ms. Fairmont, this is Irene from Dr. Terra's office. He wanted me to tell you that he and Mr. Sharp are almost done."

"I'll be there in ten minutes. Thanks." I hang up the cell and step out of the bedroom into the hall, breaking into a jog. Soon, I'll have him back. In whatever shape that comes in.

* * *

When Brant walks out of the office and toward the car, a wave of recognition and relief hits me. The weight of his shoulders, the haunted look that had appeared the day I ruined his life, is gone. His confidence is back, and I step out of the car and meet him halfway, surprised when he pulls me to him and plants a possessive kiss on my lips.

"Everything okay?" I ask.

His hand is still gripping my waist and he studies my face as if he hasn't seen it in a while. His mouth curves into a reassuring smile and I realize how long it has been since he looked happy. "We're good. Come on, we can talk in the car." He returns to my mouth without waiting for a response, my breath taken by the force of his kiss, stronger than I am used to from him, the type of kiss that guarantees a long and lengthy fuck the minute we step inside the house. He releases my waist but pulls on my hand, opening my door to the car.

* * *

"So, what happened?" I speak the moment the car is in drive, the hours of waiting and anxiety spilling out of me.

"Dr. Terra spoke to Lee and he agreed to leave."

I wait for more but he is silent, his blinker on as he waits at the light.

"And?" I finally ask.

"And he left."

I glance at the clock on the Aston Martin's dash. "It's been seven hours."

He frowns, his hands sliding effortlessly across the steering wheel as he downshifts, and the smooth motion reminds me of his hands across my skin, and the fact that we haven't had sex in over three weeks. "Seven hours?" He checks his watch. "Wow. I..." He glances at his watch again, then at the dash clock to verify. "He must have been with Lee longer than I realized."

I look away from him, out the window. "Dr. Terra didn't tell you what was involved in Lee leaving?" *For you, I'll do it. I'll fucking kill myself inside of him.* Lee's words come back to haunt me.

"No. I mean, other than the fact that Lee had to accept it. The likelihood of success is much more possible if he is a willing participant."

"So, he's gone now? Won't ever be back?" My words behave. They come out level and unaffected, like I don't care about losing him.

"I'm not cured. He's keeping me on this medication. My chances of reoccurrence are high, especially if my emotions or stress get out of control. And I'm supposed to avoid alcohol. You know that; you were there when he went through those rules."

I nod. Brant's new regimen involves lots of rules and structure and will be very different from the unpredictable life Jillian had given him. Brant's subconscious has grown used to creating additional personalities to take over when his mind feels overwhelmed. When he was young, Dr. Terra thinks it was because his brain couldn't handle the sudden pressure and expectations of his intelligence, the nonstop brain functions causing a short of sorts that resulted in another personality, one that was slower and stupider and emotionally unstable. When he was older, it happened when he was under extreme stress, or in strange situations, or anxious over something. It was no coincidence he had switched the night before his initial proposal to me. Or the days before a new product release or company merger. The likelihood of switches was amplified by the medications fed to him by Jillian—medications that increased his productivity and honed his ADHD but triggered his anxiety and stress. With the new rules, new structure, and the fact that he now knows of his condition, we are hoping for him to live a life that is relatively free of separate personas. Especially one troublesome sex machine who I already miss.

The ivy-covered walls of Windere move into view and he brakes at the entrance gate, waiting as it moves out of the way. He cups the back of my neck and threads his fingers through the mess of curls that spill over my shoulders. "You okay?"

I turn and look into his eyes, sinking into his warm and reassuring gaze. There's the man who I fell in love with. The man I want to marry. "Yes," I whisper. "I'm good."

He puts the car in park. Unbuckles his belt and leans forward. Pulls me forward until we are close. "I will be more," he says gruffly. "I'm going to be everything he was too."

"You're everything I need, Brant."

"I will be," he says, leaning forward until our lips are a breath away. "I promise you, one day I will be."

Then he presses his lips to mine and, for a moment, I taste Lee.

Chapter 87

FIVE MONTHS LATER

I stand before a full-length mirror and study my reflection, waiting for the nervous butterflies that I have been warned about. I smooth my hand over my stomach, but it is calm and quiet. I pivot to the left and all three attendees rush forward to adjust the long train and the hang of the ivory beaded fabric. I look beautiful, thanks to Hawaii's most elite wedding planner who has guaranteed every detail is perfectly coordinated to create the most immaculate tiny wedding ever had.

There will be none of society's elite here today. No fake smiles of the women I have pretended, for so many years, to like. We will be a small party of nine: Brant's parents and my own, Anna, Christine, Brant, me, plus our flower girl.

If I have any stress, it's at seeing and spending time with our parents. Brant's are still wary of me and my effect on Brant's status quo. They are still close with Jillian and don't understand why we have cut the older woman out of our lives. My parents are ecstatic at the idea of me marrying tech's most successful entrepreneur and have no knowledge of his disorder.

The door of the dressing room clicks open, and I can hear the squeal of our flower girl before she arrives, a bundle of white careening around the corner and coming to a short halt before the mirror.

"Wow," Hannah breathes, her eyes on the mirror. "You look beautiful."

"Thanks, sweetheart." I move to the edge and an attendant helps me down the pedestal stairs. I crouch before the little girl. "You look equally beautiful." I pick up her small hand and widen my eyes in admiration at her tiny cherry-pink nails.

"A lady did them." She plops down on the carpet, unmindful of her mini Dior dress. Gripping an expensive jeweled slipper by the heel and pulling it off, she holds up her bare foot and wiggles her toes at me. "Look! My toes match!"

"Very impressive." I smile. "Got your petal tossing technique down?" I pass her shoe back and watch as she pulls it on, a small pink tongue sticking out of the side of her mouth in concentration.

Once the task is complete, she looks up with a smile. "Yep!" She jumps to her feet and begins to make exaggerated tossing gestures, each one complete with a small jump.

"Awesome." I hold up my fist and she bumps it with her own, giggling.

"Where's Mr. Brant?" she asks, looking around.

I shrug, rising to my feet. "Not sure. Why don't you go track him down and escort him to the garden? We don't want him to be late for the ceremony."

She nods solemnly, the task taken very seriously. "I'll find him right now," she promises, then turns and tears through the open doorway.

I return to the dressing stage and turn back to the mirror, waiting as the attendees return to the task of preparing the gown.

"She's an adorable little girl," the woman behind me says, her eyes meeting mine in the mirror.

I nod, smiling at the memory of Hannah boarding our jet, her hands touching every surface twice before the plane took off. "She is. Adorable with a side of demon," I warn her. "Keep an eye on her; she finds trouble as quickly as she hugs." A timely crash sounds from the direction of the kitchen, and I laugh. "See?"

I point toward the vanity. "Can you pass me that box, the blue one?"

The woman passes the small box to me, and I open it, withdrawing the two diamond studs that Brant gave me at our first Christmas together. I work them through each earlobe and check myself again for any trepidation.

There's none, and I'm not surprised. I can mark the leaving of Lee as clearly as my birth, the change in our relationship greater than I would ever have expected. Looking back, it was as if our relationship started fresh that day.

"Are you ready? The groom is in the garden, and everyone is in place."

I smile and nod. "Yes."

Chapter 88

My beaded slippers softly crunch down a short aisle of crushed pink shells. The path is lined with pink hibiscus blooms that match the one tucked behind my ear. The sound of the ocean waves are set off by the steel drum band. Brant and a pastor are standing at the end of the aisle underneath the garden's pink trumpet tree, which is in full bloom, the branches heavy in pale pink blooms. The brilliant blue ocean is behind them, creating a stunning background to this moment of our love.

Each step closer is like a page turning in our lives.

Step. The night of Brant's return from the doctor's, Lee having finally left our lives. His hands on me the moment we stepped inside, a tumble of us onto the couch, his hands frantic and needy as they yanked my clothes off until I was bare beneath him. He fucked me as he never had, as Lee used to, as if he was marking me and making me his. He gripped my hair when he thrust into me. Moaned my name when he turned me over and took me from behind. He made me come with his cock, then his fingers, then his mouth, before pounding a rhythm into me that I would never forget. Afterward, he took me to the floor in the center of the great room, a fire on before us, our chests heaving with satisfied breaths as he rolled me over and took me a second time, slower. More like the Brant I loved. He whispered his love as he mended every fuck he had just broken me with. Then we slept, our limbs intertwined, and when the sun rose through the windows, he was still there. My Brant. And only my Brant.

Step. His firm and unwavering abandonment of Jillian and her removal from the Board of Directors. His adjustment of his own role in the company, now an executive in addition to running all development. The door to his office is now open to employees, two assistants keeping his schedule on track in a way that Jillian never could. He's formed collaborative teams, no longer just a one-man production factory. I love seeing him working with others, the awe in the developer's eyes when they understand the true extent of his intelligence. We were all worried about the possible loss of ability, but his therapy, while affecting other pieces of his personality, hasn't hampered that in any way.

Step. Lee is still there, pieces of him sprinkled through Brant's personality, sparkling like glitter when it hits the sun. I see it in the smile Brant now flashes, a wide grin that squeezes my heart every time it appears. I see it in the laugh that occasionally bursts out, in the cocky wink that I got last week when he stepped from the shower and caught my eyes on his naked body. Sometimes, when he watches me, I swear he is Lee, smiling at me, his eyes staring like he knows a secret I don't, like that secret is the key to my soul and I am all his to do with as he wants. I thought I would be losing Lee, but instead, I've only gained more sides of Brant.

Step. I see a dart of white fabric and the slip of Hannah's hand into Brant's, her face upturned to his as she smiled. Brant's been joining me every Tuesday at the HYA compound. He's grown to love Hannah as much as I do. Tonight, after the ceremony, once her belly is fully of cake and her toes are white with Hawaiian sand, we'll ask her if she would like to be a permanent and official member of our family. Brant's already had the attorney prepare the paperwork. All it needs is her blessing and he'll have them process the adoption. I smile at the two of them, his grin gentle as he pulls his gaze from her and meets mine. There, in the windows to his soul, I see our future. More babies, two or three from our union, maybe more from HYA. Summers in this house, winters back home, giving Windere the family it deserves.

Step. I stop before him and look into his face. I can feel my future in his intense stare, in the connection that is now iron strong. We are a team, having jumped hurdles that will make the rest of our life a cakewalk. I have lied for this man, stole for him, cheated on him with him, and sold my soul to his with our first kiss.

I love this man. I repeat, after the pastor, the simple words that interlock our lives, and feel his hand squeeze mine. Leaning forward, I close my eyes and kiss my husband.

Chapter 89 – Brant

I don't know how I got lucky enough to end up with this woman. For my soul to find her, steal her, convince her of love being enough to keep her through the rollercoaster of hell that has been our relationship. She is more than my broken self will ever deserve, but I can never let her go, she owns, whether she knows it or not, all parts of myself, every inch of my body and soul. Her unconditional love brought me to life. Pulled me from a dry, lonely existence before saving me, quite literally, from myself.

One day, I will deserve her. One day, I will fully fix myself and prove to her that it has been worth it. I will spend every ounce of effort getting to that day.

We went to the police on the night I remembered Sheila's death. I told them about the man, his tattoos, the location of his house. We drove by and found it, my memory of that day now painfully clear, as if the decades left it untouched and brand new, in a secret corner of my mind. I had hoped for an arrest, but the officer informed me that the past owner of the home, a man named Nick Coppen, had died six years after Sheila's disappearance. Evidence found in his home had implicated him in multiple unsolved cases. I left that station lighter than I had entered it, Layana's hand tight and strong in mine.

My journey in this relationship hasn't been as difficult as hers, but there were times I struggled. Thank God I didn't walk away when I suspected an affair. Thank God my heart kept an iron grip on her and wouldn't let me move. The frustration, the unknowing, the jealousy... it was grueling, but reinforced one of the first things I said to her: 'It was worth it as soon as I saw you.'

And it was. It was more than worth it.

It was the start of my life, the day my heart started beating.

Epilogue

It is all her fault. I knew she was trouble, I should have worked harder, done more, increased Brant's meds until he broke and scared her away. Had she not appeared, wormed her way into his life, then everything would be fine. Going according to plan. BSX strong, Brant and I leading it into the next millennium. Whores keeping him satisfied, the meds keeping him productive. His other personalities weren't hurting anyone; they had been keeping to themselves. Life had been good, all due to my hard work and planning. Nothing in life is given; everything is earned or taken. I earned a great deal. Took the pieces I couldn't earn. And I had reaped the rewards, as had Brant. He would have nothing without me. How could he forget that? How could he let her blind him to that fact?

I need to separate them. Because of Layana, my own sister won't speak to me, won't visit. Because of Layana, I have been kicked out of BSX like a criminal, my titles stripped, any authority I once had revoked. I built that business, slaved over it for two decades. Poured my hopes and dreams into the building's foundation, only to be locked out. If I separate them, I'll have another chance. To speak to him. Get him back to his true potential. The drugs will do that. I can help him do that.

Assemble the old team. Rehire Dr. F Rehire Molly. Maybe she can dive into Brant's brain and pull Lee back out, even if she did fail horribly with babysitting him the first time. Yes, with proper planning, intelligent design, it can all be made right again. It has to be made right again. I can't continue in this life as it is. I have nothing. I have no one.

And she ... she has everything.

Excerpt, The Journal of Jillian Sharp.

The journal was confiscated from patient's room during a routine search on March 23. Also confiscated were three white pills that appear to have been taken from other patients. Due to the content of written matter, as well as the possession of narcotics, patient will continue her involuntary admittance until such a time that there is no risk of harm to herself or others. As of the date of this report, her next evaluation will be conducted in 26 days.

Report taken by John Ferguson, Hendu Facility for the Mentally Unstable.

Thank you

Thank you, dear reader, for sticking with this story until the end. I hope you enjoyed the rollercoaster I just took you on. For me, the writing of this story was one of the most emotional journeys I have made – I left a piece of my heart within these pages. This book intimidated the hell out of me. I can only hope I did it some form of justice.

<u>DISCLAIMER:</u> Before beginning this book and, while writing, I researched DID (Dissociative Identity Disorder). I quickly realized that there were certain characteristics of DID that would make it difficult to write this story in a manner that would be most entertaining to you, the reader. So, I have taken certain liberties with the telling of this story. Please be aware that, in a real-world situation, an individual struggling with this condition might not act in the manner depicted here. If you are interested in learning more about DID, I encourage you to consult professional resources.

If you enjoyed this book, please consider recommending it to friends, sharing your reactions on social media or leaving a review. Also, feel free to check out my website to view the other books that I have available: www.alessandratorre.com.

Want more?

Join my newsletter and get a deleted scene from A Divided Heart:

Visit: subscribepage.com/adividedheartepi

Acknowledgments

Each book has its own timeline and life. This book has had two. To all of the readers who championed the original version of this book - thank you. I hope this new version found its way to you, and that you enjoyed its rebirth and expansion.

In regards to its original creation, I'd like to thank SueBee, Wendy Metz, Kiki Chatfield, Karen Lawson, Madison Seidler, Natasha Tomic, Erik Gevers, Tricia Crouch, Marion Archer and the OGs in Torreville.

For this new rebirth, a special thanks to Amy Vox Libris for her eagle eye and insightful feedback. Staci Brillhart and Laura Hildago, thank you for the vision, creation and endless back and forth communication, discussions, and edits that resulted in this stunning cover. I owe you both a hundred bouquets of flowers and all the chocolates in the world.

I don't have enough pages to thank all of the people who have helped me. To the author community - there are hundreds of you who have inspired me, supported me, befriended me, advised and taught me. Most of you will have no idea of the ways you have helped me, or the ways you inspire and help others. Thank you for sharing your knowledge, for writing great books, and for being kind and beautiful souls.

A special thank you to my team, family and support structure. You know who you are and you know how much I love you. Thank you for keeping me healthy, happy, and relatively sane.

To Torreville, I have no words, but so much appreciation for you. Thank you for staying, despite my long stretches of silence. I promise to bring you a new book soon.

To the readers who made it this far - thank you from the bottom of my heart. Please consider sharing your thoughts with fellow readers via review, social media post, or carrier pigeon. Your time and thoughts are genuinely appreciated.

Sincerely,

Alessandra

About Alessandra

Alessandra Torre is an award-winning New York Times bestselling author of more than thirty novels. In addition to writing, Alessandra is the creator of Alessandra Torre Ink, a community of over 20,000 authors - and the CEO of Authors A.I.

If you enjoy Alessandra's writing, please follow her on social media, join her Facebook reader group (Alessandra Torre's Torreville), and subscribe to her email newsletter, where she shares writing updates, personal photos, and more (sign up at nextnovel.com)

www.alessandratorre.com
alessandra@alessandratorre.com

Facebook: facebook.com/AlessandraTorre0
IG: instagram.com/alessandratorre4
TikTok: tiktok.com/@alessandra_torre

Looking for another sexy read?

Hidden Seams. A billion-dollar fashion empire is surrounded by secrets, sex and lies.

Hollywood Dirt, the New York Times Bestseller. Now a full-length movie! When Hollywood comes to a small town, sparks fly between its biggest star and a small-town outcast.

Blindfolded Innocence. (First in a series) A college student catches the eye of Brad DeLuca, a divorce attorney with a sexy reputation that screams trouble.

Moonshot, the New York Times Bestseller. Baseball's hottest player has his eye on only one thing—his team's 18-year-old ballgirl.

Tight. A small-town girl falls for a sexy stranger on vacation. Lives intersect and secrets are unveiled in this dark romance.

Trophy Wife. When a stripper marries a rich stranger, life as a trophy wife is not anything like she expects.

Love, Chloe. A fallen socialite works for an heiress, dodges an ex, and juggles single life in the city that never sleeps.

Suspense novels, written under A.R. Torre:

The Ghostwriter. Famous novelist Helena Roth is hiding a dark secret – her perfect life is a perfect lie. Now, as death approaches, she must confess her secrets before it's too late. An emotional and suspense-charged novel.

Every Last Secret. A neighborly relationship grows toxic between two couples in an affluent community - toxic and deadly.

The Good Lie. A Beverly Hills serial killer's latest victim escapes—but seems to be hiding secrets of his own.

A Familiar Stranger. A wife and mother starts to live a double life... a decision that leads to murder.

The Girl in 6E. (Deanna Madden, #1) A sexy internet superstar hides a dark secret: she's a reclusive psychopath.

www.ingramcontent.com/pod-product-compliance
Lightning Source LLC
Chambersburg PA
CBHW011846300726
48970CB00009B/2671